I0573875

A SONG IN THE RAIN
LYDIA DEYES

A Song in the Rain

LYDIA DEYES

Text and layout copyright © 2019 by Lydia Deyes
Cover artwork by Daniel Lieske
Map designed by Brianna da Silva

All rights reserved. Please be respectful and refrain from reproducing,
storing, altering, or sharing this book through any physical or electronic
medium without the permission of the author. Thank you!

This book is a work of fiction. Names, characters, places, and incidents
are either the product of the authors' imagination or are used fictitiously.
Any resemblance to actual persons, living or dead, events, business
entities, or locales is entirely coincidental. Yes, even the animals.

ISBN: 978-1-7334776-1-1

This is the 2nd edition of *A Song in the Rain*
First published in July 2014 with Tate Publishing

www.LydiaDeyes.com

My many thanks to the friends and family who read and commented on my manuscript throughout its stages of life: my writers group, beta readers, and the CritiqueCircle community. With your help, I finally have a book that I can be proud of.

*Special thanks to Patrick, Andrea, Jim, and Dan.
You guys have been my light in the darkness and without you, I wouldn't have had the courage to keep fighting.*

Fledgling sparrow, eyes of gold,
broken in a tempest night.
Darkness, thick as smoke, behold,
incites an everlasting blight.
The only hope against the scourge
must brave a battle more than might.
But should a victor soon emerge,
the hero shall restore the light.

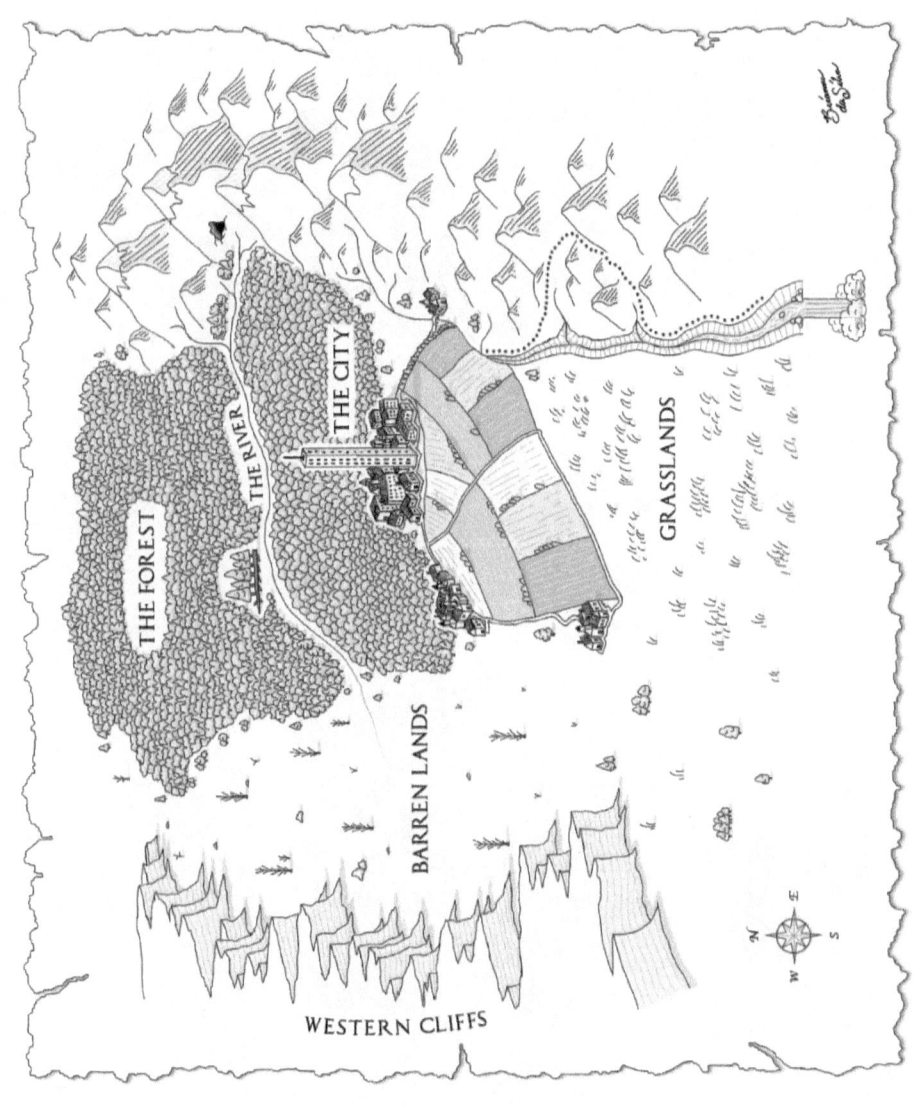

Snake

I

I was pulled out of darkness, as slowly as a leaf falling from a tree. At first I felt nothing, remembered nothing. Sensation began at the tips of my wings, tingling with warmth beneath the feathers. I tried to take a deep breath but was consumed by coughing. I tasted bitter, oaken smoke. My nostrils flared at the biting odor. Trying to open my eyes was a battle. When the lids finally cracked, they stung with heat and soot.

Where am I?

By swinging my head from left to right, I distinguished a bright, round spot in my bleary surroundings.

An exit.

As I started for it, a searing pain shot through my shoulder and my head began to throb. I stumbled, ending with my feet in the air. It took a few tries for me to right myself, half-crawling towards the light. I emerged, perched on the outer bark of a tree hollow.

The ground below me spun through a sheen of smoke, yet I could taste the fresh air. The base of my tail feathers burned from the heat, and I had no choice. I launched myself from the tree, spreading my right wing, trying to bear the burden of my left. I tumbled less than gracefully through the air. A patch of moss caught me, belly-first. Breathless, I forced myself up and kept pushing myself forward, hopping as fast as I could. I needed to get far away from the burning tree. How long did I have before it spread?

Oof!

I turned my head away from the tree to look at whatever I'd just bumped into. A gray squirrel glanced down at me with wide eyes, then returned her gaze to the tree. Her eyes reflected the flames, and her tail twitched nervously. I stood up and winced at the pain in my shoulder and head. I peered around her and saw more woodland creatures, mostly squirrels, all staring at the same thing. It looked like I was the only song sparrow here. All the animals formed a big circle around the edge of the clearing, at the center of which was the tree. Smoke was billowing from its trunk and spreading upwards into the air. Flames licked the grass at its roots, but they never caught.

That can't be normal, I thought. *Why isn't it spreading?*

The rest of the animals looked just as confused as I was. I scanned the crowd for anyone I knew, but all the faces belonged to strangers. The squirrel beside me shook her head and muttered something, but I heard no sound. I blinked. Now that I was free from the fire, I noticed the wood wasn't crackling. A limb hung at an angle, then ripped from the trunk and collapsed to the earth. The ground shuddered from the impact, but I heard nothing.

Turning to the squirrel beside me, I tugged on her fur with my beak. "Excuse me, Miss, but do you…" I stopped, breathing in sharply. I couldn't hear my own voice.

She looked at me, twitching her ears, and responded. Shaking my head, I forced myself to speak again. "I'm scared," I managed, trembling. "I can't hear anything, and I don't know where I am."

The squirrel put a reassuring paw on my back. Together with the rest of the forest animals, we watched the mysterious fire consume the tree, leaving nothing but a charred pile of sticks surrounded by an untouched field of green.

All of us continued in a daze, standing on the edge of the clearing until the last ember fizzled out. This just didn't happen. I wondered how I knew about the normal nature of forest fires, even though I couldn't remember a thing from before waking up in the flames. I couldn't even remember my own name. Reaching back in my mind yielded nothing but empty darkness. I turned my attention instead to the tree — or what had once been a tree, anyway. From the smell of burnt herbs, and because I was lying there when I woke, I guessed this had been some sort of medical center. Someone had

2

probably come across me unconscious and put me there to recuperate.

But why did it catch fire, and why was the fire localized to this one tree?

I wondered how many resources they'd gathered over time, all to be lost in a single moment.

Finally, after what seemed like eons of stillness, the forest came back to life. One by one, the squirrels began to scavenge in the wreckage, looking for anything worth salvaging. Rabbits and voles scattered through the brush, bringing back mouthfuls of leaves and roots. Woodpeckers and robins flew back and forth from the forest to the charred remains in the center of the clearing, carrying small twigs, leaves, and patches of moss. The squirrel beside me got up to join the others.

"Excuse me, Miss…" I cleared my throat, feeling as though it would somehow restore my hearing. "I want to help."

The gray squirrel stopped and turned back towards me. She stood on her hind legs, scratching her belly while she scanned the forest behind me. After a moment, she scampered past me and picked up a hazelnut. She put a paw on her chest, then on the nut.

"Hazelnut?" I guessed. She shook her head. "Hazel?" Her eyes brightened, and she nodded. When she gestured towards me, I sighed. "I don't know."

Hazel put her paw on my left shoulder, causing a burst of pain to shoot through my wing. I staggered backwards, sucking in my breath. Her face creased with worry, she sniffed my shoulder, then sat close and inspected my wing, holding it gingerly between her paws. It hurt when she moved it. She turned and said something in the direction of one of the rabbits, who hopped over. I stood, watching their mouths move; Hazel motioned at me from time to time while my wing continued to throb.

After a moment, Hazel scurried off to help the others. The rabbit twitched his ears and bounced once into the woods, looking back at me. I figured he meant for me to follow him, so I hopped behind

3

him. Now that there was no immediate danger, I was more attuned to the pain. It was hard to avoid accidentally moving my wings. I wanted to help the squirrels and other forest animals with whatever they were doing in the aftermath of the fire, but I didn't know how much good my help was going to be.

The rabbit found a solid piece of bark and carried it in his mouth as we traveled along a stream. As soon as my eyes drifted to the water, a flashback came without warning. The light was sucked out of the world. Lightning flashed, and I heard a clap of thunder so close, I was sure my eardrums would shatter. I was falling, falling fast… and then, as soon as the vision had come, it was gone. I was back on the riverbed, surrounded by silence, and I'd fallen onto my back.

What just happened? Why was I able to hear the thunder?

I guessed it was some sort of memory. I stared around me in shock.

The rabbit helped me back up, then continued on at a faster pace, glancing back at me a couple times. We eventually came across a patch of milkweed, beneath a tree whose branches stretched over the river's edge. He split the milkweed stalk into strands and used them to secure the bark onto my wing. Since I was facing the river as he worked, I focused on my reflection rather than the water, fearing another flashback. A vaguely familiar sparrow looked back at me. At first I examined his brown and black markings and fledgling fuzz, but my gaze was drawn to the eyes. Though I knew they were mine, somehow it felt as though the gold-speckled irises belonged to a stranger.

Suddenly, intense pain shot through my wings as the rabbit shifted my bones into place. He made the final adjustments and clipped the strands with a swift bite. Then, before I could react, the overhanging branch crashed and almost crushed him. He leapt out of the way just in time, landing in the river. I heard nothing as he sputtered and spat, then crawled back to the shore, grasping the edge of the branch that now dipped into the water.

What just happened?

4

My wing felt heavy and stiff and throbbed with pain, but I was so stunned, I barely noticed it.

The rabbit shook himself and looked at me warily. He twitched his ears, seeming to dismiss a thought. Turning from the river, he found a plant I didn't recognize and held out a piece of torn leaf. I wasn't sure what to do with it until he mimed putting it into his mouth. Trusting him, I chewed and swallowed, grimacing at the bitterness. He then stuffed several leaves into his own cheeks but didn't swallow them. He nodded at me to do the same, so I picked up a few smaller pieces.

He must want to replenish the supplies lost in the fire.

I was glad to do something helpful, even if it was only carrying a few things. By the time we were back to the clearing with our first haul, the pain in my head and wing were starting to fade, and so was the memory of the storm.

The rest of the day, I assisted the rabbit in gathering various herbs, berries, leaves, and roots. He used gestures to convey their purpose. Some of them helped with pain, others with stomachache. He even managed to show me a few that helped with birthing. I never imagined I'd see a male rabbit miming labor, and it sure was an interesting sight. For a moment, I forgot about my pain and laughed, but stopped short. Laughing silently was somehow even more uncomfortable than speaking.

By the time the sky began to darken, the animals had tucked the pile of medicines into a burrow and built a makeshift structure of woven branches to protect the entrance from the rain. I wandered around for a while, looking for signs of any other animals that had been in medical care when the tree had ignited. Nothing. No animals were limping or injured, and there were no bones in the ashes of the tree. I was the only one who could have been hurt. I was the only one who could have died.

Thankfully, Hazel found me before my brooding could get too dark. Since I was unable to fly, she led me to the rabbit's burrow. He didn't seem terribly happy to take me in, but didn't resist when Hazel gave him a stern look. I found a corner to perch in for the night, as out of the way as possible. I was safe, for now. I drifted into uneasy sleep, still wondering what had caused the fire, why I'd lost my hearing, and why I could remember nothing about my past.

II

When I heard the crickets, I knew I was dreaming.

Have I always been deaf in real life but able to hear in dreams?

It was a quiet night, but I was suddenly aware of every little sound. I could hear frogs peeping and croaking in the distance, breeze rustling the trees, and bats flying overhead, snatching mosquitoes out of the air. I stood with my toes grazing the burnt center of the clearing. All that remained of the tree were charred slivers of wood and ash. But as I inspected it, something at the heart caught my eye. Drawing closer, I could see an odd array of items, all lined up in a row. On the left, a snake's fang. On the right, a crow's feather. And in the middle, a wolf's claw, clean and sharp. When I nudged the items with my beak, they disintegrated into a pile of ash. I sneezed. The tiny cloud lingered for a moment as a dense, shapeless blob, then dissipated into the night. I woke up panting, with the metallic taste of blood on my tongue and silence ringing in my ears. Lying still for a moment, I tried to remember the sound of the frogs and breeze.

A few days later, Hazel convinced a pair of robins to let me watch them teach their children to fly. I followed the motions as much as I could with my wing strapped to a piece of bark. I enjoyed mimicking the motions and learned a lot during the session, but when it ended, the robins hurried their children away and left me to fend for myself. I didn't understand why they were avoiding me. I dragged my feet on the way back to the rabbit's hollow, but a commotion at the entrance made me stop short.

The entrance was charred black. A pair of groundhogs ventured inside, and when they returned, soot dusted their fur. They dragged out the limp body of the rabbit, covered in burns. He was dead.

I shook my head, stepping back. All eyes turned towards me. No… behind me.

When I spun around, half a dozen stones were floating in the air, about as high as the top of my head. As soon as I noticed them, they dropped to the ground.

What is happening? What kind of sorcery is this?

I turned back to the other animals. They had once welcomed me into their homes and cared for my medical needs, but now I saw fear in all of their eyes. Even Hazel looked uncomfortable.

"It's not my fault!" I tried to protest, shuddering when I couldn't hear my own words. "I didn't have anything to do with this. I don't know what caused the fires… I don't know why any of this is happening!" I closed my eyes, trying to shut out their fear and find peace. Instead, the fang, feather, and claw were there in the darkness. The taste of blood stung my tongue.

No one was willing to let me stay in their home after that, no matter how much I protested. They all still drew a connection between the two fires. Me. I hadn't been in the rabbit's hollow when it caught fire, but I'd slept there the previous few nights. Hazel was spent time with me at least, but even she shook her head when I asked if I could stay with her. I found new places to rest, but each time I stayed there for a few nights, it was burnt to a crisp by the same mysterious fire that didn't spread. What if there *was* a connection? Could something be attacking me?

I made a habit of sleeping out in the open, so I could get away as soon as flames licked my skin. Sometimes the fire came when I wasn't there, but each new fire came closer to catching me off guard than the previous one. I had more than a few singed feathers now, and I was running out of places to stay that weren't near the stream. I might be safer from the flames there, but not from the terrifying flashbacks.

Every time I saw flowing water, the same memory took over. Thunder and lightning seared my mind, and strange things happened. Sometimes rocks levitated on their own; sometimes an odd breeze ruffled my feathers in the wrong direction. Once, I opened my eyes to find myself on the other side of the stream and had to try to make my way back over. I hopped from rock to rock, barely able to look where I was going, afraid another accident would happen while I was standing in the middle of the stream. I remembered the first flashback and how the poor rabbit nearly got crushed by a falling branch shortly afterward. Unlike the fires, these events seemed too correlated with the flashbacks for them not to be my fault. I had no control over them, but at least they weren't nearly as harmful as the targeted flames.

On top of everything else, every night, the same nightmare haunted me. Every morning, I woke to the taste of blood. I wished I knew what the dream meant, and why all of this was happening to me.

When the moon shifted from half to full, it was finally time to remove my splint. I was excited that I could now be just as helpful as the other birds and I'd actually be able to fly on my own. I wanted to celebrate this happy moment. Hazel gathered a pile of nuts, seeds, and my favorite berries. She even hung a few sprigs of sweet-smelling goldenrod on the branches of my current resting place. But despite all of the extra food she'd prepared, despite the pleasing scents wafting from the tree, no one else came to say hello. When we took the excess food back to the community storage, I looked around, trying to meet the gaze of the other woodland creatures. The young ones stared or looked at me with curiosity, but the adults shot glances my way before hurrying their children away. Their fear and distrust hurt me. I wanted nothing more than to belong.

I looked sadly at my squirrel friend. She was the only one who showed me any kindness in this place, but I knew from her tired expression that she was sacrificing too much. The more time she spent with me, the more the other creatures avoided her, too. Between the fires and floating rocks and everything else, these animals had so many reasons to fear me. My presence was endangering them, whether I could do anything about it or not.

9

I sighed. "I can't stay here," I admitted to Hazel. Her expression fell to one of sorrow, but her eyes showed understanding. After saying those few words, the rest came bubbling out of nowhere. All my thoughts and fears and emotions rose to the surface, and even my discomfort at the silence of my voice couldn't hold them back.

"The fires are bad, but it's not just them. There's so much I don't understand… the nightmares, the flashbacks, the weird stuff that happens around me… I need to know what's causing all of it, and I don't think it's getting better with time, either. Maybe I have family out there somewhere, or at least someone who knew me before I arrived here. I'm scared, but I don't know what else to do…"

Before I could ramble on any further, Hazel pulled me close to her and wrapped her arms around me. We stood there for a couple minutes. When we broke apart again, I felt better, and though my heart was dancing on my ribcage, I felt ready.

"Thank you, Hazel," I said as I turned to leave. "For everything."

Hazel's eyes were sad, but she smiled and waved goodbye. I took a deep breath, spread my wings, and embarked into the unknown.

III

The first few leaves were falling from the trees as I flew through the woods that afternoon. For a while, everything was still. A few birds and small animals not part of the squirrel's community dipped and dodged between the trees; the breeze gently ruffled my feathers as I flew.

Eventually, I came to the edge of the forest. The sun was rising to my left, reaching its rays across the sky. Behind me was the comfort of the forest, and before me was a village of... *humans*. The word felt strange in my mind. I had no idea why I knew of these odd, two-legged creatures; I had no more memory of them than anything else from my past. Yet somehow, I felt as though the village was even more familiar to me than the forest. Perching on the branch of a birch tree, I scanned the settlement.

The line between the forest and the humans was stark. The shadowed forest floor was strewn with rocks and blanketed in patches of mushrooms and uncontrolled growth. The humans lived in an area with very short, light green grass that was browning in spots. There were a couple of short trees or bushes here and there, but white, red, and black stone-like patches and structures dominated the landscape. I could see the humans through shimmery holes in their buildings — *windows*. The word popped into my mind, unbidden.

My gaze was drawn to the dwelling nearest me. Its tall, white fence butted up against the forest; wild plants threatened to break through its barrier. An ancient, bedraggled crow was perched on the fence, not far from where I was perched. His shape was mangled, perhaps from war. His feathers were ruffled and frayed, and the eye facing me was a milky gray. As I peered closer, he shifted, revealing a missing toe on his right foot. He was so unusual, and yet...

Do I know him?

Suddenly, he flipped his head to the other side, flinging a line of saliva as he did so, and stared straight into my soul. I started, nearly fell off my perch, and flew away from there as fast as I could, keeping the trees to my left.

Barely paying attention to my surroundings, I flew until my wings ached, my lungs stung, and the shadows were longer than the trees were tall. To my right, where there had been a few scattered homes, was now a city center. I dared not stray from the edge of the forest into the bright light, with its vibrating machines and overwhelming odor. If I could hear, I was sure it would be chaotic. What deterred me more than anything else was a massive rectangular structure looming over me. I counted fourteen windows tall.

It's not safe there.

I turned back towards the trees and flew further into the forest. Just as I found a good perch and was ready to rest for the night, a chill ran up my spine. Something was wrong.

I peered through the growing darkness, able to see just enough thanks to the unnatural light of the city and slowly disappearing sun. About six trees away, I could make out a large, bird-like form slumped on the ground. After drawing closer, I caught my breath. It was a red-tailed hawk. He shifted his weight stiffly, revealing a gash on his side. His eyes were open but not focused on anything in particular. When I inched forward, just a fox's length away, they shifted towards me. Without opening his beak, his eyes pleaded for help, and his brows creased with pain. I saw no animosity in those eyes, and despite my fear of being eaten, I wanted to help him. Not so long ago, I'd been helpless, too.

Looking around for the plants I'd learned about during my time with the squirrels, I spotted a patch of lamb's ear just a few trees away. On my way over, I passed by a large spiderweb covering a bush. I plucked a leaf of lamb's ear in my beak and wrapped it in cobweb, then used the sticky strings to secure the leaf onto the injured bird's open wound. He allowed me to help without resisting, and though I could tell he was hurting, his eyes closed in relief. I nudged him up, straining under his weight, and helped him move under the canopy of the nearest bush. There were many predators in the woods at dusk, and he needed to get somewhere safer.

Grimacing, I plucked and tore open several fresh pine needles, hoping the strong-smelling tar would hide the scent of blood. The hawk moved his beak as if to say something, but I shook my head. "I lost my hearing," I told him. "I won't be able to understand you. But you should be safe here for the night." He furrowed his brow, then nodded in understanding. Standing back, I looked over my work, scattered a few leaves to hide the track where he'd dragged his wings, and perched nearby to finally get some much needed rest.

That night, I had another disturbing dream. Even though it had been nice a month ago, hearing in my nightmares now felt eerie. I spooked at every rustle and snap, and this time, at the hiss of a snake. Tonight, my dream was different from the repeating vision of the feather, claw, and fang. I saw only a strange, murky darkness — like smoke, but heavy, crawling along the ground.

The smoke reminded me of the odd ash cloud that always formed from the three objects in my recurring dream. If I listened intently, I thought I could hear whispers in the smoke, but I couldn't understand them. My feathers pricked my skin. Then I noticed a slight change in the cloud. There was a track. It was as if an invisible snake was winding through the darkness, both a part of it and different from it at the same time. Curious, I moved closer. The smoke parted around me as I waded towards the path of the snake. But when I reached where the track had been, I saw no sign of the slithering creature on the ground. Instead, I saw pawprints! They looked like they belonged to a squirrel or rat.

Suddenly, I realized the smoke had been billowing behind me while I was focused on the tracks. It loomed high above me, then crashed over me like a wave. Engulfed in darkness and surrounded by whispered screams I still couldn't understand, I woke up.

The sky was dark when I opened my eyes, even though it was just past sunrise. The heavy clouds filled me with dread. As the first raindrops splattered my head, I had another flash of memory — lightning, falling, thunder. I heard the rumble from the past just as I felt the one in the present. I trembled with fear. I needed to get out of the storm. I glanced at the bush where the hawk was hidden. He was watching me. Once we made eye contact, he turned his head to stare at the massive building at the edge of the forest. I followed his gaze upwards. Lightning flashed, illuminating the side. Something moved in one of the windows, the second from the top.

Is that... a bird?

When the sky flashed again, whatever it was had disappeared.

I looked back at the hawk and cocked my head. "Should I go up there?" He nodded. I hesitated for a moment but was soon convinced by another drop landing on my head. Maybe there was a way to get inside before the sky erupted. The massive building was more imposing than anything else nearby, but the promise of shelter was too strong to resist.

As I approached the window, I noticed every pane at this elevation was covered in dust and grime. The raindrops left thick trails behind them, but they were so dirty, I still couldn't see in.

How could I have seen a bird before?

I examined the corners of the eaves but couldn't find any opening. I saw a few vents in the wall, but they were completely clogged with what seemed like a mixture of mud and grass. The sky vibrated with thunder again. Desperate, I landed on the sill, pecked on the glass, and cried out as hard as I could.

"Hello? Is anybody in there?" I cursed my lack of hearing.

How can I know if I'm shouting loud enough, if there even is anyone on the other side to hear me? Would these city folk speak my language, whatever that may be?

"Can I come in? Hello?"

14

I was about to give up and find a less dry but more reliable alternative when the window suddenly slid up. Startled by the sudden movement, I nearly lost my grip on the windowsill. Nothing but a dark, empty room was before me. There was no time to hesitate as fat raindrops began to smack against the glass and splatter the floor inside. It was too late to go back. I plunged into the mysterious room.

IV

The window slammed behind me.

Magic?

I was immediately overcome with an intense feeling of safety, even though nothing about this room and its strange window seemed safe and I was now trapped.

Well, might as well move forward.

I hopped along the floor, taking in scents of dust, oak, and dried grass as my eyes adjusted to the shadows. Before me was a large wooden door. Light filtered in through a chipped gap on the hinged side, as well as the crack at its base. The latter might just be large enough for me to squeeze under if I tried...

Before I could finish my thought, the door swung wide open on its own, blinding me with light from the hall. After blinking several times, the flash faded into a softer tone, and I stood face-to-face with another sparrow. She had a thin scrap of blue fabric tied around her leg, barely more than a thread. Her eyes were wide, but not with fear.

Excitement?

I was so stunned that when she spoke, I didn't think to shake my head like I had with so many animals over the last several days. I just stared blankly, trying to remember where I knew her from. When she paused and spoke a second time with a furrowed brow, I shook myself back into the present. "I can't hear you," I said, the phrase becoming something of a mantra. "But... do I know you?"

The sparrow's eyes shifted, and her head drooped slightly. Then she tilted it up again and motioned for me to follow her. I felt like I should trust her, but I still couldn't place where I knew her from.

Why does she seem so familiar?

"Um, before we go too far," I said, recalling my friend outside, "there is an injured hawk hidden in a bush out in the forest. Can he come inside, too?"

She cocked her head, then called behind her. A moment later, a fox scampered into the room. I nearly fainted in fright.

How could a sparrow be friends with a fox?

The fox stopped when her eyes met mine, but she shook her head and bounded towards the window. She didn't pause; it opened for her just before she reached it. Worried I'd just given up my friend as a meal, I watched as she scurried down the black metal staircase. The rain poured harder, and I fought against the memory itching to surface. I watched the fox's red tail disappear into the forest, then her head reappeared, with my friend in her maw. The fox climbed back up the stairs, much more carefully this time. She returned and released him, and I breathed out the sigh I'd been holding.

"Will you be okay?" I asked him. When he nodded, I relaxed. I stole a glance at the fox; she was just licking her paw. I noticed she also had a blue piece of fabric, this one loosely tied around her neck. I was curious but couldn't think of a simple yes-or-no question to ask about it. "Okay," I told the sparrow. "I'll follow you now."

The too familiar sparrow led me from the room to a long hallway, and a thousand thoughts and questions spiraled through my head.

Who is this sparrow? Where is she taking me?

From the corner of my eye, I caught glimpses of the same mysterious dark smoke from my dreams. Whenever I looked directly into the shadows, though, there was nothing there.

What is this place?

As if in a trance, I could do nothing but move forward, following the familiar stranger as we passed by rooms on the left and right. Sometimes a door would creak open to reveal dim light in an adjacent room. I thought I could see flashes of various creatures — a

17

squirrel's tail, a raven's claw, a glimpse of blue fabric — but none lingered long in my line of sight. We wound through hall after hall.

Finally, we turned into a room and were suddenly within a paw's reach of a lynx and raccoon having a discussion. The lynx looked far older than any animal I'd ever seen. He seemed to have shrunk over the years; every inch of his fur was wrinkled and gray. He dismissed the raccoon, who scampered out the door with a backwards glance at me.

The sparrow beside me exchanged a few words with the lynx, then turned tail and left me alone with him. I shivered and took a step back. *Have I just fallen into a trap?*

"Hello, Sheer," I heard in my head. I shrieked and stumbled backwards. The voice was deep and somehow sounded coarse and soft at the same time. *"Don't be alarmed. I can help you."*

"What in green grass was that?" I cried, forgetting for a moment that I couldn't hear the words coming from my beak.

"My name is Samuel," the lynx said, this time moving his mouth at the same time as I heard the phrase in my head. *"I'm sorry to scare you. I normally do not use this ability, but I wanted you to be able to understand me."*

Every fiber of my being shook, and I wasn't sure what to do. Here was a creature who could speak to me in a way I could hear, yet it was so terrifying, I didn't know if I wanted it to continue. Had he called me by name?

What name?

A stack of parchment beside the lynx fluttered, even though the only window in the room was closed. He glanced at it, then back at me. *"Don't be afraid, young one,"* Samuel continued. *"You're safe here. I know this method of speaking is strange, but I can help you learn to communicate in other ways."*

I struggled to put the hundreds of questions racing through my mind into words. "Um, what did you call me? I was so startled, I…" Now that I'd gotten started, they wouldn't stop coming. The breeze

18

that had rustled the papers picked up, pushing against my feathers in sync with the whirlwind of thoughts and emotions rushing through my mind. "How come you can speak in my mind? What is this place? Who is the sparrow who led me to you? And…"

"Hush, now. A racing mind won't do you any good if you can't keep up with it. Close your eyes, take a deep breath."

I followed his instructions, recalling the feeling of safety I'd experienced when first entering the building. After a few breaths, the breeze calmed, and I felt more in charge of the thoughts in my mind. I tried again. "You said my name… what was it?"

"Your name is Sheer. The other sparrow is your sister, Violet. She thought she'd lost you in a storm and has mourned your loss since. Do you remember the storm, Sheer?"

Thunder shook the window beside us, and I heard the rumbling in my head, a vivid memory of a storm long forgotten. "Yes," I replied. "But I don't want to. The flashbacks keep coming, and I can't control them. How do I make them stop?"

"You can't make them stop," the lynx said, shifting closer to me and lying down so our eyes were level. I saw nothing but kindness in them. *"But you can make them stop hurting."*

"How?"

"As with any fear, you must face it. You're strong, Sheer. You're strong enough that you push the memory away each time it comes… but avoiding trouble won't destroy it. You have to allow the memory to finish."

I gulped, but I felt I could trust him. Thunder shook the panes beside us again, and this time I shivered and closed my eyes, allowing the memory to take hold.

A song sparrow, barely a fledgling, flapped his wings desperately through the storm. Dirt turned quickly into mud as rain pounded the ground. Thunder clapped, and it seemed like the whole world vibrated with it. A tree, just a wing's breadth away from the young bird, incinerated with a flash of lightning. He began to fall. Deaf and blind, he plummeted as if drained of life. He barely reacted when his wing struck the edge of a branch. After he landed in a murky puddle with a thump and splash, he didn't move. Moments passed. A final flash of light revealed the shadow of a squirrel moving towards the limp body as the storm moved on.

I opened my eyes. For a moment, all I could do was stare into nothing. Lightning flashed outside, but the memory didn't come back again. I sighed with relief. "I saw myself," I told Samuel. "I think I know how I was injured. And how I lost my memory."

"Good!" Samuel's eyes twinkled. *"Now, I do believe you asked another question in your flurry of words. Would you like to restate it?"*

I nodded. "What is it about this place? I feel… safe here. Even before meeting you or Violet or anyone, even when the window closed and it seemed like I was trapped. Why?"

"Ancient magic," he responded, *"that I learned over the decades. I've been given the gift of a very long life and have devoted much of it to studies that build upon my early experiences with humans. It's much too advanced for me to explain, but trust that this place is the safest place you could be."*

Could it be safe enough to protect me from the fires? "Why? Why do you want to help me?"

Samuel's eyes twinkled. *"First, because I'm the guardian of the animals who live here, on the thirteenth floor. Your sister is one of them, of course."*

I creased my brow in confusion. "First? Is there another reason?"

Samuel was quiet for a moment before answering. *"Do you ever feel that you're different from other creatures, besides the fact that you're deaf?"*

20

I stared at him in shock. "H… How do you know?"

"What do you feel makes you different, Sheer?"

"Well…" I shuffled my feet. "I think my eyes aren't normal for a sparrow, for one. Everyone keeps looking at me weird."

The lynx nodded. *"Anything else?"*

I looked into his eyes. I trusted him, but the fires and the strange things that happened around me were what drove me out of the squirrel community. I didn't want to lose out on a chance to have a new place to live. One that was safe and sheltered from the rain I hated. One where someone *knew* me, had known me before everything had gone wrong.

I can't tell him about those. Not yet, anyway.

I started to shake my head, then remembered one more thing.

"You were able to help me with the memory of the storm… could you help me stop dreams, too?"

Samuel furrowed his brow. *"What kind of dreams?"*

I told him about the recurring dream of the snake's fang, crow's feather, and wolf's claw that turned to dust when I tried to touch them. I told him, too, about the more recent dream about the black smoke and the snake's trail through it, and how upon inspection the trail became pawprints. When I was done, Samuel closed his eyes. After a pause, he spoke again.

"Fledgling sparrow, eyes of gold, broken in a tempest night. Darkness, thick as smoke, behold, incites an everlasting blight. The only hope against the scourge must brave a battle more than might. But should a victor soon emerge, the hero shall restore the light."

Samuel opened his eyes. *"That is the second reason I want to help you. It means this,"* he continued, then repeated the same four sentences, word for word. I blinked.

"You said the same thing twice," I said, confused.

Samuel stood up and stared straight into my soul. He glanced at his paws and muttered to himself, then seemed to remember I couldn't hear him. *"Young sparrow, you shouldn't joke about these things."*

I faltered, thrown off by the sternness in his voice, which still resounded in my head. "I don't know what you mean," I managed to say. "What did I do wrong? You really said the same thing twice."

"Right now, I'm speaking in my own language," Samuel said. *"It's called Montin. When you first came into this room, you were speaking it, too. I thought perhaps you had learned it somewhere. But now, you're telling me that it sounds the same to you?"*

"The same as what?" I asked, not sure if he was playing a trick on me.

"Kisalan," he replied. The voice echoing in my head sounded agitated. *"The language of the songbirds and small forest mammals, which took decades for me to learn? The language your sister speaks?"*

"I guess so? I don't know."

The old lynx sighed. *"You have many gifts, Sheer. That prophecy... I think it refers to you. I don't know exactly what your dreams mean, and I don't know why you have this gift of language. Of one thing I'm sure, though. The darkness you've seen is a symbol of the evil that you must defeat, just like in the prophecy. The snake, crow, and wolf must be the enemies you will someday have to face. I'll ensure that my scouts report any strange happenings regarding any of those creatures. Hopefully, you will have dreams that are more detailed in time. Dreams that can lead you to the evils and quench them before they grow too strong."*

I yawned. The night was at its peak by now, and so much had happened today, I felt overwhelmed. Finding a mysterious building with magic windows. Meeting my sister. Discovering a clue about my past. Learning that I could apparently speak and understand two languages…at this point, Samuel's words barely registered in my mind.

22

"That's enough for today," Samuel said, jolting me awake. *"You need rest. I'll call your sister back and have her show you where you can sleep. Let's talk more tomorrow."*

"Okay." I was thankful for the promise of sweet, sweet sleep.

"Oh, but one thing first. Here." I blinked and focused my eyes on his paw as he used his sharp claw to sever a tiny sliver of blue fabric off the larger piece tied around his neck. *"You're a member of the thirteenth floor now. The doors and windows will always open for you with my magic. And this special fabric signifies that you're one of us. You'll know that you're safe from any predators that wear this color, and they'll know that you're a friend. You should ask a squirrel or mouse to help you tie it. Just tell them I sent you."*

"Thank you, Samuel," I replied, grasping the fabric in my beak. My heart skipped a beat as I felt its rough texture against my tongue. I finally had a place where I belonged. I just needed not to mess this one up.

V

My head was throbbing when Violet returned to the room. She beckoned for me to follow her. A door opened for us on its own, and I wished I knew how it worked. I could ask her, but how would I understand the response?

Maybe I'll ask Samuel later...

When we entered, though, all thoughts of my disability left my mind. The room was filled with shelves, all piled high with branches. Every sleeping bird in the room was some variety of sparrow. My sister gestured to an empty sprig.

"Will you stay here, too?" I asked, feeling weary and very alone.

In response, Violet landed on a nearby branch. I noticed scratches that perfectly matched where her toes touched the wood. It made me feel better to be close to my sister. Before I knew it, I'd drifted off to sleep. For the first time since I could remember, I had no dreams that night.

Feeling extremely rested the next morning, I followed Violet out into the hall. We flew to an ornate archway, which led to a cavernous room in the center of the thirteenth floor. Inside was an enormous rectangular table, around and upon which sat a plethora of creatures. I was sure I'd never seen so many animals so close together, even before losing my memory. Most of them were birds fluttering around the room, but I also saw lynxes, foxes, and other mammals. I spotted wild cats, raccoons, badgers, and ferrets among them. The motion of all these animals was overwhelming, and I had to close my eyes to stop the room from becoming a spinning blur. When I opened my eyes more slowly, I adjusted to the chaos and took note of the details. Everyone wore some sort of blue fabric, and everyone was getting along. I was nervous at first, but none of the predators seemed remotely interested in having me for breakfast. Food was set before everyone: mostly roots, seeds, and berries, and fish or prepared meats for the carnivores. I wasn't sure where the meat came from, but the energy in the room told me it certainly wasn't from members of the community.

Across the way, I saw my hawk friend. He perked up when we made eye contact. His eyes bright, he shuffled his way over to me with a giant grin on his face. His wound had been cleaned and patched up by someone more professional. When he bent his head down and turned to eye me, I couldn't help feeling amused. Guessing at what he wanted, I touched the top of his head with my own. Pleased, he jumped up, nodded to my sister, then hopped back to his own meal.

"Do you know him?" I asked Violet. When she shook her head, I wondered if he'd known about this place before we came. He'd encouraged me to investigate, after all. He seemed like a good bird.

"Your friend is very amusing," I heard inside my head. I jumped, then turned to find Samuel behind me.

"You scared me!"

"I'm sorry Sheer, I didn't mean to. It must be hard to have one of your senses missing, and I can't pretend to fully understand. I'll try not to startle you next time." I nodded, not wishing to dwell on it. I picked at my food, still not used to so many different scents in one place. I tried to ignore the frequent glances I was getting from around the room. Why did my eyes have to look so different?

Now that I knew he was there, I felt the rumble of Samuel's voice when he spoke again. *"You may be deaf, but your other senses are strong. You were able to recognize your hawk friend from across the room before he saw you. Not many songbirds can say as much."*

I had, hadn't I? "His wound was patched up. Do you have a healer?"

"Yes," Samuel responded, his eyes twinkling. *"My granddaughter Anna is the best you'll ever meet."*

My heart lifted. Maybe I could put my limited knowledge of plants from my time with the squirrels to good use, and perhaps learn even more from her. The feeling sank quickly.

How will I learn anything more complicated than a plant's general usage?

Forcing my thoughts to veer in another direction, I paused. "What's his name?"

"Your hawk friend? His name is Barrie."

"I wish I could've asked him that myself," I admitted, gulping down the last seed, "but how would he have told me? Or anyone else's name, for that matter? I got lucky before when I met a squirrel named Hazel…"

"If you're finished with your breakfast," the lynx replied, turning towards me, *"I can show you."*

Curious, I followed Samuel out of the hall. He brought me to the same room where I'd first met him and padded over to the far wall. There, he picked up a dark rock, then what looked like a large, flat, cream-colored leaf.

"This is graphite," he explained, *"and this is parchment. Many, many years ago, I lived with humans. They use these to communicate with each other when speech would not suffice."*

"You lived with humans?"

"Yes," he replied, pausing to make several marks on the parchment. *"Now, the human written language is far too lengthy and complicated for many animals to find useful. It takes too long to write down simple ideas. I came up with a unique, simpler language and taught it to all who live here and were willing to learn. Even though I've taught myself to speak multiple languages, not everyone*

can do the same. *Of course, you'll have a much easier time talking to the other animals because of your gift of language, but you'll still need a tool for understanding complex concepts and unique words like names. For the rest of the animals here on the thirteenth floor, a shared written language is a simple way to ensure everyone can communicate with each other. This marking here means…"*

Then, to my dismay, he spoke plainly. I heard nothing in my head. "Um… Samuel? Could you repeat that?"

He did, the same way. When my face fell, he finally spoke in my head again. *"I know it's hard, Sheer, but you must realize that you cannot rely on my ability forever. And though the written language is a powerful tool, it's not a tool everyone knows how to use, nor is it good for all situations. I'll teach you to write, and I'll speak in your head for a time, but you must learn to comprehend speech even when you have neither available to you. Do you understand?"*

I hesitated, but as much as I wanted to avoid thinking about it, Samuel was right. Nodding slowly, I asked, "Can I try again?"

Samuel's eyes brightened, and he sat up straight. Putting his paw on the marking, he spoke again. I studied his face, his mouth, the movement of his lips, but I still couldn't grasp what he was saying. He wasn't using exaggerated motions, as I'd grown accustomed to when talking to Hazel. He wasn't nodding or shaking his head either, the two universal gestures I relied on so heavily when asking questions.

"I can't do it," I despaired. "I can't understand what you're saying."

"It's okay," Samuel said, gingerly lifting my beak with his claw turned sideways. *"This marking means 'family.' And I'm thinking that perhaps as we begin this journey of learning, it may be easier for you to learn from other birds, like your sister and your friend, until you have progressed more."*

I picked at a splinter on the floor. "Maybe."

Samuel called out into the hall. A moment later, the door swung open again. I was still not quite used to all the magical elements of the thirteenth floor, but I didn't have long to dwell on it. Both Violet and Barrie came into the room.

"This will be good for you as well," Samuel said, his voice echoing in my head, even though his speech was directed at Barrie. I appreciated that. *"You can learn the written language along with Sheer. I need both of you to help him,"* he continued, turning to Violet as well, *"by voicing out the words that I write and say. Speak naturally, without excess motions."* Finally, he faced me again. *"Alright! Let's get started."*

After Samuel wrote two characters on the parchment, Violet was the first to speak. I tried ever so hard to understand. All I could tell was that she seemed to say the same phrase more than once. I asked Samuel whether this was true.

"It's odd hearing you switch between languages," he admitted. *"When you're alone with me, you seem to speak my native tongue; yet, when you're with others, you're speaking your own."* I noticed his mouth remained still, and I wondered why he didn't want to share this information with my friend or sister. Was this gift something to be ashamed of?

He shook his head, then continued to speak, this time out loud as well as in my mind. *"Yes, she repeated her phrase. Do you know what she was saying?"* I shook my head. *"That's okay,"* he replied, *"it will take time. Try watching Barrie say the same phrase."*

I felt closer to Barrie than to my sister. It was partly because of how strange it was not to be able to recall my own sibling, but mostly because we shared experiences. Both of us had been injured and could've died if left alone. Of course, I almost died multiple times even after being rescued, but that was something else entirely. At least I was safe, for now, from whatever might be targeting me. There had been no sign of fire so far, and that was good.

Yet, despite the deeper feeling of connection, watching Barrie was no better than watching Violet. He was simply speaking to me as if I could hear, and I felt my entire body droop in disappointment. I would never be able to learn. How could I? I tried anyway, and as he repeated the phrase, I tried to take note of the emotion expressed in his eyes. I did recognize it, but I couldn't connect it with words. It was hopeless.

"Sheer, they were saying 'thank you,'" Samuel told me when I shook my head again. *"Would you like to try another phrase, or would you like to see the same one again?"* He gave me no other option. I wanted to give up.

I let out a deep breath. Something about Samuel's sincerity gave me just enough fuel to keep going, though not enough to get my hopes up. I opted to see the same phrase again and, already knowing what they were saying this time, tried to form a connection between the two birds to match their body languages and expressions with the words. I could see no distinct similarity. Several times I wanted to stop, but Samuel pushed me on. We cycled through multiple phrases, each one repeated twice by both my sister and friend, but none of them clicked. I was learning the written language bit by bit from Samuel's scribblings before each spoken phrase, but I still felt more lost than ever. When we were tired and hungry, he finally drew the session to a close. Together, we wandered back into the great hall with the massive table.

At dinner, I was overwhelmed and lost. All around me were a couple hundred animals, involving themselves in conversation I couldn't understand. Samuel wouldn't speak inside my mind, and even if I'd known enough of the written language to have a discussion, everyone was so caught up in their own conversations that no one was interested in me. Even Violet and Barrie were having a lively chat while I picked at my food. I felt completely alone, despite being surrounded by others. When I was finished with my medley of grass seeds and berries, I left the table without a word to anyone and retreated to my perch in the sparrow room. Even the door seemed reluctant to open for me.

VI

That night, I had another dream. I sat on my perch in the dark, listening to the sounds of the building and city. The door creaked, the eaves settled, and a muted drone of human life outside came muffled through the window.

Is this what it sounds like all of the time?

Then there was a whistling. It was like a strange and unfamiliar breeze. Different, somehow, from the breeze I'd heard in my dreams before. The sound rose and fell in waves that chilled me to the bone.

I rose and followed the sound, flying silently past all of the sleeping sparrows. Down the hall, left, right, and right again. The volume and pitch intensified as I drew closer to the source. When I made it to Samuel's room, the old lynx was sound asleep, despite the howling. The strange wind rattled his window panes, screaming to come in. The sky was dark beyond the clear glass, filled with dense fog that was darker than night. It moved and frothed like liquid. When I approached, the window swung open of its own accord. I was sure the wind would rush in, knocking over everything in its path, but… nothing stirred. It whooshed and howled, but I felt nothing at all.

Then, with no control over my actions, I began to sing. The language, strange to my ears, flowed from my throat like a beautiful stream. Somehow, I was singing *color*. It was the most colorful song, the most beautiful song, and it lifted my heart. Then, as quickly as it had begun, it was over. The wind was gone, and the sky outside shone a dull blue, with warm light radiating from the city itself. I spotted a star in the sky, and I heard nothing more than the gentle creaking of the old building.

I woke up early, refreshed and ready to take on the day. I didn't know what to make of my dream, but I was glad it was so much nicer than the nightmares that had haunted me since waking in the burning tree. After breakfast, I flitted over to Samuel's room to see if he had anything planned for the day.

"I thought we could go outside while you focus your studies on reading expressions and body language," he said. *"I believe it may help if you're not trying to learn to write at the same time. We can explore a bit and meet some new animals neither of us knows."*

Streaks of rain made rivers on the dusty window. Despite the promise that my flashback had been conquered, the thought of falling water still filled me with dread. And besides, how could I know I wouldn't still be a target for fires out there, outside of Samuel's wards? "Can we do something else?"

He looked, too. *"Ah. Well, it's only drizzling. You can ride on my back if you don't want to fly..."* Upon turning back to see my expression, his eyes softened. *"Okay, Sheer. We can stay inside today. Would you still be alright with learning expressions from animals you don't know?"*

I nodded, relieved that we wouldn't need to go out in the rain. Besides, though Barrie was my friend and Violet my sister, I didn't know them very well either. To call them complete strangers wasn't much of a stretch, and I had nothing against meeting even more new animals. Still, I worried today would be just as unproductive and frustrating as yesterday. Pushing the negative thoughts out of my mind, I focused instead on the colorful song from my dream, drawing inspiration from it.

"Think of it as learning to hear without your ears," Samuel said as he led me into the hall. *"You must use your heightened senses to make up for the one you lack."*

Samuel introduced me to several new animals on the thirteenth floor. Each one gave me awkward side glances as he did so. I knew they were looking at my flecked eyes, though I could tell they were trying not to. I tried to ignore them; with Samuel beside me, I was sure they'd eventually accept me. At least here, Samuel's magic protected me from the fires that had driven me away from the squirrels, and since my first day here, no other strange things had happened. Besides the dreams, of course.

Reading the expressions of strangers was a far greater challenge than I'd expected, but that was the point. They were all instructed to say a single phrase, and I had to guess what it was.

After several failed attempts, we moved on to a wiry ferret who looked at me with beady eyes. I saw a cocky glint in them. The way he drew his paw back slightly… I felt as though his phrase was not only spoken to me, but directed at me. It was a question, I was sure, but when his brows didn't raise and his head didn't tilt, I knew it had been phrased almost as a statement. Either that, or it wasn't genuine.

Was he mocking me?

"Yes," I replied, hoping I was right. "It's true I cannot hear. But I'm learning to understand speech regardless."

The ferret's brows furrowed, and Samuel shifted on his paws. I'd made a mistake. Both of them met my line of sight, then immediately looked away, as if they were ashamed. Instantly, I knew what the question really had been. I quickly added, "And I have no idea why my eyes look different."

The ferret's mouth turned up in a smirk. He looked to Samuel, who was beaming. The old lynx spoke to me without his voice echoing in my head, and I knew he was proud of me. His eyes were gleaming, and he was standing tall, with his head held high, eyes focused on mine. I realized even though I didn't know exactly which words he'd used, I was still able to determine the general meaning of his phrase. That gave me hope. I'd been so focused on trying to understand exactly what others were saying, I'd blocked myself into a corner. Once I learned to write, I could use that method for specifics.

With that revelation, I was able to broaden my strategy. Instead of trying to make out every word, I focused on *how* someone was speaking, and I gave answers that applied to a broader range of possible prompts.

A fox's eyes darted to my foot, where my little piece of blue fabric had been tied. His eyes were happy and encouraging.

He must have welcomed me to the group.

"Thank you! I'm happy to be here."

A pair of mice subconsciously brushed their paws on their bellies, and their gums moistened with the slightest hint of saliva. That one was tough — perhaps they asked if I like cheese or what my favorite food was. I decided to play it safe with, "I'm sure cheese is your favorite, but I like sweet berries!"

A rabbit's eyes closed for a microsecond longer than a normal blink, along with a head tilt and softer ear posture. I thought for a few moments before it clicked.

He must have asked something about sleep or rest.

"I slept well last night, thanks. What about you?"

I surprised myself and Samuel by quickly picking up on phrases and responding readily. I noticed that animals used minuscule movements in their bodies and faces during speech far more often than I would have thought, had I not been looking for them. I saw the inner meaning of sentences that could've been sarcastic, or that meant something other than what they may have seemed to someone who focused on the surface. I could finally communicate with others, almost normally, and it filled me with joy.

Barrie and I took up writing lessons again now that I had a foundation for communicating beyond "yes" and "no" questions. We branched out to learning general objects, and it was much easier to learn the written words for those. Sometimes Violet joined us, even though she already knew how to use Samuel's written language. I marveled at Samuel's innate understanding when he explained this was backwards from how he normally taught the language. *"I knew it would've been impossible for you to learn to read body language if you were focused on individual words,"* he said in my head one evening, when I was worn out from the day's lessons. *"But you*

needed to figure that out for yourself. Now that you have, I think you'll advance much more quickly."

Samuel was right. I did start picking up on speech more quickly, even surpassing words we were learning in his lessons. When we were still working through the words for various plants, I'd finally improved enough in understanding speech to ask my sister something I'd wanted to know since I'd found her.

"Violet, where are our parents?"

My sister hung her head. "I'd barely learned to fly when mom and dad disappeared," she said, motioning with her wings and toes to help ensure I understood. "They went out to find food one day and never came back. I looked for them, but they were gone."

My heart fell. Not sure what else to do, I rested my head on her shoulder. "I'm sorry you lost so much of your family. I'm here now, though."

"Thanks, Sheer," Violet said when I lifted my head. "They were your family too, though. Do you remember them at all?"

I shook my head. No matter how hard I searched in my memory, I couldn't recall anything about them. It was sad that they were lost, but it was hard to miss someone you never knew. Samuel felt more like family to me than anyone else, even more than Violet. His kindness, knowledge, and wisdom were how I imagined a grandfather would be. I didn't know what I'd do if I lost him, the way Violet had lost our parents.

Between the writing lessons and practice with interpreting facial expressions and body language, I spent time with Samuel's granddaughter, Anna. Though, I strongly doubted she was really his granddaughter. He was much older than any lynx should ever be, and great-great-great-great granddaughter was probably still ten times too few. Regardless of how distantly she was related to my mentor and the guardian of the thirteenth floor, she was just as kind and thoughtful. She barely blinked an eye when he told her I could speak Montin as well as Kisalan.

34

Is she used to strange things like this, since Samuel can practice magic?

I took an interest in how various plants and medicines were used to treat illnesses, and Anna was delighted to teach me. She handed me an entire stack of papers she, her grandmother, and many other ancestors had written over the years of working with animals on the thirteenth floor. I stayed up every evening reading through it, a page or two each night, until the last rays of sunlight faded from the windows. When I got stuck on a word, I took my own piece of charcoal and made a tiny mark next to it. In the morning, I asked Samuel to help explain it. Details like vocabulary were still much too difficult to understand from body language.

"You know, Sheer," Anna said one day when I was halfway through the pile. "Even though not many animals need help in a safe place like this, there is still always someone in need. Especially out there." She pointed her nose to the window. It was a clear day in the late afternoon, but I'd grown so accustomed to the safety of this building, I was afraid to leave it. When I was living with the squirrels, fire had found me wherever I stayed for more than a night. If someone or something was targeting me, would they find me again once I was outside of Samuel's protective wards?

Stop being so ridiculous, I told myself. *We won't be out for nearly that long.*

Anna cocked her head and waved her paw in front of my face. "Sheer, you okay? You spaced out there for a moment."

"Hmm? Yeah! I'd love to help."

The window opened as we approached, and fresh spring air wafted in. It carried scents of flowers and grass mixed with the stinging, acrid smells of the city. I breathed in deeply and sighed. It was wonderful. Anna used the metal staircase beside the building while I flew down beside her. Flying outside in the sunlight felt so much better than flying and hopping around inside the building. We found several individuals and small communities in need of help, including a turtle with an injured foot and a clan of frogs that had all eaten a bad batch of flies.

35

I recounted my adventures to Barrie at dinner that evening, still exhilarated from the fresh air. Then I remembered how this had all started. "Is that how you knew where to go when you were injured?" I asked him. "Anna's expeditions outside the building, I mean."

He nodded. "I'm glad you were able to understand. I don't think I would've lived through the night without your help," he said, gesturing with his wing. "You dressed my wound before Anna did, and you got into the building. Without you, the only animals to find me would've been the ones wanting to eat me." I bowed my head, but he bent down to look into my eyes. "Why did you help me, anyway? You could've left me alone." He clenched his talons. "I'm a predator. If I had been well, I could have — would have — hunted you. But you helped me."

I shrugged. "I know what it feels like to be alone and wounded. And I know what it feels like to be feared. It's not a good feeling."

Barrie stared into my eyes, and I averted my gaze. "I'm not afraid of your eyes," the hawk said, standing tall. "I think your eyes make you special. Plus, they make it easy to pick you out in a crowd." He leaned down and playfully touched his head to mine.

As the days and nights passed, I watched the forest bloom in bright colors, then dim to brown. The first snowfall brought frost and cold, but we were all safe and warm inside. By early spring, I actually enjoyed talking to other animals. The act of speaking itself was still odd, so I kept my own words to a minimum unless I was with my friends. Though I could read the expressions of others, feeling the vibrations in my throat but hearing no accompanying sound was unpleasant and unnatural. As for comprehension, I excelled. I no longer needed Samuel to translate in my head, but his presence was a comforting anchor. He gave me confidence and the assurance that even if I grossly misunderstood someone, he was there to help me.

All the animals under Samuel's guardianship started to feel like one big family, but I still struggled to find my place in it. Even though I'd been accepted as a member of the thirteenth floor, none of the other animals would willingly approach me on their own or think to tell me news about the community; except for my sister, friend,

36

and mentor, of course. The other animals were still afraid of me, just because I looked different from them. At least they didn't know about the fires. I couldn't bring myself to tell Samuel about the experiences I'd had with the squirrels. What if word spread and they kicked me out of the one place where I felt safe? I tried to participate and socialize with the other animals, but though they didn't turn me away, they didn't go out of their way to include me either.

One night in mid-spring, a couple of mourning doves celebrated the hatching of their first chick. Everyone else woke to the shrill yells of excitement and went to congratulate the new parents when the first baby poked a hole in her egg, and watched as she slowly cracked open the shell while the moon rose in the night. All the way through, I stayed asleep on my little perch. It wasn't until the next morning that I heard the news. Violet, Barrie, and Samuel apologized for not coming to get me… they were too caught up in the excitement themselves to think of me.

By the time I arrived to see the little one, the crowds had thinned. The baby was already wearing her own scrap of blue fabric, and the parents wanted some privacy. I was ashamed. How could I miss such a wonderful moment in their lives when we shared a home? Despite the thrill of learning that never seemed to fade, my heart cried desperately for a change from the silence that smothered me during the day. My dreams, sporadic since coming to the thirteenth floor, were my only refuge from the quiet.

VII

A few nights after the hatching of the mourning dove, I had a new dream. Of course, it wouldn't be complete without the presence of the mysterious, pulsing darkness. This time, a sliver of the strange smoke broke off and formed a snake — a fully rendered cobra, not just a fang or trail. Taken aback by the contrast in detail to my previous dreams, it took me a moment to realize the end of her tail morphed into a rat's. She slithered past me, oblivious to my presence. Beyond her, I could see vague forms of dozens of small creatures that reminded me of monkeys. Though I couldn't make out too many details, it seemed they were all perfectly identical. They weren't a part of the darkness itself; rather, the darkness coalesced into dense links around them, chaining them together. The snake watched over them with a cruel eye, clearly in control.

Did she enslave these creatures?

As she passed beyond where I could see, the darkness lost all of its shape, slowly turning into a huge cloud of dust. When it settled, the crow's feather, wolf's claw, and footprints of a sparrow remained in her wake.

What could this mean?

Then I heard the whispering of a breeze, too quiet for me to make out the words. The image shifted, and I was suddenly flying north over the city, faster than a falcon. The wind cut my face and ruffled my feathers while the building I called home vanished behind me; the sun was just barely starting to peek over the horizon. Below me, the city transitioned first into cultivated fields, then vast grasslands. The mountains looming in the distance drew closer and closer, until I was directly above them. A massive rift in the ground cut through them and led off into the distance.

Suddenly, I was no longer flying — I was falling. Spiraling towards a river at the bottom of the ravine. I spread my wings to slow my fall, but it had no effect. I clenched my claws and shut my eyes, bracing for an impact, but it never came. I woke up just before I hit the water. My feathers were ruffled as though I'd actually been plummeting from the sky. I closed my eyes in relief, struggling to regain control of my breathing.

When my heart finally stopped pounding against my ribcage, I opened my eyes to see Violet watching me.

She tilted her head in concern, and I read the gentle creases around her eyes. "Are you okay, Sheer?"

"Yeah," I said, trying to form my voice into what I hoped was a whisper. I didn't want to wake the other sparrows. "Bad dream."

"Do you want to talk about it?"

I thought a moment before I responded. "Yes," I finally decided, "but I think I should tell Samuel. Want to come with me?" Violet's eyes brightened, and she nodded. Together, we slipped out of the sparrow room. Dawn was on the horizon, so I knew Samuel would already be awake.

After I recounted my dream to Samuel, he stared at his paws for a long time before responding. *"This is very strange indeed, Sheer."* He raised his head slightly to look me in the eyes.

It had been a while since Samuel had spoken inside my head, so the echoing voice caught me off guard. *He must believe this is something important.* "Why? What does it mean?"

"Well, I can see that the snake's strength has increased significantly since your last dream, even from the limited scenes you've described," he said. I felt the rumbles of his throat in time to the echo in my head, so I knew Violet was able to hear as well. *"If the vision is true, then she has enslaved at least a dozen of those odd... monkeys, did you call them? I haven't heard any news from my scouts of such a thing yet, but this needs to be stopped before it gets any worse. I think the second part of your dream is exactly what we need. We should follow that path and head for the mountains."*

39

I stepped back. The prophecy Samuel had told me rushed to mind. "She's real? But I don't want to fight. I'm not ready! I'm just a sparrow. How would I defeat a cobra? Especially since I can't hear… it's not like I can expect her to sit still while I try to read her body's expressions. And…"

"For one who complains about how weird it feels to talk, you talk an awful lot when you're anxious, Sheer."

I clapped my beak shut, and heat rose to my face.

"Anyway, it doesn't matter if you're ready or not," the lynx said, standing. *"The snake won't wait for you to be properly prepared, and neither will the others. If the darkness in your dreams signifies evil, as I believe it does, we need to take advantage of what information we can glean from them to stop the evil from spreading. We have a lead, and the time is now."*

"The others… the crow and the wolf?" I remembered the old but menacing crow I'd seen before I arrived at the thirteenth floor, and I shivered. I didn't even want to think about facing a wolf. The claw in my dreams was terrifying enough by itself.

"Yes. I know you don't want to join this fight, Sheer, but your dreams are absolutely key in getting us a step ahead of them. You and I are in a position to keep the knowledge of this evil between us and destroy it before it affects the rest of the world. But focus on the snake, for now. The others have not changed in your dreams beyond their tokens, so I believe she must currently be the greater threat."

"But shouldn't we come up with… an army or something? You don't expect me to fight her all by myself, do you?"

"No army. Not yet. If we try to recruit other animals to our cause before we truly need them, panic could spread, and that has never done anyone any good. Even if that didn't happen, assembling an army would attract too much attention, too soon. There must be a connection between the three creatures in your dreams, so I do not want to risk alerting the other two before we have a chance to defeat the first. No, we should keep this quiet, for the protection of the thirteenth floor. But you will not be alone, Sheer. I'll go with you."

I shook my head, still unwilling to face the danger so suddenly placed before me. "It's not safe for me out there!" I cried without thinking. "Whenever I stay in a place for too long, any place other than here, this mysterious fire just… keeps coming for me. I'm *safe* here. I don't want to go out someplace where the fires could come back." As soon as it was out, I held my breath.

I shouldn't have told him, I shouldn't have told him…

Samuel was quiet for a moment. *"Do you really think that you can be safe here forever, Sheer?"*

"I…"

"If you're indeed the object of this prophecy, I have no doubt that something was targeting you before you came under the protection of the wards of the thirteenth floor. And I have no doubt that whoever is targeting you will find you again someday. When that day comes, you must be ready. You've been incredibly lucky, young sparrow. Don't push your luck. Strength doesn't come from nowhere."

I hung my head in shame but breathed out a sigh of relief at the same time. Samuel hadn't said he'd banish me from the thirteenth floor because of the fires that haunted my past.

"You could stay here where it's safe… until it isn't anymore. Or you could prepare yourself properly to protect yourself when the time comes. That includes eliminating potential threats before they become impossibly dangerous, such as the creatures in your dreams. If we don't take care of the snake now, do you think her acts will never affect you? What about the animals she's enslaved already? Don't they deserve a chance at safety, too?"

I knew what the *right* answer was, but that didn't make it any easier to choose. I couldn't bring myself to look Samuel in the eyes. My body started to shake, and fears raced through my mind.

"Calm your mind, young sparrow. Trust me, and trust in your own strength. Look at what you have accomplished since you arrived here!" The voice in my head silenced, but the vibration of Samuel's voice didn't. I looked up from my feet to watch his expressions.

"You can communicate without your ears," the old lynx continued. "You've made friends, and you've been a huge help to Anna on her expeditions. You're stronger than you think, Sheer, and you can train to be physically stronger on the journey."

He projected his voice into my head again. *"As for your safety, of course I'll take extra precautions. I wish you had told me about this problem before, but that doesn't matter now. It only proves that this evil is real and dangerous. Not just in general, but dangerous to you specifically. Someone must know about the prophecy and want to prevent it from coming true."*

Taking a deep breath, I knew he was right. I was still afraid, but I knew I could trust him. "Can we bring Barrie along with us?"

Violet shifted beside me, and I turned in time to see her speak up. "I want to come, too." She turned to look me in the eyes. "I lost you once, Sheer. I don't want to lose you again."

"Yes, Violet," Samuel said. "Of course. Sheer, if Barrie wants to join us, he may. Friends you can trust are great assets to have close by." Sending his voice to echo in my mind again, Samuel emphasized, *"Don't tell anyone else. We shouldn't alarm the others unless it's necessary. I'll tell Anna. If we don't return in two phases of the moon, she'll tell the others what happened. Until then, I'll ask her to say that we are out giving you more practice for understanding speech."*

"Okay," I relented. "When do we leave?"

"Tonight. Violet, Would you tell Barrie? The two of you should get some rest before we leave."

As Violet left, Samuel spoke to me again. *"Now, to keep you safe. I can place a ward on you, Sheer, like I did on this space. But in order for it to work, I need to know exactly what was happening. Keep no secrets from me."*

I explained what happened when I'd stayed with the squirrels. As I explained how I'd woken up in the flames, how the fire had killed the rabbit, and how each new resting place I found ended up in ashes, I was glad Violet wasn't listening. She already felt terrible for losing me for so long, and I didn't want her to know exactly how difficult my life had been before I found the thirteenth floor.

When I was finished, Samuel frowned. *"You said the fire never spread beyond the tree or burrow?"*

I nodded. "I don't know what it was… it felt like it was only coming after me."

"That is dark sorcery indeed," Samuel said. *"It reminds me of a myth of a terrible vulture made of shadow. In the stories, it uses fire as its weapon to destroy its prey. But that's only a tale, and I've never seen it nor heard reliable counts of its existence. I don't know what could really be happening here. I think it's safe to say, though, that you were definitely being targeted. I'll place a protective ward on you that should prevent this. There are other ways to find a creature besides this sorcery, so you won't be able to hide from them forever. Still, it should give you some time to prepare and grow stronger."*

Samuel's voice left my mind, and his words shifted to a much deeper rumbling. I stood perfectly still while he chanted. He paused to breathe a few times but otherwise barely wavered. His eyes pinched shut as he concentrated for what felt like an hour. When he finished, all of his muscles shook from exhaustion.

"I don't feel any different." I stretched my wings and legs.

"Well, you aren't supposed to feel anything." Weariness leaked into the voice resounding in my head. *"We'll just have to trust that it worked. If anything happens, I'll be with you, and I will do all I can to keep you safe while we figure out a different solution. Now, get some rest. When it's time to leave, I'll come get you."*

VIII

Samuel, Barrie, Violet and I left in the dead of night, when the city was completely still. For the first time since arriving on the thirteenth floor, I was leaving it for a reason other than helping Anna provide medical assistance to those in need. Despite my trust in my mentor, I worried about the fires.

Will Samuel's wards on me protect me the same way as the building has so far?

We headed to the forest and snuck around the outskirts on our way towards the southern fields to avoid being spotted by the humans. It wasn't the most efficient route, but we were able to cross through the residential areas by the time the city gleamed with the glimpse of dawn. We were much safer in the large fields, but we still had to be careful to avoid the humans and their machines.

During the day, Barrie flew high above us as a lookout. He pretended to search for prey even when he was full, circling slowly in the air. The rest of us kept under the cover of the tallest crops; Violet and I rode on Samuel's back, since we could move more swiftly that way. We slept next to hay bales at night.

In the evenings, after the humans left their fields and before the nocturnal hunters came out of their dens, we had a few hours to rest and train. Samuel instructed all three of us on proper fighting techniques. We scuffled on the ground, dipped and dodged between stalks, and practiced diving motions. Between Barrie's perspective, Samuel's sense of hearing, and my uncommonly accurate sense of vibrations, we had a full range of senses to steer away from humans and predators. The distant mountains grew closer every day.

Now that we were on the move, I started having dreams again. Each night was the same: the nightmare began with the dark cloud and snake, and ended right before I hit the water after plummeting from the sky. The day finally came when we walked out of the last human field and into wild, uncultivated grasslands. That time, my dream was different.

Though it started out with the same pulsating shroud, that was where the similarities ended. The snake that emerged was in such incredible detail, I could make out the glint on her individual scales, the folds of her hood, and the fork in her tongue. She not only had a rat's tail at the end of her body, but whiskers on her face as well. And this time, she saw me.

The cobra hissed in my direction, flaring her hood. Then she settled, looking off into the distance. She turned and slithered away, and as she did so, the smoke behind her materialized into a strange blue creature, like a tiny monkey. There was only one this time, but I could clearly see all of its details — the aquamarine fur, the chains of darkness so dense they looked like writhing metal.

When the creature had passed, out of the smoke materialized another: this time, a sparrow. She was a pale brown, and still barely a fledgling. The young sparrow followed the rat-snake and tiny blue monkey as if in a trance. She was hopping instead of flying — perhaps she didn't know how. The way she was walking was unnatural, mimicking the snake's movements as the cobra swayed left and right. When she briefly faced me, her expression was blank and her eyes were glazed over. Then they all disappeared into the smoke and the crow's feather drifted down from the sky, mangled and torn. The wolf's claw appeared beside it when I drew closer. It was so shiny, for a moment I thought I could see a part of my speckled eye in its surface.

I opened my eyes. I felt strangely calm despite what I'd just seen. I hadn't woken up panting or feeling like I was falling, and that was a pleasant change. It was still dark, so I waited until the sun's rays peeked over the horizon and Samuel stretched awake before telling him about my dream.

"Perhaps the details of the cobra and the monkey creature are more refined," he said with a yawn, *"because we are getting closer. The sparrow is new, but I'm not sure what to make of it. Do you think you can make the dreams come to you even when you aren't sleeping? Perhaps we can use the clarity to track the snake."*

I hadn't thought of that. Why would I want to subject myself to the nightmares, even when I was awake? But if we needed to find her, and we could use the detail in my dream to determine whether we were going the right direction, maybe it was necessary. "How would I do that?" I asked as I settled onto his back.

"Try closing your eyes and clearing your mind, as if you were sleeping," Samuel said. I was grateful that he considered my inability to read his expressions from behind him and projected his words into my mind.

"Okay, I'll try that."

Clearing my mind was a challenge. With my eyes closed, my other senses kicked into an even higher gear. I could feel Samuel's slightest movements. The gentle breeze shifted direction from time to time, changing the intensity and identity of scents around me. The crisp grass, sweet flowers, and earthy ground delivered wafts of smells. The flowering grass made me salivate, and I could taste remnants of juice from the berries I'd eaten at dawn. Though I was in the middle of Samuel's back, I could feel the vibrations of his throat as he spoke softly with Violet to pass the time. I quickly learned that trying to ignore the distractions from my three active senses was fruitless. Instead, I acknowledged each scent that tingled my nostrils, each breeze that ruffled my feathers. When I opened my thoughts to exploration, I was surprised to find how easy it was not to dwell on them. Soon, I had entered something like a trance. I was fully awake, but each thought was only briefly acknowledged before it was lost in the flow. I didn't chase the thoughts; I just let them go. That was when the dream came.

I opened my eyes to find myself inside an enormous, hollow tree. No wind was rustling the leaves, but I could hear the trickling of water from somewhere. It was dark, but there was an eerie ambient glow. I could see no source for this light and determined it must be a

46

function of the vision itself. Regardless, it allowed me to see the cobra in front of me, surrounded by the mysterious smoke. The young sparrow's eyes were glazed over as she stood stiffly beside the snake. The tiny monkey slave was nowhere to be seen. Between me and the two creatures was a large bowl, with an unpleasant scent. The snake mixed in an herb I'd never seen before. A bat fluttered into the space, and the cobra reacted. She spit her venom at him, causing him to fall to the ground. She slithered over, then mercilessly stripped a wing and tossed it into the pot.

Shaking with disgust, I tried to pull myself out of the dream, but the vision suddenly shifted. The only thing that remained was the ever-present shroud of darkness. Now I was looking at the precipice of a mountain, upon which stood two wolves, their pack behind them. The larger of the two was standing closer to the edge, looking out into the distance. The smaller one had dark fur, though not quite black, and sported a scar. It stretched over the left side of his face, originating at the base of his ear before passing through his eye and running down his muzzle. He was staring intently at the larger wolf. It was this smaller wolf, not the larger one, that was wrapped in the mysterious smoke. Before I could discern his intentions, the image cleared and I was again on Samuel's back. I sensed we'd stopped, and I opened my eyes.

Before us, the earth seemed to split in two. It was the ravine from the dream that started us on this journey. Samuel stood with one paw on the left side of a crack, and one to the right. Beyond where he stood, the crack widened until it was so vast, no creature could have jumped over it. The split itself twisted and turned, and when it vanished over the horizon, it seemed to end further to the right than where we currently were. To the left of it, the way onward followed the canyon's edge and sharp turns. Rocky hills and mountains bordered the ravine, forcing the path to meander through them. To the right, the path seemed gentle enough, an endless sea of grass like the one behind us.

I flew over to where the ravine was wider and saw that the drop was too steep for Samuel to climb down. The land we stood on jutted out over the trench like a natural bridge. Far below us, a stream trickled into the bottom of the crevice. It gained speed and momentum as it continued into the distance, fed by tributaries and brooks that made their way through a labyrinth of holes in the rocks, or steep waterfalls from distant mountain snowmelt. I knew we'd have to choose a side path. Even though Violet, Barrie, and I could fly, we couldn't leave Samuel stranded on the wrong side.

"In your dream, you flew over the mountains, correct?" the lynx said, voicing the fear deep inside me. The path to the right looked so much safer and could provide all of us with food.

"Yes, but…"

"That is the surest sign we have. We should not lose faith in your dream's direction yet." Without a further word, Samuel lifted his paw and started down the path to the left, which wound in and out of the mountains.

IX

"I managed to have a dream on purpose," I told Samuel as we left the point at which the ravine began. "Or a vision, I guess. What would you call it?"

"That's great, Sheer! I'd probably call it a vision."

"A vision, then," I agreed, recounting everything that had happened. When I'd finished explaining, I paused. "Do you think we somehow triggered the wolf? It's just... I've never seen the entire wolf before. Do you think someone is still targeting me despite your magic, and sending the wolves after us?"

Samuel thought for a moment. *"I don't think so. In your vision, the wolves didn't see or acknowledge you, right?"*

"That's true. The darker one was only looking at the larger one."

"I think we are just close to them. Let's hope they are only passing by. As for the part where you did see the snake, I think it just confirms that she's gaining strength, and that we are drawing closer." We continued on, though I noticed Samuel picked up his pace.

Over the next few days, we traveled with no incident, though the sky became laden with dark clouds. It hadn't rained since we'd set out to find the snake, but it was foolish to think we could make it all the way there without a storm.

When the first crash of thunder warned us of the coming downfall, we sought shelter in a mountain cave. Even if I hadn't been afraid of the water, it was too difficult to see or fly outside, and the path was muddied and slick. The rain didn't let up for three days, and we were hungry. There were scattered grass seeds and insects for me and Violet, and mice for Barrie and Samuel, but not enough for any of us to be fully satisfied.

To pass the time, I tried to conjure more visions of the snake, to no avail. Every time I managed to clear my mind and receive a vision, all I saw was the pack of wolves, the scarred one's detail increasing gradually each time. This scared me, and I could tell from the others' faces that it frightened them, too. I stopped telling them what I saw, but they knew.

We could only practice combat so much before becoming physically exhausted, and I could say the same about my attempts to see the snake. When we'd tired ourselves out, Samuel told us stories of his time with the humans. His echoed thoughts in my mind allowed me to drift away, not forced to focus on understanding his words. Besides, his tales were full of quirks and nuances I was glad to be able to hear. He told us how his human had found him and rescued him from poachers, and how they'd worked together to destroy a man possessed by evil spirits. While Violet and I listened, rapt, to his every word, he explained how the thirteenth floor had come to be.

When it finally stopped raining, moving on was bittersweet. We needed to continue onward towards the snake and find fresher sources of food, but I'd enjoyed listening to Samuel's stories. As Violet and I rode on Samuel's back and he carefully plodded along the muddy path, I kept conjuring visions. I was able to draw upon them much faster now. Sometimes the vision came when I wasn't even trying; I'd just blink and find myself in the middle of a vision. One moment I'd be traveling with my friends, and the next I'd see the darkness, hear sounds, and it would seem like I'd been transported into a completely different place. But I was getting good at dismissing the visions, too. All it took was a shake of my head, and I'd be on Samuel's back again.

I hoped the wolves would pass by and allow the snake to return, but the opposite was true. If the path took us farther into the mountains, the image of the wolves came more into focus. If the path took us up to the very edge of the ravine, the wolves came more into focus. I could tell the larger wolf was one of the leaders, and the younger one was likely his son. Beyond that, I knew without a doubt they were getting closer.

We'd been traveling alongside the ravine for a particularly long stretch when another accidental vision came. This time, though, I saw the wolves from a distance, rather than the close-up perspective I'd grown accustomed to. I blinked, trying to understand why I felt something else was different. I swiveled my head, trying to pinpoint what it was — and then I realized. The darkness, and the temporary ability to hear, were both missing.

Without those…

"Barrie?" I was suddenly hyper-aware of the silence of my voice in the real world. "What do you see on the cliff there, behind us?" He looked, then glanced down at me from his lookout point, his eyes wide with fear. This was no vision. The wolves were real.

I closed my eyes and cleared my mind, hoping to see whether they'd spotted us. Immediately, I saw the murky smoke, wrapped around the young, dark wolf… who looked straight into my eyes. He turned and gave his father a terrible glare, and the two of them sprung forward. Pulling myself out of the vision, I saw that the wolves were now on the move. "Run, Samuel!" I shouted. "Run! The wolves are coming!"

Violet dove to cling to Samuel's back beside me as he launched forward, picking up speed. Barrie flew over the ravine beside us. We sped down the crooked path, Samuel kicking rocks into the canyon. As we drew to a point where the road wound again into the hills, Samuel skidded to a stop. Another wolf pack was bearing down on us from that direction. I could feel the vibration from their paws hitting the ground as they made towards us at full speed. The two packs joined edges, then slowed down and crept towards us. We were trapped. In front and to our left were angry wolves. To the right, an outcropping of the mountain range blocked the way. Behind us was the steep ravine. Samuel's paw slipped on the edge, but he regained his footing. I could almost see the thoughts spinning through his mind. He shuddered.

"Samuel…"

Before I could finish my thought, Samuel took a deep breath, then launched himself off the edge, taking me and my sister with him. Out of shock, we both let go. The scarred wolf pounced forward and managed to snag Samuel's fur, leaving a long gash on the lynx's hind leg, but it was too late. The wolf had to stop to balance himself, his prey lost.

Violet, Barrie, and I dove to follow Samuel as if we were of one mind. We grabbed the skin at the scruff of his neck and pumped our wings as hard as we could in a desperate attempt to slow his falling. He crashed into a wispy tree and grasped at its branches, but it ripped from the canyon wall. I lost my hold on Samuel right before he hit the water, my fear of the substance temporarily drowning out the fear of losing my mentor. He cried out in pain; the impact with the water stripped patches of fur off his legs and belly. I had to dip and dive to catch up with the other three as they were swept away in the current. Samuel's head drooped, and Barrie struggled to keep it above the water. Gasping, the three of us scanned the banks for a way out. When I looked ahead, my heart dropped. The water ended in a clean line. A waterfall. Beyond it was more of the ravine.

How did the rest of the ravine form if the river plummets in the middle? I wondered, but had no time to dwell on it.

"Come on, Samuel, wake up!" I shouted, hoping my words carried over the sound of the water. "You have to swim!"

Samuel kicked, slowly at first, then with more vigor, fighting his fatigue with incredible willpower. Violet, Barrie, and I refused to leave his side. We pumped our wings, attempting to slow his speed down the river while he tried to move sideways. But now, the current was too strong. I could feel the shift in Samuel's shoulders when his rear claws grazed the bottom, but he couldn't get a grip. It wasn't enough, and we all toppled over the edge. As we did this, I felt a mixture of terror and awe. The waterfall appeared to be endless. It went down and down into a hole in the ground, until it disappeared into a cloud of billowing steam. Before any of us could react, the hole swallowed us up, and we plunged into darkness.

X

We fell for an incredibly long time in the pitch blackness beside the waterfall. It was terribly cold, and we were all soaking wet from the spray. Every new droplet of water that touched me caused me to shiver in fear.

"Are you okay, Samuel?" I asked. When I heard no response, I considered the vibrations of the air from the powerful waterfall, and shouted instead. "Samuel! Are you okay?"

"Yes…" he responded. *"If you ignore being soaked to the bone and uncontrollably falling to who knows where."*

"Violet? Barrie?" I strained my eyes in the darkness, but I couldn't see anything.

"They are here, too," Samuel's voice echoed in my mind. Though I breathed a sigh of relief, I felt incredibly lonely, unable to see my companions. My mentor, my sister, my friend. I was glad to know they were here, but worried I might never get to see them again.

Then it happened. The darkness gave way to light, and suddenly we were surrounded by a world of bright colors… in what seemed to be a large underground cave. The waterfall impossibly rounded and slowed, and we rode gently into a calm pool at the bottom.

There must be magic here.

Exhausted from our long plunge, we dragged ourselves out to dry. Everyone looked fine despite the ordeal, though dripping wet and gasping for breath. "It's good to be able to see you guys again," I said to Violet and Barrie.

My sister and best friend merely nodded in response, but I knew what they meant. "Good to see you too, Sheer."

53

For a moment, we recovered in stunned silence. The walls of the cave were lined with glowing plants that produced enough light to make it seem like a cloudy day on the surface. The waterfall that defied physics ended in a gentle, bubbling brook, which circled around the entire perimeter of the space. It stayed at the same level, despite constantly being fed with more raging water. We were surrounded by foliage of all imaginable colors and shapes. Some plants had huge, leathery, yellow leaves behind which Samuel could easily have concealed himself; others had hundreds of tiny, spiky, red ones barely the size of a beetle. Dozens of species of fruit I'd never seen before hung heavy on each and every bush and tree. And in the middle of all of this was an enormous tree, stretching taller than the building with the thirteenth floor, all the way to the roof of the cave.

"Have you ever seen anything like this?" I asked Samuel.

He shook his head. "I've seen magic, Sheer, but nothing like this. Keep your wits about you. I don't like it." Then he suddenly ducked low to the ground. *"Hush,"* he said, projecting his words into my mind since I couldn't read his expression anymore. *"Something's coming."*

I kept my body still and stared out above the grass. Then I saw what Samuel had heard. In the distance, a line of strange blue monkeys, just like those in my visions, were approaching. They moved in an odd march, their footsteps perfectly in sync. We watched them continue on their way, passing before us from the right, and I thought perhaps they hadn't seen us. But just as they'd made their way off to our left, they stopped.

One monkey, the one in the front, split off from the group and sniffed the air. She drew closer to us, and I could tell she was about three times my size. Stopping short, she stared directly at Samuel, then pointed at him and called to the troop. The way she spoke was unfamiliar and rigid, and I couldn't understand exactly what she'd said. As all of them turned in unison to look in our direction, my heart pounded against my chest. We'd been spotted.

Since hiding did us no good anymore, Samuel rose up and warily approached the creature. She was clearly surprised by his size and stumbled backwards. I couldn't see what he was saying from my perspective, but I supposed he must have asked to see the leader of this strange place. I shivered.

What if the snake is here?

The monkey bent to the side, spotting me behind the lynx, then bent the other way to look at Violet and Barrie on his other side. When our eyes met, I felt as though I somehow knew this creature. She looked back at Samuel, then nodded and motioned for him to follow her. Without any apparent command, the rest of the monkeys immediately turned and continued off in the same direction they'd been traveling before.

Samuel beckoned for the rest of us to follow the blue monkey. She led us to the central tree, up a spiral staircase on the outer side that seemed to be a part of the bark itself. She took us to the very top. The tree was so huge, even the highest branches were large enough for Samuel to straddle comfortably. After seating us on a branch, she left. Several minutes later, she returned, panting from the second climb, with a large bark slab piled with a variety of fruit. Each one was enticing, colorful, and split in half, ready to eat.

Realizing how hungry I was, I picked an oblong one with a hole in the center. It was covered in spikes, with soft yellow flesh on the inside. I was about to take a bite when Samuel's voice echoed in my head. *"No, Sheer!"* he barked. *"We don't know what this fruit is. We shouldn't trust it. Let's just wait and see whether we can meet with the leader of this place. I want to get to the bottom of all of this."*

I chuckled, since we seemed to be quite literally at the bottom of the world, then sat back to wait. As I tried to think of something to do to distract me from my aching stomach, I remembered that I'd been unable to see the cobra in my visions due to the presence of the wolves. Now that we were far away from the wolves, maybe I had a better chance. I closed my eyes, finally willing to have the vision I'd been waiting for. To my surprise, it came immediately and was more vivid than any I'd ever had before.

I saw the snake, as clearly as if she were right in front of me, surrounded by the same mysterious smoke. I could see each of her individual scales, every flicker of her tongue, every twitch of her eyes and tail. The sparrow beside her was also in full detail. Her eyes were clouded over, and as she stood, her body slowly wavered from side to side. I distinctly heard the soft rustling as the snake's scaly body shifted against the ground, and I shivered. It felt unnatural to hear something so precisely.

The snake was still in the hollowed tree, which I'd seen before, but suddenly seemed *too* familiar. A tiny blue monkey came into the space, trembling in the presence of the snake. He bowed deeply, but she coiled quickly in front of him, flaring her hood and casting him in shadow.

"What are you doing here, ssslave?"

"Lady Nyoka," he said, trembling. His voice was peculiar, a much higher pitch than I would have expected from a mammal, even a small one. *Then again, my only frame of reference is Samuel.* I dismissed my thoughts and focused on the vision as the monkey creature continued. "I'm sorry to intrude. There are some strange visitors from the Upper World here. We have given them the traditional welcome and, upon request of the lynx, promised your presence. One seems different from the rest. His eyes are odd."

The cobra settled back, thinking. Then she responded, flicking her tongue as she spoke. "Thank you, Mathiasss. Thisss isss indeed very interesssting. You are disssmissssed."

"Thank you, Lady Nyoka." The creature then left with another solemn bow.

"Come, my apprenticcce," hissed Nyoka, turning to the sparrow. "We have sssome visitorsss to greet."

"Yes, Mother." Even though it was only two words, the sparrow's voice was so sweet and beautiful, I wished I could hear more. Before I had the chance, my vision ended.

Back in the real world again and surrounded by silence, I was stunned at what I'd witnessed. I shook my head to clear it and spun to face my companions. "The snake… Nyoka. She's here! And the sparrow seems to think Nyoka is her mother."

When I turned back around, Nyoka was already slithering up the wooden staircase. Her so-called apprentice wasn't far behind, oddly mimicking the side-to-side slithering motion. As Nyoka's head crested the top of the stairs and she slithered onto the large branch where we rested, everyone stood at rapt attention. Violet hid behind Barrie, and Samuel widened his stance defensively.

When the snake spoke, her words and body language were so different from other animals I'd met, it was difficult to understand her. I'd learned a little about her body motions from this last vision, but I could still barely guess what she was saying: "Welcome to my world."

Turning at the gentle rumbling of Samuel's voice, I watched him speak a word of greeting. He was careful to appear friendly, though I knew he was apprehensive. I wondered whether Nyoka was speaking Kisalan or Montin. Samuel hadn't implied he knew any other languages, but I didn't think either would be the native language of a snake. Perhaps she'd also learned to speak a second language? *That would make sense,* I realized, *since all of her slaves are monkeys, and because her apprentice is a sparrow. She probably speaks Kisalan.* I glanced over to Violet and Barrie; they didn't seem to be having any trouble understanding her. *Definitely Kisalan.*

When I turned back to Nyoka, she flared her hood in defense. Samuel must have spoken her name, which she hadn't provided. "That doesn't matter," Samuel replied to her comment, dropping nearly all pretense of friendliness and gesturing instead to the blue monkey behind us, and to the dozens walking around below. "You have surrounded yourself with helpless slaves that do not belong here. Where did they come from?"

I tried to pay attention to their conversation, but I was suddenly overcome with another vision. I tried to push it away, but it was too strong. When I submitted to it, I was surprised to be in the same place. Everything was moving in slow motion. I saw Nyoka, surrounded by the murky darkness that was pulsing with strength. She had the rat's tail and whiskers again. Her stance threatened

Samuel, and the strange smoke around her tried without success to wrap itself around him. I saw my sister, my friend, and the tiny blue monkey. As I watched, the latter began to transform. Her skin peeled off her, revealing a different body underneath. First a beak, then feathers, then wings, then slender feet. She'd taken on the form of a sparrow that strongly resembled an older version of my sister. Time slowed even further, and I could feel my heart's individual beats even as I heard her name whispered by a sudden breeze.

Reika. Mother.

XI

The vision faded. Nyoka lost the rat's whiskers and tail, though I knew they were merely hidden; Reika was once more a tiny blue monkey slave. I wanted to save her from this, but I didn't know how. She'd been lost for so long, she clearly didn't recognize me or Violet. Had she lost her memory, like I had? Or was it suppressed? Completely forgetting I was in the presence of an enemy, I called out to her.

"Reika?"

My enslaved mother, Nyoka, and my friends all turned to face me. Violet's eyes widened, recognizing the name, and she spun her head from side to side, seeking our mother. The cobra coiled tightly in fear and anger, and the others' eyes read curiosity and confusion. None of them knew who I was speaking to — my mother didn't recognize her own name. My heart clenched in my chest. I knew how that felt.

"Reika," I repeated, locking eyes with her enchanted form. "Mother?"

Suddenly, my mother's body transformed, just like it had in my vision. Fur turned to feathers, muzzle to beak, arms to wings. In a matter of moments, she was her true sparrow self, free from bondage. She shook her head and stared at her surroundings, then at her wings, her toes. She glanced at me and Violet, her eyes flashing with joy before settling on Nyoka and shifting to fear.

I turned back in time to see Nyoka rise up swiftly, fanning her hood to its fullest and preparing to strike. She moved so quickly that her "apprentice," who was standing immediately behind her, startled and began to fall from the large branch where we were all perched. The helpless sparrow barely even flapped her wings to save herself. Nyoka halted, now distracted. I remembered that in my visions, the

59

young sparrow had never flown — and now she never would. She was falling to her death.

Before anyone could react, Samuel leapt from the branch, plummeting after the sparrow.

"No!" I shouted, but it was too late.

Because Samuel had jumped after the sparrow so quickly, he was able to catch up with her in mid-air. Deftly maneuvering despite his age, he stretched his neck and snatched her in his mouth just before hitting the ground. His front legs touched down first, and he crumpled upon impact.

"No!" I shouted again, as if I could rewind time. I flew down to where he'd landed. The dirt was stained red, but from the left side, he seemed uninjured. "Samuel! Are you okay?"

The ground vibrated with his groan. Samuel opened his jaw and coughed. The sparrow tumbled out, shaking her feathers. She stood, dazed, looking from side to side.

"Samuel?" I repeated, pushing against his muzzle with the side of my beak.

"I need to get to the river," he finally responded. He spoke through gritted teeth, and I was glad he could echo his words inside my head. Without that, I wouldn't have been able to understand anything other than that he was speaking — though that was certainly a good sign. The old lynx grimaced as he pushed himself up, then yelped and collapsed again. *"I need to wash the wound,"* Samuel said, trying to stand again. I flew to his right side, wishing I was strong enough to help. He trembled as he rose, revealing his broken front limb. Part of his bone was sticking through his skin, and his fur was clotted with blood. Horrified, I recoiled from the sight. I closed my eyes and nearly retched.

Suddenly, the air smelled different. A breeze wafted past, crisp and clean. I opened my eyes and gaped. Samuel was gone. So were my friends, the tree, and all the strange foliage. I spun around, taking in my surroundings.

A vision? Not now!

I tried to shake myself from it, but nothing happened. I let out a shout, but no sound fell on my ears. This wasn't a vision. This was real… but how?

I was standing atop a massive pile of rocks. On my left stretched a long lake, waves sloshing at my feet. On my right, a dry ravine wound through the landscape until it disappeared into the horizon. I looked up, and my heart stopped. Those were the mountains we'd passed through before falling down the waterfall. I could even see the precipice where we'd been cornered by the wolves. My eyes widened in realization. This wasn't a lake; this was the river. There must have been a landslide that collapsed into the ravine, forming a dam.

But if this was the river and the precipice was to my left, then where was the waterfall? I launched into the air and flew south for a while, but I couldn't see the hole anywhere. It had been buried by the landslide.

No! I thought. *How will I get back to them now?*

Pushed to haste when I remembered Samuel's state, I picked away at the pile. I clutched clods of dirt, pebbles, and stones in my claws and flew them to the side. After minutes of frantic motion, I was exhausted. Somehow, the pile looked even larger than it had when I started.

I landed back on the rocks, panting and trying to think of another way. How had I gotten here, above ground? None of my dreams or visions had physically transported me, but this hadn't been a vision at all. Then everything clicked. Memories flashed through my mind, each one faster than the last. The tree branch that had nearly fallen on the poor rabbit back when I lived with the squirrels. The levitating stones. The piles of papers in Samuel's room that had moved without any wind… and once before, I'd transported myself, too.

Samuel had taught me how to control my visions and issue them upon command. Could I put the same energy into these rocks and tear apart the landslide that plugged the hole for the waterfall? It was a massive task, but I had to try to control my elusive ability.

I stared at a small white pebble in front of me, memorizing its shape, hairline crack, smudge of gray. When I couldn't look anymore, I tried to recreate the feeling that had driven me here. Transporting myself above the waterfall was the most powerful thing I'd accidentally done so far, and I needed that power again. I knew what had caused it: the shock of seeing my mentor nearly die, then suffer terrible pain, was far stronger than any fear of water or thunderstorms could ever be.

Grimacing, I forced myself to picture the bone sticking out of Samuel's leg. I thought about how he'd injured himself trying to save someone associated with the enemy. How he could be bleeding to death from that terrible wound, and how I could do nothing to help. I thought about how much I wanted to help him, how much I needed him to survive. I thought about how I needed these rocks to move if I was ever going to see him again. I thought about my sister and friend, and my newfound mother, so suddenly lost again.

Something small nudged my right foot. I peeked open my eyes.

Yes!

The tiny rock had moved. I didn't know exactly how I'd done it, but I'd moved it with my mind. With that success, I redoubled my efforts. I didn't need to move the rocks much, just enough to destabilize the dam. I just needed to clear a way for the water to push through and fall down the hole again.

Not wanting to lose my focus, I closed my eyes and concentrated. I didn't open them for hours, but I felt an occasional shift beneath me. When the light behind my eyelids had dimmed and my head was pounding from strain, I risked another glance.

Very little had changed, and at first I was disappointed. Then I saw the pile I'd made. To the right of the original landslide was a small cluster of rocks the size of a berry bush. Though it wasn't much, I puffed up with pride. *I* had done that. With my *mind*. I took a quick sip of water, ate as many berries from the grassland side of the ravine as I could stuff in my stomach, then settled down on a branch protruding from the cliff. There was no more time to take breaks or rest — my friends needed me.

This time, I shifted my target and broadened my focus. Rather than memorizing pebbles, I imagined the bottom of the landslide crumbling apart and fixated on that image. I pushed past the blossoming pain in my head, using it as fuel.

My friends are in more pain than me. They are in danger, and I need to help them.

The air shifted to a pleasant cool as the night progressed, but I disregarded the temptation of sleep. Acknowledging every distraction and dismissing it like Samuel had taught me for conjuring a vision, I entered a sort of trance. Time seemed to fly by without a care. The sun rose, turning my eyelids red, but I still didn't open them. It fell, and rose, and began to dim again. I felt hungry, thirsty, and exhausted. My concentration faltered when I nearly fell off the branch from weakness. Just as I opened my eyes to catch myself from falling, something caught my eye.

Blinking away drowsiness, I was sure I was imagining the tiny vortex on the water's surface. I shook my head and stared at it, then at the wall of dirt and rocks the landslide had created. It still looked massive, but I could see crumbled piles of rocks at the bottom from my work. A small stream of water trickled through the blockade.

Is that all?

My heart faltered, and my head bobbed again. I couldn't keep this up much longer. Then I felt the vibrations. At first I thought it was my stomach, but when the branch below me began to shake, I stretched my wings and shot into the air. I watched in amazement as the entire mass of rocks shifted, spraying water over the top. With a massive rumble, it heaved and collapsed. Rocks and dirt cascaded to either side, then the center of the mound began to cave inward. The landslide crumbled and fell. The water poured in as soon as there was room, accelerating the collapse. The waterfall was back.

XII

When the chaos had settled and water was flowing freely, I knew it was time. I dove straight down into the hole, avoiding splashes from the water, which still sent shivers of fear through me.

Despite my fear, I was so exhausted that I nearly fell unconscious on the way down, and was startled awake by the light at the bottom. When the water leveled out, I was shocked to see how much the lack of water had affected the world below, after just a couple of days. I spotted my mentor and friends crawling towards the water. All across the cracked riverbanks, dozens of small blue monkeys, just like the form my mother had been imprisoned in, were doing the same. Samuel's leg was red and swollen, and he looked pale, but he was alive.

His eyes brightened when he saw me. He stepped forward to speak but stumbled and grimaced in pain. He didn't need to speak, though, nor project his voice into my mind. The way his eyes bored into my soul said more than words could ever have expressed. Even though I hadn't mentioned anything, he must have seen the change in me.

You're ready. You know what you need to do.

We'd come here for one reason, and especially now that Samuel had been hurt, our mission had been delayed long enough. When I looked around, though, Nyoka and her "apprentice" were nowhere to be found. I breathed a sigh of relief.

Despite what Samuel thinks, I'm not quite ready yet.

Before I could help anyone, I needed to take care of myself. I couldn't be much help if I collapsed from exhaustion. Surely, if the snake lived down here, there was something safe to eat. The trees were mostly barren, but after searching thoroughly, I found a brown bush with a single withered nut left. It was a perfectly consistent blue, with a hard outer shell. Starving and desperate to eat, I reached for it but then drew back my beak. Samuel had warned against eating anything in this world.

I took a step back and saw a few beetles crawling on the bush, eager for the same fruit I'd almost picked. New fruit was forming before my eyes, and beetles continued to swarm. I recognized their patterns from the true Earth above and knew they were safe for me to eat, even if the fruit might not be. I snatched as many as I could before they touched the fruit and gobbled them up. Full of renewed energy, I flew back to the river for a drink, then looked around me. It seemed the greatest need was for water.

Using large, stiff leaves, I brought water from the river to slaves too weak to crawl to it. Already, the trees and grass seemed to be stretching with joy, drinking water through their roots. Fruit was sprouting on the bushes and trees at an amazing rate, and leaves that had been shriveled and dry were now crisp and green. I marveled at the different rules that seemed to govern this world. While I was looking around, I spotted Nyoka's apprentice wandering among the bushes. I couldn't see the cobra anywhere, so I moved over to help the sparrow. Samuel had risked his life to save her, so she must be worth taking care of.

I led the sparrow to another blue nut bush near the base of the tree, which was already nearly bursting with fruit and beetles, and spiders who were desperately weaving webs all over the bush to catch the influx of insects. She ate while I kept watch, hoping Nyoka would reveal herself. I'd rescued my mother, but hundreds of other slaves still needed to be freed. I knew that to rescue everyone, I'd first have to face the snake herself.

Nyoka did appear, slithering out of the roots of the tree. She saw me and moved towards me, more slowly than usual. Her tail twitched strangely, and for a moment I saw the whiskers and tail, and the murky dark smoke that permeated all of my dreams and visions. The image was gone in an instant, but I knew now was a good time to strike.

I looked around for something, anything, to work with. My claws and beak alone wouldn't be enough to defeat her; she'd kill me with her venom. I didn't want to resort to my newfound power. It had helped me get here, but it was slow, and the potential for strength scared me. I'd nearly killed the rabbit with the falling branch... *though,* I thought miserably, *he didn't make it anyway, in the end.* Shaking the image from my mind, I went back to searching for a weapon. I spotted a tree that held large, spiky fruit. *Perfect.* I flew over to it as Nyoka approached me, the young sparrow following along behind her.

I grabbed the fruit and tugged, but it was stuck! Its stem was too strong. I pulled with all my might as Nyoka wound herself around the tree in my pursuit, leaving her apprentice on the ground. The fruit finally came loose, but its release shook the tree. Nyoka slipped from where she clung to the trunk, and the fruit flung out of my claws. Instead of hitting the snake as I'd intended, it fell onto the sparrow and burst open. Orange goo oozed out all over her brown feathers.

Nyoka retreated back to the roots beneath the massive central tree. I flew down to the sparrow, apologizing as I picked pieces of fruit off her head, but I stopped when I saw she was unconscious. I called Violet and my mother to help. Barrie would've scared her, though he would have meant well, and Samuel was injured. Together, we wiped off as much of the sticky goo as we could while she came to.

The sparrow shifted, then blinked. Her eyes weren't clouded anymore, and the lost expression on her face was all too familiar. "Who are you? Where am I?" She looked into my eyes for answers. I understood her fear upon waking in a strange place; I'd embarked into the unknown only about a year ago, but it felt like so much longer.

"Hi. I'm Sheer," I said. I wanted to explain how I knew how she felt, how I'd been through the same thing, but I found there was no need. When I looked into her eyes, it seemed she already knew what I would say, before any words left my beak.

"It's all right now, dear," Reika said. "What is your name?" My mother's body language brought back so many memories... memories from when I'd known nothing about myself. I realized I still didn't know much about my past, besides the storm that had started it all. At least now I had a sister and mother.

The sparrow closed her eyes. "It's been so long," she replied. "It's hard for me to remember." After a moment, she opened her eyes and said a single word, but it wasn't enough for me to interpret from her expression or body language. Confused, I looked to Violet.

My sister hopped forward and used her beak to scrape symbols in the dirt. *Amery.* It was a beautiful name.

"Amery," I repeated.

Her eyes shimmered with joy. "Yes! That's my name. The snake…" Her joy vanished, replaced by fear. "Oh, the snake!" She twisted her head around frantically.

"Hush now," my mother cooed. "You're with us now."

Amery didn't look convinced. She started to talk fast, with body motions that conveyed fear, but not specifics. I looked to Violet, confused. She graciously motioned out the key words I was missing: potion, memory, force, trance.

I closed my eyes for a second, recalling Amery's motions and piecing them together with the new information. When I opened them again, I understood what she'd said. "She frightens me. She feeds me a potion and… I don't know much, really. I can't remember what happens between the feedings. I must have been in some kind of trance."

My empathy mixed with a pang of jealousy. Amery may have had a patchy memory, but I had nothing from my past. I pushed away the feeling and looked at Amery with glee, implying she was free, free from the spell. She looked back at me with an equal sense of delight, which morphed into determination. "I want to defeat her," she said. "I want to free everyone else."

I shook my head. "No, you need to recover. I need to do this."

"Are you going right now?" Violet asked, turning to me.

"Yes," I replied, facing the roots under the massive central tree. "It's time. You and Barrie should stay here… I'll call out if I need you to come after me." Before I had time to hesitate, I pushed myself forward. The snake would pay for enslaving so many.

Once I ducked under the root structure, my eyes took a while to adjust to the darkness. As I entered the center of the hollow tree, though, enough light was filtering through cracks in the outer shell for me to see. I gaped in awe. Even though I'd seen the room in visions, it was much more massive in real life. I refrained from simply gazing at the inner side of the bark that made up the walls of the lair. I was here for one purpose, and one purpose only. Though I was afraid of power and still afraid to fight, Nyoka was evil. It was time her reign came to an end.

The cavernous hollow, though huge, was mostly empty. I saw a few withered stores of herbs and other potion ingredients. A large pile of snake fangs and dried fruit was stacked against one side. A mouse hung by its tail, far above my head; I wasn't sure if it was dead or alive. I shivered and shifted my gaze to Nyoka. She was splayed out on a decently large rock off to one side. Her skin was gray, and I guessed she was in the process of shedding it. She was convulsing, and her body was thrashing against the rock.

Seizing the opportunity, I darted over and pinned her head down with both my feet, pressing my toes into her hood. I knew I wouldn't be able to hold her down, but if she tried to strike, I'd move with her. I remembered Samuel's lessons and tried to predict all possible retaliations. Yet… she didn't try to fight back. She just lay there, as if I wasn't even in the room. Not sure what else to do, I asked her, "What are you doing?"

I closed my eyes and conjured a vision of my surroundings. I needed the temporary ability to hear to understand her response. "I am… not really a snake," she said. "I use a… potion to appear as one. During the drought, all… of the herbs I need… for the potion were withered… and I could not make the concoc…tion. It has been se…everal days since I ha…ave taken it, and I'm… turning back…

back… in…" The convulsions overtook her, and she couldn't say any more.

"I know," I said, releasing the vision from my mind and finishing her sentence. "Into a rat." Even as I said the words, her skin began to molt. She was shedding it, but with it, her entire identity as a snake. Her body bulged under the scales, and as the skin peeled, a rat's nose and whiskers were revealed. Ears popped out, then her front paws. The uncovered skin puffed out with fur. Nyoka was once more a rat.

XIII

My vision blurred, my head pounded, and I felt as though I was going to be sick. The walls of the hollow spun around me. I fell backwards, losing my hold on the rat. I'd never conjured a real-time vision before... and probably shouldn't try it again. The blurriness and nausea faded as I blinked and shook my head to clear it.

After several deep breaths, I fought off the dizziness. I noticed how the shafts of light that shone through the cracks in the outer bark wall never wavered. There was no wind in this underground cave. Back on the surface, the light and shadow would constantly dance. I realized I'd fallen away from the rock where the rat was lying still, and flew back up beside her.

"Why, Nyoka?" I asked. "Why force Amery to follow you, and call her your apprentice? Why turn into a snake? Why enslave all those animals as blue monkey creatures... and how?"

The rat glared at me with beady eyes. Now that she was a mammal, it was much easier for me to understand Nyoka's body motions. "Why?" she replied, no longer convulsing. "I was always in the gutter, kicked and spat at, looked down upon. It was about time something changed. I wanted to be the one on top for once."

"Maybe you had a rough history, but that doesn't mean these other animals deserved this!"

"That's life," she spat. "You don't get a fair one unless you make it yourself."

"I know how it feels to be looked down upon," I said. After hearing Nyoka's explanation, my own sense of loneliness and frustration rose above all else. Staring at my feet, I continued. "Everyone on the thirteenth floor is afraid of me just because I look different from them... and they don't even know my past. If they did, they would be even more afraid, for reasons I can't control.

When I was with the squirrels, fire would just burn every place I tried to stay. It even caused the death of someone who was helping me."

I looked into Nyoka's eyes. "But despite all of this, I still found a few who do care for me. In fact, I think they care more for me *because* of my troubles, and because I try to push past them. Don't you want that? If you gave up this nonsense, maybe they'll give you a chance, too."

The rat picked at her paws and didn't speak for a while. When she looked at me again, the expression in her eyes was completely different — sad, even. "I do want that," she said.

"It's never too late to change," I pressed, my heart beating faster with excitement. *Could I really help her, without fighting her?* "You can still reverse this."

"You know," she mulled, "I didn't feel so strongly about wanting this power until... well, I'm not really sure what caused it, exactly. All I remember is that before, I didn't have any strength to help myself." She held her paws close to her chest, then spread her arms. *Freedom.* "And then I did. I suddenly felt more than capable, and I knew how to do all of this." She gestured to the dried potion ingredients around us.

I tilted my head, confused. "What caused the change?"

Nyoka stared at the ground for several minutes, then met my eyes again. "I don't know where it came from; a strange, cloudy darkness just appeared in front of me. It looked like black smoke, but heavier, settling and crawling on the ground. It whispered to me with a thousand voices I couldn't understand, but it felt powerful. It felt *good.* I approached it, and... it went *into* me. That's when I got this knowledge, this power."

It took me a moment to comprehend her, but her tendency to use excessive paw motions and dramatic facial expressions helped, and I was able to piece it together. Once realization settled, my heart pounded in my chest.

What if it's the same smoke I've seen in my dreams?

71

Nyoka shifted, and I turned to watch her speak again. "I liked it at first," she said, stretching out her paw and admiring her claws. "I felt strong, independent, like nothing could stop me." She looked into my eyes. "But then it started to take over. I think it had more control over my actions than I did. At that point, I was scared. But I couldn't fight it." The rat tucked her face into her paws. She continued talking, but I couldn't understand anymore. All I knew was that she was ashamed.

I relaxed. Somehow, Nyoka was free from the grasp of whatever had been controlling her. I drew closer to her and awkwardly wrapped my wing around her shoulders. "It's alright now," I said. "Whatever it was, it's gone. You still have time to undo all the things you've done."

When Nyoka raised her head, I remembered the troubles I'd experienced before the thirteenth floor. "I told you about the fires… Samuel, my mentor, thinks someone was targeting me. Was that you?"

The rat shook her head. "I have no idea what you're talking about. I don't have any ability to track someone or send fire their way."

I sighed. The danger was still out there somewhere, and I wasn't sure how I'd ever find it. I could solve one problem now, though. "How can we free the other slaves?" I asked Nyoka.

"I think you already know how," she replied.

I thought for a while. "For my mother, all I did was say her name."

"Twice. You said it twice," she said, holding up two digits on her paw.

"Is that all? But do you even know all of their names? How will we rescue all of them?"

"There is another way," Nyoka replied. "You used it on Amery. I call it the … fruit." I had no idea what name she'd given the fruit, but she wouldn't know the written language, so I didn't bother to ask. The name didn't matter anyway. I remembered which fruit had brought Amery out of her trance: the one I'd tried to use to harm Nyoka when she was still a snake.

"The fruit? How?"

"I had to put some sort of safety into this world. Just in case something went wrong with the potions I used on myself. When I controlled the minds of the slaves, I forbade them from eating it, but it should still work."

This was getting more and more confusing. "Wait, what do you mean, *you had to have it here?* Did you create this world?"

Nyoka nodded. "The darkness that went inside me was very powerful. With its help, I could control and shape matter, make an entire miniature world exist in this cave. I lured unsuspecting creatures into it and morphed their bodies to all be the same diminutive forms. It felt *good* to have so many under my rule, even if they weren't willing. Too good."

I closed my eyes, trying to understand all of this. It was starting to make more sense, but I still had questions. "If you've already turned back into a rat, then why are the slaves still in their cursed form?" I asked, opening my eyes again.

"Their form, my own, and Amery's submission are all from potions infused with dark magic, but different varieties. They all needed to be renewed at different intervals — my own with every few sunsets, Amery's with each phase of the moon. Theirs, though, only needed to be applied once in a lifetime." As she said this, the ground rumbled. Dust fell from crevices far above, and the mouse hanging by its tail swung stiffly. "We need to move quickly," Nyoka said, jumping to her paws. "Now that my power is gone, I think the world might be collapsing. Let's go!" She scurried out the door, and I flew to follow.

When we emerged from the hollow tree, the light plants lining the cave walls were flickering and fading. Barrie and Samuel had joined my mother, sister, and Amery. Samuel stood on three paws, keeping his injured leg off the ground. All of them looked at me with matching expressions of concern.

"Sheer! There you are! Something's happening... what do we do?" Barrie asked. "And who is that rat?"

"It's Nyoka," I replied. "She's not an enemy anymore. I don't have time to explain right now. The world is collapsing, and we need to save all of the slaves and get out of here. Can all of you help get the…" I looked helplessly at Nyoka, and she repeated its name for my friends. "Right," I continued. "That fruit, from the trees? It's the spiky orange one that fell on Amery. If we feed it to the slaves, they'll be freed from the spell."

We all came up with a system. Without commands to guide them, the cursed slaves had gathered by the water and sat idly as dust fell like rain with every tremble of the ground; we would have to take the fruit to them. Samuel bit down hard on the shell until its insides oozed out, then Barrie carried it over to the riverside. From there, Violet, Reika, Amery and I filled our beaks with the soft fruit and distributed it to the slaves, while Barrie went back for another heavy haul. Nyoka scurried across the grounds, finding and freeing the slaves whose names she knew. As we worked, more and more animals were freed and our team grew exponentially. Most of them were small mammals or birds like squirrels, mice, sparrows, and pigeons, but a couple of foxes and feral cats were there as well. Once we had a rhythm going, it didn't take long until there were more animals helping than enslaved. Soon all of them were free, back in their original forms.

"Come, everyone!" Nyoka said, standing midway up the stairs etched into the tree so all the animals could see and hear her between tremors. "Follow me, there's a back way out!"

Nyoka led the way to a cluster of thick grass at one end of the massive underground cave that housed this strange world, and pushed the stems aside to reveal a hidden tunnel barely large enough for Samuel to squeeze through. She paused when she reached it and turned to me. "I had nearly forgotten that this was here," she admitted. "It's been so long since I came down this way." The ground shook again, and rocks cascaded down the cave wall.

"Let's get out of here," I told her, "and leave all those memories behind."

The rat nodded, and the edge of her mouth turned up in a smile. She turned and scrambled up the sloped path, leading the way out.

Crow

XIV

When we emerged on the surface, the light stung my eyes. I didn't realize just how dim it had been in the tunnel. As I looked around, I smelled the soft, fresh grass and wildflowers. The rest of the animals popped out of the tunnel single file, then spread out, swarming like ants and relishing in the fresh air. It was good to be back in the open again, this time on purpose. It was time to go home.

Some of the enslaved animals scattered, but most had nowhere to go and decided to follow us. Reika, Amery, and the dozens of animals who'd been freed from their cursed forms didn't know which way to turn, even if they'd been to the thirteenth floor before. It had been too long since they were first trapped underground. Thankfully, we had a team of navigators — if Samuel or I faltered, Violet or Barrie could identify landmarks and get us back on track. The landslide gave us a nice slope to climb out of the ravine. After that, we stayed on the side with the meadow. It was slow going, since Samuel was injured, but I was more than happy to move at his pace. I was just glad he was still with us.

Violet and Nyoka helped me find the right herbs to mix into a poultice to help prevent infection where Samuel's bone had broken through his skin. Barrie helped me wrap his leg with fresh leaves and strands of milkweed stalk once we came across a patch, which would hopefully prevent further damage until we could get back to the thirteenth floor and the more advanced medical supplies.

That first night, we rested under the moonless sky, staring at the stars until we fell asleep. No wolves haunted my dreams. When I woke to ground adorned with tiny droplets of dew, I savored the warmth of my family and friends.

For most of the journey, Amery rode on Samuel's back. During breaks, my mother and I put aside time to help her learn to fly. Reika seemed to enjoy the opportunity to teach another young one, since she'd missed that crucial time in my life. She knew all sorts of exercises I wouldn't have thought of: jumping off a low tree branch, balancing on a swaying stalk, or hopping from rock to rock without touching the ground. At first Amery was clumsy and often fell, but she eventually mastered flying, landing, and taking off. Her skill grew, and she was soon a brilliant flier. I watched Violet and Amery's shadows race along the ground and dance in the fields as they flew together.

After many long days of traveling, when the moon was over halfway full, we finally reached the outskirts of the city. Home was within sight.

Climbing the stairs to the thirteenth floor was a challenge for Samuel, but soon we'd arrived safely. My mentor arranged for a feast to welcome the newcomers, then immediately went to see Anna. We all hoped she'd be able heal his broken leg. I stayed with him in the medical room until it was time for the feast.

When I entered the great hall in the middle of the thirteenth floor, a mouse that worked in the kitchen stood up and looked at me, getting my attention. "Someone donated a gift of rare sweet berries for your meal, Sheer," he told me as I approached. "Would you like them along with your seeds?"

"Yes, thanks! Do you know who it was?"

"No," he said, shaking his head. "I just heard about it from…" Here, he said someone's name, but I would need him to write it down. Since the commotion was growing and he needed to get back to serving the feast, I didn't bother to ask.

"Alright," I replied. "Could you thank them for me, then?" He nodded, then scurried off to the back room.

It had been a very long journey, and I was exhausted. Once I polished off my seeds and the delicious berries, I excused myself and left the merrymaking to rest and ease my growing headache.

To my frustration, I was unable to drift off to sleep. When everyone else had dozed off, I flew to the herb storage and grimaced as I chewed on some chamomile, hoping it would help, then returned to the sparrow room. I shifted on my feet, shuffled my wings, and changed my head position all night long. When the sun's rays filtered in through the window, I still hadn't slept.

I remained on my perch, anxious for the sleep I so desperately needed. My stomach hurt, but not from hunger. I squeezed my eyes closed, trying to shut out the light and fall asleep. My friends and family were probably worried, but no one bothered me.

I was unable to sleep, unable to eat, for two whole days. My entire body ached. The last night, I forced myself to get up and walk to Anna's room, since I couldn't fly at that point. I had to know what was wrong with me.

I don't know how far I got before I collapsed.

My mother, my sister, Amery, or Barrie, whose room was next to ours, must have heard me fall. I vaguely felt myself being lifted by familiar talons and carried off.

At some point, I was brought to Anna's room. I felt like I was lying on my belly, on a bed of grass or moss. That was when the dreams started — or were they hallucinations?

The first was a view of the room from overhead, as if I were a spider in the corner. I immediately noticed I could hear, just like I could in my visions and dreams, though this perspective was new. Rain tapped against the window pane, and wind howled outside. I recognized the lynx healer herself, as well as many other animals standing around a bed. On the bed, a sparrow lay with his wings and claws tucked tightly against his body. It took me a moment to realize the bird was... me. The bird was — I was — breathing irregularly, tossing my head back and forth. Was I dreaming? Samuel was there, talking so quietly to Anna that I couldn't hear him over the rain. My sister, Violet, and my mother, Reika, stood at my side. They looked worried. Amery got along well with them, so I wasn't surprised to see her there, too. Barrie was pacing back and forth from the door to the window, sometimes on his feet, sometimes in the air.

Suddenly, Reika jumped up. "The prophecy! Don't you remember? The one about the healing tree with all its different fruits.

81

I used to sing it to you, Violet. Barrie, you must have heard it, too. Maybe it holds a clue?"

"How so?" Violet asked.

"Remember the first verse?" Reika responded. "Over the mountain and into the sun, two song sparrows are flying along. They follow a falcon, quite a strange friend; going toward what seems to them, the world's end."

That's not how the prophecy went, I thought. *What kind of bad nursery rhyme is this?* But as soon as the thought crossed my mind, it was gone again, and the dream continued on.

"Perhaps we are those song sparrows," my mother was saying. "Barrie is almost like a falcon, I mean, technically a hawk, but these things aren't based on technicalities. We must fit the prophecy! We are meant to go to the tree of healing!"

"Maybe you're right," Violet responded, nodding thoughtfully. "The last part of the third verse… 'they have to save a friend of theirs, whose life depends upon apples and pears,' seems pretty accurate."

"I agree," Barrie added, "but I only hope we can get the fruit in time to heal Sheer."

"But there are only two sparrows in the song," Amery interjected. "There are three of us."

"Oh, you're right!" Violet said. "How do we know who is supposed to go?"

"Amery, I think you should go instead of me," Reika suddenly said. "I'm getting too old for this, and I want to stay here by my son's side."

The two young sparrows piped up together. "That works." Violet, slightly older than Amery, turned to Barrie. "We'll all go, together. But how will we know where to go? Does the song say anything about where to find the mountain?"

Barrie shook his head. "No, the prophecy doesn't say, but I know where to find it. My mother showed me once. Follow me! We should leave now, before he gets any worse." Despite their confidence, I was confused. *This doesn't sound like any prophecy I've ever heard of,* I thought. *If it's even real, how do they know it's meant for them? Why would apples and pears save anyone? What is the rest of the prophecy?*

Before I had a chance to ponder the subject any longer, the dream shifted. I was now watching a very old crow. A dark shroud of mysterious smoke furled around him. He had one good eye; the other was cloudy, focused on something far off to his left. One of the toes on his right foot was completely missing, and his feathers were ruffled and frayed. He opened his chipped beak, and his throat shook with a warbled, crackly voice. He looked oddly familiar.

Was this the crow that attacked me after I left the squirrels?

When he spoke, I was surprised he had a thick accent. "You've given 'im the poisoned berries, yes?"

"Yes, sir, Spike," a gander answered, the dream's scope shifting to show the new creature. The smoke curled towards him but didn't envelop him. "I have done as you commanded. Please, may I now see my mate and goslings, as you promised?"

The crow shook his head vigorously, flinging a line of saliva through the air, which landed on the gander's beak. The latter shuddered but retained his composure. "No!" Spike shouted. "Not 'til the sparrow is dead. Y'see, Gander, I've got to answer to the grea' Nivek. If I fail... if *ya* fail... neither of us will e'er see the light of day again. Forget all my other plans; we'd both be dead. Ya hear? Ya'll stay here, with me, 'til it's done."

Nivek? I had no more time to wonder about who this *great Nivek* was. The scene changed, and I once again saw my friends and sister. I watched them fly toward a mountain so tall, most of it was covered in mist. Then the vision did something strange: I saw two things overlaid at once, as if both were slightly transparent. I was still watching the two sparrows and hawk, but I now saw another snapshot of myself, too.

I could hear myself moaning in pain, but the voice sounded like it belonged to a stranger. I appeared to be suffering from a seizure. From my mouth bubbled foamy saliva; my body was shaking violently. It was strange to be looking down at myself. I felt disconnected from my body. I felt nothing, but I watched myself writhe and squirm as if I were in incredible pain. That scene faded, and the images of Violet, Amery, and Barrie became clearer.

XV

"Wow," Violet exclaimed when they neared the mystical mountain. "I've never seen anything like it!"

"Few have," Barrie replied. "They have to know exactly when and where to look. It's usually covered with fog so thick, it's impossible to make out. You can only see it for an hour a day, just as the sun is rising."

Amery exhaled. "Amazing!"

"My mother knew another hawk who just happened to chance upon the mountain at the right time of day after a long and unsuccessful hunt," Barrie said.

"You're lucky to have a mother with such good connections," the older sparrow commented.

"Sheer's lucky to have you as a friend," the younger one added.

"I suppose so," the hawk replied. "I hope we can save him. He's a good friend to me."

As I watched them in silence for a while, I found it difficult to remember who these animals were. Was my memory fading? I couldn't even remember ever meeting the older sparrow, though the younger one seemed familiar for some reason. Was it her voice? I could no longer recall her name. Thankfully, I still remembered Barrie, but... how had I met him? And who was this Sheer they were talking about? I certainly didn't know *him*. What was happening to me?

While the three strangely familiar birds continued on their quest to a place I didn't know, to save someone whose name I didn't recognize, I heard a crackling voice no louder than a whisper. Somehow, even though I didn't recognize the voice or see the speaker, I knew it was a crow.

"Not long now," he was saying. "Not long, and Nivek'll be satisfied."

I refocused on the strange birds: two small and one large.

Where are they going, and why are their faces full of worry?

"Wake up, sleepyheads!" the largest was calling. Drowsily, the other two rose from their perches. To wake herself up, one of the small birds sang a verse of a strange song. It seemed to inspire her, to encourage her to move onward.

"There's a garden along the way," she sang. "In the middle is a great tree, bearing fruit that heals, night and day."

What an odd nursery rhyme. What kind of tree bears magical fruit?

They flew on, sometimes singing various verses of what must have been the same song. By midday, they'd flown to the top of the mountain. After saying something about a moon, they went to sleep in the middle of the day. When they woke, an entire range of mountains and valleys rose from the mist. Venturing across the landscape after a hearty meal, the trio continued their desperate journey in the dark.

When they'd descended into a densely forested valley, many white birds swooped up from the trees.

"Owls!" whispered the youngest bird, hiding behind the largest. As soon as she said the word, I was able to connect it to the white bird... but I struggled to keep it in my mind.

Why is this word so hard?

One of the owls, whose eyes were faded, spoke. "Whooo comes into the realm of barn owls?" I tried without success to remember what *barn* meant. Was it a type of tree? Or perhaps somebody's name? Or maybe it was the pale color that patched their faces. If not, then the color had now escaped me, too.

Why is my memory fading?

86

"It is I, Barrie, and my two friends," said the larger bird. "We wish to pass through — or over — your forest in search of the healing tree," he explained. This caused a change in tension. It seemed the occupants of the forest were afraid of this bird, but now that they heard his business, they were comforted. The two small birds looked confused, and I was relieved not to be the only one.

The large bird offered no explanation, but the owls allowed them to pass peacefully through. All three were followed closely by fearful eyes, but no one did anything, and the trio made it through without any more trouble. When they reached the edge of the forest, they were exhausted. The two small birds rested in a bush near the ground, while the larger one chose a high branch as his perch.

In the morning, they all woke up early, ate breakfast, and moved on. Ahead of them stretched more hills and valleys, but in the distance, the ground seemed to shimmer.

What could that be?

As they drew closer, the shining ground revealed itself as an immense body of water. I hated it. *Why?* I couldn't remember. One of the small birds called it a sea. It was sparkling, full of silvery scaled creatures that splashed in the sun. The largest bird swooped down, but they kept slipping out of his grip. Giving up, they moved on.

They went across the shining sea, flying until the sky was a dark color — something between the night sky and the color of the shining sun. I tried for a while to remember the names, but nothing came to mind.

At this point, the birds began to search for land. They were tired from constant flight in unpredictable winds that bounced off the waves. They looked all around, but it was a long time before the youngest bird spoke up. "Barrie, is that... land ahead? I can't quite make it out," she asked.

The largest bird looked and exclaimed, "Yes! I think it is! Let's head in that direction. I don't see anything closer." With renewed energy, the three birds flew toward the promising earth and found it to be true. They collapsed in a tree and promptly fell asleep.

When the older small bird woke, the other two were still sleeping. Now that morning light allowed her to see further, she gazed around at her surroundings. She focused on a tiny speck in the distance but couldn't determine what it was. I had a strong feeling it was somehow important, that it had something to do with me, but I couldn't remember why. Besides, they kept mentioning a friend who needed to be healed... I wasn't sick. I was only dreaming. I didn't feel like I was in pain or ill. In fact, I couldn't feel anything at all.

Suddenly, I was concerned. Shaking my head, I tried to wake myself up, but it didn't work. I shrugged. It didn't matter. Besides, I wanted to see what these birds were trying to get to, and how their adventure would play out.

Apparently, the smudge in the distance was important after all. When they got up, the trio made a beeline for it. They flew much faster now, sensing they needed to finish quickly — I had no idea why. I couldn't remember why they were going there in the first place.

I was watching them fly toward the slowly growing speck on the horizon when the image became slightly transparent. I saw a second image at the same time, overlaid over the first. It was very strange... something I was sure had never happened to me before. In the invading image, I saw a small bird just like the ones flying to the smudge. He was lying stiffly on a bed of something that looked soft. He was very, very ill. He was dying.

The second image faded away, but the first remained muddled. I blinked, trying to make it clear again, but nothing happened. It was impossible to distinguish between the two small birds, and all the color had drained from the image. Still, I could tell that the three birds had drawn close to their destination: an enormous tree bearing multiple kinds of fruit. It was surrounded by other single-fruit trees, in turn surrounded by vines of many different varieties. Around the entire circumference was a boundary made of wood. I couldn't remember what it was called.

Each bird took a different kind of fruit from the big tree and quickly turned around, beating their wings even harder for the return journey. I'd have hoped to see the end, but suddenly my vision went black. I felt like I was falling through darkness, increasing in speed the further I fell. Everything was dark, and very cold. Suddenly, I felt completely alone. I wished those birds had gone on the journey to save me, to keep me from falling in this terrible place.

No, I thought, *don't be selfish.*

I couldn't remember if I'd been dreaming or awake before. Was I dreaming of falling now? I entered an even deeper state of confusion as I continued to plummet through the dark and cold. Soon, I lost all sense of what it meant to be conscious. I couldn't even remember who I was, or what existence was.

What does life feel like?

I couldn't remember, but it felt vitally important to the scrap of memory that clung to the recesses of my mind.

What is memory? What is time?

The words meant something to me, but I couldn't remember what. I was hopelessly lost in confusion… hopelessly… something…

But then something warm and gritty that tasted like clay slid down my throat and I began to feel warm again. I stopped falling through darkness and felt as if I was being lifted up instead.

I blinked and opened my eyes. Before me were my mother, sister, and friends.

Barrie jumped up and rushed over to me. "Sheer, you're alive!"

I weakly smiled at him. "Yeah, I guess I am."

"You should rest, Sheer," Anna told me.

I tried to nod, but my head felt like stone. I was about to close my eyes when I saw a flash of white out of the corner of my eye. When I moved to stand up straight, Anna gently pushed me back down with her paw. Still, I was able to glance towards the door. Gander had wandered into the room, and a few other animals were peeking through the doorway behind him. Gathering what little strength I had, I spoke, hoping my voice was loud enough for him to hear. "You don't have to report back to Spike, Gander. We can help you. We can protect you and your wife and goslings."

The blood drained from the skin around the goose's eyes, and he stared at me in shock. I couldn't think straight enough to explain. "We'll discuss it later," I told him. "Just... just know that we're here for you." Exhausted, I let my eyelids droop closed. I felt a cool breeze follow my friends and family as they left, and I knew Gander and the other onlookers must have gone as well. Never in my short life would I have imagined feeling so grateful to drift into dreamless sleep.

XVI

Over the course of the next several days, stragglers wandered in and out of the medical room and my friends paid me several visits, but I spent most of the time alone. Finally, it was my last day in the infirmary, and I was looking forward to spending time with them again.

"How are you doing?" Samuel asked for the dozenth time when he limped into the room. He still couldn't use his right front leg. An infection had taken hold despite the precautions I'd taken before we journeyed back to the thirteenth floor. Anna's care was helping, but it was a losing battle. His leg was swollen and red; the wound itself was bursting with yellow pus that smelled horrible. He sat down, and I could feel his groan vibrating the air while his granddaughter tended to his injury.

"More worried about you than myself," I replied. "Your leg is getting worse."

"This may be true. I've survived many things in my lifetime, though," he said. "Sometimes you just have to take things as they come. It does no good to worry over things we cannot control." The rumble of his voice calmed me.

"How old are you, Samuel?"

My mentor laughed. I saw his chest heaving, felt the puffs of air, but heard nothing. "Old," he replied. "Plenty old. You could say that my blood is infused with magic. I was young once, of course. I was barely an adult when this building was built. Do you remember the stories I told you while we were on our way to the snake?"

"I do!"

"The humans I lived with wanted a safe haven for the woodland creatures this city displaced. They built this building, and they taught me how to be a guardian, a keeper of the peace. When their time came, I took my place at the head of the table."

The old lynx went silent, looking down at his paws. He didn't move for several minutes, but I sensed he had more to say.

I cleared my throat. "Samuel, did you have something else you wanted to talk about?"

"Well… yes. One of my scouts has returned with news from the northeast," he said, nodding to the door. "They found a cave filled with mist and smoke, buried deep inside a mountain." Samuel glanced at the door, then switched to projecting his voice in my mind. *"Birds of all kinds have been disappearing around it for the past year. The number has grown enough that the animals in the vicinity have started to notice. Some of them claimed to have seen crows coming and going freely."*

"The crow from my dreams is the one who planned to poison me," I said quietly, suddenly remembering the visions I'd seen while I was sick. I didn't know how much of the dreams were true, but I knew that part was. Gander's reaction had confirmed it. "Do you think the same crow is involved in this, too?"

"Undoubtedly. Even though the snake is no longer a threat…"

"Or a snake."

"Right, I keep forgetting that she's a rat now… you'd think since I see her daily, I'd stop referring to her as we did when she was just in your visions." He chuckled, then shook his head. "No matter. Even though Nyoka is no longer a threat, we cannot forget the other two creatures in your visions. Nor can *you* forget that someone was targeting you. it's even more obvious now. As you said, Gander poisoned you, under Spike's command. Perhaps the crow was the one behind the fires as well."

I nodded solemnly, ashamed that I'd completely forgotten about them until now. None of the usual nightmares had haunted me since escaping the underground world, and I hadn't thought to force one ever since the ill effects of conjuring one in the presence of the transforming snake.

92

"Whoever is behind it," Samuel continued, *"they have started to burn a chemical made from the sap of the poppy flower. It makes animals more susceptible to the cave's pull. I'm not sure what else they're mixing into it, but it seems to be especially potent for birds. I've instructed our head meal coordinator to mix ground coffee and other herbs into each meal here just in case, which seems to combat the effects enough, as long as everyone keeps their distance from the cave. Unfortunately, I do think we've lost some of our members to its pull already... so far, no one has returned. I'm not sure how well the mixture will work when an animal gets too close, since the potency of the drug increases as you draw nearer. But even if it weren't for the drug, there are now reports of strange sounds emitted from the cave entrance. More and more birds are being drawn in every day from a mixture of the two effects."*

After pondering what he'd said, I looked into Samuel's eyes. "What should we do?"

"I don't think *I* am going to be of very much help, Sheer."

Nodding, I rephrased my question. "What should I do, then?"

"Well, I'd start with investigating," he said. Again, he switched to projecting his voice in my mind, and his mouth didn't move along with his words. *"Keep it quiet so no one's alarmed without reason. Find out what's going on, and make it stop. If you can, bring back those who have already fallen under its spell. If this goes much further, we'll have to prepare the thirteenth floor for more serious evasive maneuvers. I don't want to lose any more of our avian members."*

I sensed the importance of secrecy and the weight of the task, and blinked my affirmation.

Samuel bowed his head slightly in thanks. "You'll need help — don't go alone."

The next morning, I flew into the grand central hall for breakfast instead of eating mush with obscene amounts of water in the infirmary. As soon as I entered, all eyes turned on me. I could tell they were whispering about me… no one had ever been poisoned on the thirteenth floor before. Now they had one more reason to be wary of me, besides the fact that I just didn't look like everyone else. It was just like when I was at the squirrels… at least this time there had been no collateral damage. Besides Spike's threats towards Gander, anyway. I could feel their fears and prejudices radiating from their expressions, but I did my best to ignore them. I flew freely to the end of the table. Barrie, Reika, Violet, and Amery were there — they didn't shy away like everyone else, but their postures still gave away their wariness. Their thoughts were an indistinguishable mixture of caution, pity, and delight to see me again.

"Sheer!" Barrie exclaimed, the expression in his eyes a diluted version of the feeling displayed by his outstretched wings. "It's so good to see you out and about!"

"Yeah," I replied, landing next to a small plate of seeds and berries set out for me. I pushed aside the berries, offering them to my sister instead. "Violet, you take these. I don't think I can eat berries ever again."

"Oh! Of course, Sheer," she replied. "I'd offer you some of my seeds, but I've already eaten them all…"

"You can have some of mine!" my mother interjected, practically shoving them towards me.

"No… I'm okay," I said. "Really. This is more than I've been eating the last few days."

While we ate, I told them about what Samuel had said. About the cave, and the drugged gas, and the mission to stop whatever was going on.

When I'd finished, Reika spoke up. "Did you say this started about a year ago?"

"Yeah, why?"

"It's just… that's when Comfrey disappeared," she said, nodding for Violet to write the name on one of the pieces of

94

parchment kept handy on the table. I blinked, not sure what she meant. But when I met Violet's eyes, they gave it away.

Dad.

"Do you really think he could be there?" Violet asked.

"I don't know," Reika replied. "It's been so long since I've seen him. But if there's even a small chance he's there, a chance we could rescue him, I want to go."

"Me, too!" Violet exclaimed. "Even if he's not there, to think of all the other animals that could be captured..."

"Maybe my parents are there, too," Barrie added. "They're also missing. I don't know where else they would be."

"I don't know what happened to my parents," Amery added. "Nyoka kidnapped me before I hatched, so I never knew them. But I'll come and help — you'll need everyone you can get."

I nodded, thankful I didn't need to convince my friends to help me. Looking around at the other animals of the thirteenth floor, who were still keeping as far away from me as possible, I knew this was as big as the crew was going to get. Samuel couldn't join us with his injury, and he needed Anna here to take care of him. Hopefully, the five of us would be enough to get to the bottom of this.

XVII

Following Samuel's instructions, we picked up the antidote from the kitchen, and Anna gave Barrie one of the few lanterns the community owned, to bring on our journey. We left the thirteenth floor that evening and flew through the cool summer night breeze, the bag of coffee strapped to Barrie's leg. When the sun rose, we could see a mountain rising from the mist ahead of us. I gasped — it was the same mountain Amery, Violet, and Barrie had flown over in my dream. I turned to look at them, but none of their expressions indicated they recognized the place. I was slightly disappointed. That part must have been nothing more than a dream. It had certainly been an interesting story, though. Maybe it helped keep my mind active long enough for Anna to obtain the antidote.

As I turned my head back forward, I gaped once again. The sun's rays settled on a brilliant field of red flowers growing in the sandy soil beside a lake. I remembered what Samuel had said about the cave of smoke, and called to my friends.

"That's what they make the drug from! Look..."

Below us, an entire flock of pigeons was scattered among the flowers. They seemed to be tending to them and picking ones that were ready to harvest. They didn't look up at us; they were hyper-focused on their task.

Those birds must be working under the crow's control, I thought. *Magic, perhaps, or under the influence of the very drug they're helping to produce.*

I looked to Barrie, but he shook his head. "We need to conserve our energy and our supplies," he said. "We don't know what we're about to get ourselves into. We can come back for them later." Nodding reluctantly, I gave the pigeons one last look as we passed overhead.

The mountain was large and seemed closer than it really was. By the time we reached the entrance of the cave, the blazing sun was high in the sky and my wings ached. Barrie cautiously led the way into the hole in the mountain. It was much cooler inside, protected from the early summer heat by the shadows.

"Ignore the noises that come from inside," I reminded my friends, recalling Samuel's warning. "It's a lure." I almost wanted to hear them myself, to know why they were so attractive to so many birds. The smoke, which smelled a lot like the flowers used to create it, was so thick, the lantern only shone a few feet ahead of us.

"Amery," I called, choosing her since I thought she was the most vulnerable. "Come here and eat some of the coffee powder before we go any further."

She did as I asked. I followed suit, then handed the bag to Barrie. He dipped his beak deep inside and handed it to Violet. As she was about to swallow her portion, I felt the very air tremble. Something big was approaching, and fast. Then I saw the Beast. It was an enormous reptilian creature, with thick, armored skin and spikes from its head to its tail. Each of its four legs were as thick as Samuel's entire body. I'd never seen anything like it — this sort of creature shouldn't even exist.

It came out of the smoke so quickly, I had no time to react. It snapped its jaws around my beloved sister, coffee and all, and she was gone.

Violet was gone. My heart stopped.

I was shocked, but to save myself, Amery, my mother, and my friend, I had to act fast. We'd just arrived, but I already knew we were in too deep.

"Fly! Come on, follow me and get out of here!" I shouted to my remaining companions. Amery, although stunned from what had just happened, rushed to join me. Reika and Barrie, on the other hand, were sluggish. Maybe Barrie hadn't had enough of the coffee mixture; maybe his incredible hearing made the strange sounds more effective on him. My mother hadn't gotten a chance to eat any of the coffee… she was feeling the effects of the smoke. Instead of heading for the exit, to fresh air and an escape from the terrible Beast, they followed it as it led them down into the cave.

"Stop!" I shouted, but they disappeared into the smoke. I wasn't ready to lose my best friend or mother, especially so soon after losing my sister. Calling to Amery, I followed them; I hoped I might still be able to save them.

We passed over the broken lantern. Barrie had dropped it along the way. I had neither the time to grab it nor the strength to carry it, so I let it be and braced myself for the coming darkness.

To my surprise, fire flickering in the depths of the cave was reflecting off the rocks all around. It provided just enough light that, as we drew closer, my eyes adjusted to the darkness. Amery's unsure movements and squinted eyes told me that my enhanced senses had helped, too. She couldn't see a thing. "Keep close to me," I told her. "Follow the sound of my wings. Focus on them instead of the sounds from the cave."

There was a sort of natural bridge up ahead. It spanned an enormous hole in the ground that plummeted into the earth as far as I could see. As we neared it, I could see the silhouettes of dozens — no, hundreds — of birds perched on the edge of the bridge. I could barely make out Reika and Barrie's forms approaching the crowd. A bird split from the line and plunged into the depths. Another bird fell, then another.

Suddenly, several Beasts tramped from the side of the cave across the bridge, swinging their tails back and forth. They must have reached some sort of capacity; they were forcing all the birds to dive to their deaths prematurely, to make room for more victims. We were too late.

I felt two large birds approach me and Amery from behind. I began to despair but tried to fly faster.

"No!" I cried. Everything happened at once, and the world seemed to move in slow motion. Reika and Barrie were knocked down into the pit. The two crows behind us caught us in their talons.

They were taking us back towards the entrance, and all I could do was watch as my mother and best friend fell. "No!" I cried again. "No!"

XVIII

Hoping my silent words could somehow save them, I cried out their names in my desperation. "Reika! Barrie!" I cried out my sister's, too, even though I knew she was long gone. I could feel the movement of the crow's belly as he had a conversation with the other, but I didn't care that I couldn't hear them. I didn't care what happened to me next. How could I tell Samuel I'd failed? How could I go on living without my family and friends?

Amery and I were dumped on the ground, but I didn't even have the strength or willpower to get up. Then I recognized a mangled talon in front of my face.

Spike.

I peeked out of the corner of my eye, turning my head slightly sideways so I could just barely see both him and the crows who'd captured us.

"I thought I told you not to harm him!" Spike narrowed his one good eye. I didn't even care anymore that I couldn't hear his interesting accent. I was content to barely cling to the conversation.

"I didn't, sir," the crow beside me protested. He was so close, I could feel his chest move as he breathed. "I promise. He's faking it."

"We'll see. Take the girl away. We've got no use for her," Spike ordered.

The crow behind Amery bowed his head. "Yes, sir."

Amery squirmed and bit at her captor, to no avail. When she was dragged away, I found the strength to rise. She was the only friend I had left. I had to follow them; I had to protect her. Samuel had risked his life for her — I couldn't let that be in vain.

"There, see?" my captor announced triumphantly, pointing his wing in my direction. "He's fine."

"So he is. Sparrow," Spike addressed me, "I know what you were trying to do." He tossed the bag of coffee before me, now slick with saliva from the Beast who'd swallowed my sister. He stood tall, with his chest puffed out, and gestured with his wing to an invisible giant. "You think those reptilian monsters came from nowhere? I need that blood… *avian* blood… to bring them back. Yet you come traipsing in, trying to mess up my whole operation!"

I said nothing. Instead, I stared at his two-toed foot, refusing to look him in the eyes.

He was killing birds to create the Beasts. I shuddered in disgust. *How could someone do such a thing?*

Spike continued slowly, tapping his toe with every other word. Without looking at the crow, I wasn't sure what he was saying anymore. I assumed it was some kind of threat. I refused to budge, and after a while, the tapping stopped. He shifted his body to face the crow beside me.

Suddenly, my captor swiped his beak toward my right wing. Before I could think about what was happening, a cold piece of metal was clipped over my feathers. I immediately felt the added weight. I wouldn't be able to fly with this thing on. I stumbled forward, off balance, and cringed from the pinching sting. My captor pushed me along toward a cage. It was about three times as tall as the crows, and four times as wide on both sides.

The crow forced me through the gate, then closed and locked it behind me. I noticed the bars of the cage were further apart on the top than on the sides. That was my only chance of escape. But even if I did manage to squeeze out that way, I wouldn't make it very far with the clip weighing me down. Besides, I was being watched.

I had little hope. I was still beset with grief, but I knew submitting and giving in to my pain was no way to avenge the death of my only friends and family. No. All of this was Spike's fault. I had to defeat him. I closed my eyes with the setting of the sun, hoping I'd be able to come up with a plan before morning.

In the middle of the night, I felt a soft breeze near the ground, and coughed because of the dust. I opened my eyes and peered into the darkness until I saw a pair of glinting eyes.

Amery. She's alive!

Peeking over at my guard, I saw that he'd dozed off. "How did you get away?" I whispered to Amery, hoping my voice wasn't too loud. "And what are you doing here? They'll catch you again!"

She gave me an incredulous look that probably meant something like, "I came back to rescue you. What else would I be doing here?"

I shook my head and nodded to my clipped wing. "They'll do the same to you if they catch you." Flapping my wings, I tried to indicate that she should leave. I didn't want them taking her away again. Surely, the second time she wouldn't be so lucky.

Amery stared into my eyes, not wavering. After a moment, I released a sigh, then directed my gaze at the wider openings above me. When I turned back to her, she had a glimmer in her eye.

She flew up to the top and squeezed through the bars. She started to climb down with her claws and beak but lost her grip. A dust cloud rose up around her when she fell. It must have made a sound, for the sleeping crow stirred.

We held our breaths and remained completely still. I watched him mumble something like, "Don't let them get away," then go back to sleep. We were safe, for now.

I turned back to Amery and gestured to my clipped wing. I desperately wanted this thing removed.

Amery responded by pulling it off with her beak and claws. My wing ached afterward, but I was free. I stretched, and we climbed up to the top, using our wings for balance. We squeezed through the wider gaps and looked around for the quietest way to escape.

The crows might hear our beating wings and wake up if we flew, so we hopped from branch to branch and tree to tree until we were far off. Then we headed through the forest in the general direction of the city, towards home.

We stopped to rest around midday. Amery had gotten sleep the previous day; she stood watch so I could close my eyes without fear.

While I napped, I had a dream. As soon as I saw the mysterious black smoke, I knew the visions were coming back again. I saw the place I'd just left, and Spike arguing with my guard.

"How could ya let this 'appen, Bruce?"

"I fell asleep, sir. I didn't think he could escape, sir." The guard cowered in fear.

"Less ya gi' me a good reason t' spare ya, I'll end yar life 'or this. I needed t' know who 'e was!" Spike spat.

"Th…There is one thing you could use to find him again," the crow pleaded.

"What? Spit it out, ya moron!"

"His eyes… they're different. They're flecked with g…" he said, but he didn't get to finish.

Spike lashed out at the guard, raking a sharp talon across his face. "How could ya not tell me this b'fore?" he demanded. "Yar tryin' t' tell me tha' we captured th' bird from th' prophecy, th' only one Nivek cared 'bout? Th' one I tried t' poison, but 'e survived? And ya moron let 'im go?"

"I didn't know!" Bruce cried, blood dripping from his beak. "I swear, I didn't know!" When Spike went to attack again, Bruce shrieked. "Wait! Please, wait! There's one more thing."

"What?" Spike demanded, lowering his talon. "It bett' be good."

"The coffee mixture they used."

103

"You best git t' the point, Bruce," Spike warned, flexing his claw.

"There's only one animal who could find coffee in the city and not get caught by the humans."

Spike's eyes narrowed. "Ya think I don' know the lynx is a part o' this? We've tried attackin' th' boy from th' inside already, for Nivek. But now it's personal. Tha' bird almost ruined my plans! I wanna kill 'im myself, and that dumb ol' lynx, too. I bet there's tons of avian blood ripe for th' takin', tha' he's keepin' safe. But we can't take on th' thirteenth floor, with all 'is wards! Not withou' an army."

"I'll get your army!" Bruce shrunk back, trembling. "Please, give me another chance."

"Fine. If ya can do tha', I'll spare yar life, Bruce. But if ya disappoint me..."

"Thank you, sir. I won't disappoint you. I promise, you will have your army."

XIX

Awakening with a start, I looked for Amery in a panic. When our eyes locked, I shook my head swiftly. We couldn't go back to the thirteenth floor... not now that Spike had a plan to kill me. I told her what I'd seen. She had an uncanny way of understanding me, so it was nice not to have to use as many words.

"The crow," I said simply. "We can't go back."

"But Sheer, he'll attack even if you don't return," Amery said, catching on to what I meant. "And when he does, he'll murder everyone there!"

I shrugged. None of them would want anything to do with me anymore, anyway. Not when they learned we lost Barrie and Violet and Reika, and had ultimately failed in our quest.

"Sheer!" Amery scolded, her brows crossing in anger. "They may not be the friendliest towards you, but they don't deserve to be abandoned! What would Samuel say?"

I flinched. I didn't need to be reprimanded by her... what did she know? She'd only recently arrived on the thirteenth floor, and one of its new members was the rat who'd kidnapped her. She should care even less about them! But... she was right. If my mentor knew I'd rather run away from the thirteenth floor than put myself in the hands of Spike and his army, he'd never forgive me.

I grimaced and looked at Amery, though perhaps not entirely willing to listen to her plan.

"We go back and prepare everyone for battle," she said simply.

Samuel had intended to keep the thirteenth floor safe, and free from spreading panic, by shielding the common creatures from too much knowledge of the dangers lurking in the world. But now that had to change. We could no longer keep them in the dark. If we did, all of them would die without even knowing what had happened. Amery was right, again.

Unable to argue anymore, I consented. We stretched our wings, took off, and flew onward towards the city.

Upon our return, the window opened for us as always, but that was where the hospitality ended. Amery took it upon herself to explain that our mission had been a complete failure. There was no grand feast, since there was nothing to celebrate. Not only had we failed to rescue any of the animals from the smoke, we'd lost Violet, Reika, and Barrie as well. Just thinking about my family and best friend made my heart ache with sadness. Though Amery had given the news, all of the members of the thirteenth floor stood tall and stern, glaring at me. They finally had a real reason to hate me. The cats hissed and lowered their ears, the sparrows looked away, and the others narrowed their eyes. The words *freak, weirdo,* and worst of all, *traitor,* shone in all eyes that met mine. It stung, and the names echoed over and over again in my mind as if I'd heard them firsthand.

You don't belong with us, their stances shouted, and my mind took care of the rest.

Why don't you go back to the cave of smoke and finish what you started? You should be the one at the bottom, not Barrie and Reika.

Why didn't you look out for your friends instead of yourself? No one wants you here. Just go away.

My thoughts put words to their expressions, dragging me down. I tried to push through the crowd, to get to Samuel, to someone who cared about me. No one moved. They wanted me to know how much they hated me. My mind continued to make up what they were saying, the worst ideas rising to the top before I could consider otherwise.

Why doesn't he speak?

You're a freak. You shouldn't even be alive.

106

If I were you, I would kill myself.

I tried to keep my eyes on the floor, but I could feel everyone glaring at me. As much as I knew I needed to help them, to warn them, their hostile eyes bored holes into my soul. The words I imagined them saying sunk deep into my flesh, harsher than any wound. They were angry and afraid; they thought I was some sort of demon. I started to shove.

Ignoring the pecks and even more hate-filled looks I got in return, I pushed harder, squeezing through gaps and pecking at the sides of larger animals who refused to budge. More than anything else in the world, I needed to get to Samuel.

After what felt like a lifetime of negativity, I finally made it to his room. I stopped in shock. It was completely bare. Spinning around, I rushed to Anna's room, picking up speed through the less crowded hallways on the other side of the building.

I flew so fast into the room, the door slammed against the wall in its attempt to get out of my way. Samuel wasn't here either, but Anna was tending to a young rabbit with a bent ear.

"Where is he?" I demanded, landing on the floor. "Where is Samuel?"

When Anna looked at me, her eyes were red from exhaustion. Her coat was rough and unkempt. Her mouth was turned down, and her whiskers drooped. She closed her eyes and shook her head solemnly. "I'm sorry…"

"No," I moaned. "No, it can't be. He was fine when we left!"

"The infection was spreading, Sheer. You know how hard it is to treat something that severe. I did everything I could."

"No," I repeated, shaking my head and stepping back. "No, no, no!"

My confidence shattered, and my hopes drowned; I couldn't bear it any longer. I stumbled forward and flew out the window, up to the roof. A few pigeons were perched there, but they took off as

107

soon as they saw me. I was completely and utterly alone. I wallowed in my grief, alternating between crying and screaming and sitting still until the sun began to set.

Amery came up to check on me. I didn't look at her; I just stared into the sunset. It wasn't fair. Why did such beauty exist in such a cruel world? How could the sky be such fantastic shades of orange and pink, the weather so warm and calm, when everything had gone so wrong? The cold sadness inside of me contrasted starkly with the painted sky and warmth of the summer evening. My senses of sight and touch tingled with delight, but all the negative thoughts threatened to push out the good ones.

I can't hear the crickets chirping. I can't hear the river rushing, nor the humans bustling about. I can't even hear myself speak. What kind of life is this?

I wish I had died in the storm, before I lost my memory.

I wish I had died in the fire, before any of this started.

I wish I had died from the poisoned berries. At least Gander would've been reunited with his family.

I wish I had died in the cave of smoke with Reika and Barrie and Violet.

Everyone I love is dead.

Who is left that cares if I live or die?

Amery came closer and sat next to me. I sighed. *Amery is the only one I have left. If I had to have only one… why couldn't it be Samuel?* I knew I should go back inside, since it was getting dark, but part of me didn't want to go. I wanted to watch the end of the sunset. I wanted to watch the last of the sun's rays vanish, like all of my hope. I wanted to embrace what might happen if I stayed out alone.

Not saying anything – not that I could understand without looking at her – Amery stayed silently beside me until the sun had almost completely disappeared from the horizon. I looked straight ahead at the last fading shades of orange as she finally stood and began to head back. Then she stopped, and I couldn't help glancing up at her.

Her eyes softened in relief when I met her gaze. "Don't worry about the other animals. I'll tell them what we know. I'll prepare them for what's coming. You should come inside and rest. It's not safe to be alone out here after dark."

I shook my head. With a cracked throat, I made my decision. "No, Amery. That's not your responsibility. You don't need that kind of weight dragging you down. I'll tell them. it's my duty and my responsibility now, not yours."

"All right," she responded. "But you need to rest first. You've been through a lot. Please try to get some sleep."

I nodded, then followed her back into the building, into the sparrow room. For a moment, my gaze lingered on Violet's empty perch. I landed on it, feeling the grooves where her claws had worn into its surface. I missed her. Trying to push the thought from my mind, I hopped to my own familiar branch. I closed my eyes and struggled for several minutes to put up a mental wall against the derogatory thoughts that continued to seep into my mind, to no avail.

At some point, I must have fallen asleep from pure exhaustion. When sunlight began to filter through the dusty window, it felt as if I'd only just shut my eyes. I sighed. It was time. No matter what the others thought of me, I had to do the right thing. Samuel wasn't here to guide them anymore, and they needed to know about the coming battle. Whether they chose to take my advice or leave it, it didn't matter to me. At least I would have warned them.

XX

As soon as I entered the great hall during the communal breakfast, I was overwhelmed by the hostile glares. I tried to ignore them, but their fantasied meanings jumped to my mind again. I flew to the head of the table, to Samuel's empty place. If anyone hadn't been staring before, they were now. I closed my eyes, hoping if I couldn't see them, the thoughts would go away.

"Listen!" I cried out, hoping by opening my throat more, my voice would project across the room. "Please," I begged. "I know this is hard, and I know you don't trust me, but there's something that you all need to hear." I peeked through my eyelids to gauge the expressions of the crowd. Most of the animals continued to look at me with suspicion, but some had adopted an expression of curiosity. I continued with urgency, shifting my focus from one attentive creature to the next, ignoring the ones still glaring. "I know that I could never replace Samuel, and I'm not trying to. I know you're all anxious about what will happen to the thirteenth floor without him. But we have something much more dangerous to face, and we need to work together to fight it. A war is coming to our doorstep. A crow named Spike is planning on amassing an army to get past Samuel's wards and attack the thirteenth floor."

Many animals stood or fluttered into the air and spoke out of fear and anger. "Hush!" Anna shouted from the back of the room, so loudly, I could feel the reverberations of her voice from the walls. "Listen to him!"

I nodded to her in thanks. "We have to prepare," I continued. "We can't let them win this battle. Are there any scouts that can look to recruit anyone who can join the fight for us?"

For a few moments, no one moved. Then a couple of hawks, wild cats, and rats came forward. Nyoka was among them. After acknowledging them, I addressed everyone else. "In the meantime, I need all of you to be careful until the time comes. Even if creatures

110

appear to be on our side, it's always possible they are spies for the enemy, trying to find easier ways to get past our guard. Don't disclose any information about our plans to newcomers that I haven't screened."

I hesitated for a moment, then closed my eyes to conjure a vision of the room. Last time, when Nyoka was transforming from a snake to a rat, procuring a vision in real-time had drained my energy and left me dizzy. I didn't want to take it too far, but I needed to know everyone in the building could be trusted.

When the image appeared, everything was gray and blurry except for the animals. None of them, not even Nyoka, was surrounded by darkness. I almost opened my eyes, then Gander wandered in.

Has he spoken to Spike, even after I told him we could help him?

A few wisps of the mysterious smoke clung to his feet like chains, but they didn't encompass his entire form, nor did they go inside him. I dismissed the image. I felt a bit lightheaded, but the feeling was fleeting. I made a mental note to keep this type of vision no longer than I just had, then left my post at the head of the table.

"You do realize," I prodded as I approached the spy, "that Spike has probably been lying to you?"

Gander nodded and looked into my eyes. "I know… but I had to try. I had no other choice!"

"Do you know where he was keeping your family?"

Gander replied with a simple phrase, then his head. *The cave of smoke. They're dead.*

My heart fell. "Oh. I'm sorry."

"I don't know what to do! He can't hurt them anymore at least, but if I stop helping him… I don't know if I'll ever be able to step outside this building again."

"There is one thing you can do," I said solemnly. "Do you think you can continue to see him but switch your allegiance? Can you give him reports that are only partially true and instead divulge his plans to us? When this is all over, he'll be defeated. He won't be able to hurt you."

Gander's eyes expressed pain and sorrow, but a desire to trust. "Do you really think so?"

"Of course," I responded. "He's after me, too, you know. Defeating him is partly an act of self-preservation."

"Partly? What's the rest of it?"

Revenge, I thought. *Revenge for killing everyone I cared about.*

I knew that wasn't the best thing to say right now, though. Out loud, I simply said, "He's evil. His reign needs to come to an end."

"Okay, I'll do it."

Several days later, Nyoka returned with a few dozen small mammals and birds from the forest. None of the other scouts had any news, and Gander didn't know yet when Spike would attack. Many of the animals Nyoka recruited had lived close to the cave of smoke and wanted to help defeat the mastermind who'd lured so many to their deaths. None of the other squirrels or rabbits I'd lived with were interested in joining a fight for me, but Hazel had agreed to come.

"Hazel!" I said as soon as our eyes met. "I haven't seen you in so long! How are you?"

Hazel smiled and waved, then nodded to signify *good*.

I rushed forward and gave her a hug, wrapping my wings around her and leaning my head against her shoulder. "I can read expressions now! I'm very good at it. Try me!"

"Oh! I'm so glad to hear that, Sheer. Did you find your family?" My high spirits plummeted faster than a drop of rain. Hazel's eyes creased in concern. "Is something wrong?"

"I found my sister and my mother," I replied with a sigh. "But it wasn't long before I lost them again. This time, for good."

While Hazel and I reminisced, everyone else sorted into different rooms for battle training. No one really knew what they were doing, but many of the thirteenth floor members had made visible improvements in strength and dexterity in the last few days. They were nowhere near ready to fight against Spike and his crows, but they were more coordinated and capable than they had been before.

I took a break from supervising the activities and flew down from the thirteenth floor, to the outskirts of the forest. I spotted a red beetle with beady black eyes sitting on a branch.

Perfect.

With a battle looming on the horizon, I couldn't push down the skill I'd developed at the waterfall anymore. We needed every advantage we could get. After looking around to make sure no one was watching, I concentrated on the beetle, trying to bring it to me with my mind.

To my surprise, the beetle shot towards me at incredible speed and attacked my head. I shrieked, and Amery flew down from the window to help. She snatched the beetle out of the air and held it down with her claw, gentle enough not to crush it.

Amery looked at me with wide eyes. "It's speaking fragments of Kisalan," she said. "I don't know where it learned our language. It's asking you not to eat it." She looked to the beetle, her eyes furrowed. "Sorry," she continued, turning back to me. "*He's* asking you not to eat *him.*"

"What? Um… okay," I said, not sure whether to address Amery or the beetle. I'd spoken to many different kinds of animals, but none of them had ever been potential meals. I wondered if that was how

Samuel and the other predators felt all the time. A pang of grief wrapped around me. I missed my mentor.

"I don't know if he has a name, or what it is," Amery said. "He just keeps saying he's poisonous and doesn't taste good. It's possible his *name* is Poison... oh, it is?"

"Okay, *Poison*," I replied. "I'm sorry I tried to eat you. You can release him," I continued, looking up at Amery. "I've definitely lost my appetite."

To my confusion, Poison didn't fly off. "Now... he's asking if you're in league with Spike," Amery explained.

"No," I told him. I didn't want to reveal anything else to this beetle that could speak the language of songbirds.

Amery listened to the beetle for a moment, then looked at me. "He said, 'Danger! War! Bad plans that crow has.' I think he's on our side."

I pondered the words, then addressed Poison directly. "What do you know about the crow's plans?"

"He says he knows Spike tried to kill you," Amery translated. "He also says he came here to ask if you needed help in battle. Should we trust him?"

I quickly conjured a vision and immediately dismissed it when I saw he wasn't surrounded by darkness of any kind. There was no residual dizziness, and I breathed a sigh of relief. "I think we should," I told her. "We could use the help. What exactly can you do for us?" I asked, turning to the beetle again.

How much could a tiny beetle do?

"He plans to gather up all of his kind, and all the fruit bats in the region. He says he's known them for some time."

Now, that sounded like a modest proposal. "I accept your help, Poison. Please bring the bats and beetles as soon as possible." With that, the beetle zipped away at a speed I'd never have expected of such a small creature. I shook my head in disbelief and hoped he wouldn't get eaten along the way. Amery and I flew back to the thirteenth floor, still marveling at the strange encounter.

XXI

In my dream that night, I was far away on a deserted island. I saw Spike, surrounded by the mysterious dark smoke to which I was so accustomed. He uttered a loud "Caw!", which could probably be heard for miles. He'd begun recruiting his armies. I wondered where Bruce was, and whether he was also recruiting. Then I noticed something Spike hadn't: a stray crow among the reeds, watching him.

Somehow, I knew it was Spike's niece. *Rebekah.* I didn't know how this information came to me, but I accepted it as true. Regardless, she wasn't enclosed by darkness, so I knew I could trust her. She slipped away from her hiding place and crept to a neighboring island, then flew low to the mainland. There, she was joined by a ruby-throated hummingbird. She nodded to the tiny bird, who then chirped sweetly. Her shrill voice carried far and was answered by a swarm of hummingbirds rising from their places in the fields. Rebekah was calling her own army to fight against her uncle's.

I woke up, startled. We had to find this crow and her flock of hummingbirds, so we could join our forces together. If she tried to attack Spike on her own time, the effect wouldn't be as great as if we all worked together. Determined, I flew to the great hall, where breakfast was being served. I asked around if anyone knew someone who could fly far and fast. Eventually, I was directed to a peregrine falcon, fondly referred to as "Swift."

"Would you be willing to do me a favor?" I asked, taking a brief moment to explain the situation to him.

"Of course, Sheer." He polished off his fish and took off with a burst of speed. I was slightly taken aback, uneasy that I'd so suddenly become well known among the members of the thirteenth floor. Everyone seemed to know my name.

116

I shook off the feeling, now revived with energy. We'd soon have four armies bound together. Nyoka led the modest group of birds and mammals from the forest, Poison was coming with beetles and bats, and Rebekah would soon arrive with a flock of hummingbirds. Amery, Anna, and I led the members of the thirteenth floor. We might actually have a chance in this battle. Spike would be caught off guard when he arrived to find not only the existing members of the thirteenth floor, but three additional armies.

Gander pulled me aside when I was leaving breakfast. "I know when Spike is coming," he said. "But you're not going to like it."

"When?"

"Four days. He's finished recruiting all the crows for miles."

My heart started to race. We may have had the numbers, but we didn't have much strength or coordination yet. I'd hoped we would have more time to prepare. "Four days! That's so soon! Have you heard anything about Bruce and the recruitment he was going to do?"

"No, I haven't heard anything."

Swift returned on the third day. With him, he brought not only Rebekah and her small but feisty hummingbirds, but also Poison and his huge army of beetles and bats. Swift had crossed paths with the other scouts on the way back, and they'd returned empty-handed. It didn't look like anyone else would be joining us before the battle. They had a night to rest. Thanks to Gander, I knew Spike was planning on attacking at nightfall the next day. I tried my best to get sleep, but anticipation and anxiety kept me awake most of the night.

It was an hour before Spike was supposed to attack. Everyone gathered in the great hall. Most were anxious, but some were excited. None of us had ever been in a war before. I began instructing the leaders in turn, hoping my voice was loud enough for all the other animals to hear. I'd been planning with each leader individually in private, trying to coordinate how we'd work this out, but now

117

everyone needed to hear. We all needed to be in tune with each other, to work together, or else we'd fail. There would be no secrets on the thirteenth floor.

"Poison," I began, "I want beetles behind every door. Attack the crows' faces first. Try to blind them if you can." I waited for Poison to translate the message to the swarm of beetles. When they all took to the air, I hastily added, "Don't go anywhere yet! Everyone should know what everyone else is doing."

The beetles settled down again, so I continued. "Bats, be prepared on the ceiling. Surprise them from above and distract them. If you can, wound them and get them out of the building." All of the bats shook their wings in acknowledgment. Many of them yawned. "Perk up!" I called. "I know it's early for you, but we all need to be as alert as possible when Spike's army arrives."

I turned to the flock of brightly colored birds, with Rebekah at the point. "Hummingbirds, I need you stationed evenly throughout the thirteenth floor. You may be small, but you're fast and have long, sharp beaks. Use them."

Finally, I addressed the entire room. "And for the rest of you, use your natural talents. Use your claws and teeth, talons and beaks. Remember the training you've had over the last few days. We're not vicious, like Spike — let's hope for few casualties. But do wound your opponents. The best way to defeat them is to injure them and get them out of the building. When they're weak and coming a few at a time, they won't be able to get past Samuel's magical wards. It's only when they come in strong droves that they'll be able to enter the building."

Looking around at all of the animals, I felt honored that they were willing to give me such rapt attention. "Alright," I finished. "Now all we have to do is wait. Go to your positions. Do not loosen your guard!" As all the animals filed out of the great hall to wait for Spike's army, I turned to where Amery stood beside me. "Dim the lights." Since we knew our way around the building, we had an advantage in the darkness.

We didn't have to wait long before the building began to tremble. *What is that?* I looked at Anna beside me, whose face was morphed into fear. *What did she hear?* I peered down the hall, but there was nothing but shadow. Then two red eyes opened in the middle of the shadow. It was far too large for a crow. My heart felt like it sank into my gizzard. *A bear!*

I turned my head from side to side and could see more. That explained the shaking building: they'd scaled the brick exterior. "Bears!" I shouted. "He brought bears!"

So that's how Bruce helped.

The enormous grizzly bear closest to me swatted away the beetles and bats, unaffected. He rose on his hairy hind legs but had to stop short to avoid putting his head through the ceiling. He opened his gigantic jaw, baring his long, yellow teeth, and roared. I felt the vibrations shake the walls, then his saliva land in my face. I fell backwards out of the air. The bear didn't see me, but charged straight for Anna. The lynx healer was frozen in fear.

"Run!" I shouted, but she didn't hear me. I had to take matters into my own claws. I flew onto the bear's head, clutching at his face. He was so much bigger than me, I could only aim for one eye at a time. I grabbed onto his thick fur, holding on as he spun around and tossed his head violently in an attempt to fling me off. He sank to his belly, pawing at his head to get rid of me.

I hung on for as long as I could, but he was strong and soon shook me off. Anna had brought her wits back together, though, and was fleeing to the great hall. The bear took up almost the entire hallway, and I was pushed along as he pursued her. I managed to right myself and fly ahead of him once he entered the much larger room in the center.

I flew beyond Anna, who had turned to face the oncoming bear, but didn't know what to do to help. I was much too small in comparison. I watched as the bear charged, my focus unwavering. Suddenly, he fell backwards with an earth-shaking impact, as if he'd run into an invisible wall. I drew closer to him and found him unconscious.

119

Did I do that?

If so, I'd somehow kept him from moving. Was this the same ability that had helped me shift the landslide at the waterfall, just in reverse?

I didn't have much time to ponder how I'd immobilized the bear. There were struggles and fights all across the floor. Anna had control of this area, for now.

As I exited the great hall, I looked around at the devastation. Walls were crumbling, animals I knew were slaughtered everywhere, and the bears and crows outnumbered those we had left. I flew through the crowds, scanning the battle for areas where our own forces were most severely outnumbered. My mysterious power had finally come in handy.

XXII

First, I came across a rabbit and mouse fighting against four crows all by themselves. One of the crows had caught the mouse and was gripping her by her tail. The crows didn't hear me approach and were caught off guard when I used my body, plus a bit of help from my ability, to push them over. The one holding the mouse dropped her, and she sunk her teeth into his leg. The rabbit gave each of them a swift kick to the chest, sending them flying into the wall and falling unconscious.

As soon as those four crows were gone, two more filled their place. I knew the mouse and rabbit could handle them now, so I moved on to a fox who was cornered by a bear. I used my ability like I had in the great hall. It worked — the bear stopped moving, standing frozen like a statue. The fox was able to get on top of it, gaining the advantage.

While I continued to help in unfair fights, I began to search for Spike. I needed to fight him and end this battle, but I couldn't find him anywhere. I flitted from one struggle to another as swiftly as possible, like a shadow.

Next I saw two falcons, pinned down by yet another bear. This time, I used my power to lift the bear off them for a moment. They squeezed out and attacked the bewildered bear without questioning how it got there. They were too caught up in the action to care, and took advantage of their new position.

I moved on to help Amery and a couple other sparrows, who were far outnumbered by crows. The crows saw me, and I joined in fighting against them. With more claws and beaks, and my own added tricks to hold back the crows' attacks, we managed to gain the advantage and defeat them. Amery and the two other sparrows knew nothing of my power but thanked me for my assistance. I simply nodded and went to help another struggling group.

121

I came across another lynx, cornered by two nasty bears, and used my power to halt them.

Two crows were pulling a rat in opposite directions. I plowed into one, freeing the rat, who bit into the wing of the other. Again, I was thanked, but again, all I did to respond was give a curt nod.

A few beetles were being chased by crows, who were snapping at them. One crow managed to catch the beetle he was chasing and chomped down hard. He then went after another. I flew in front of him, distracting him, which allowed more beetles to come in and help. I repeated the maneuver for the other two crows.

A bear was preparing to rip off a bat's wing. I jumped onto his face, clawing at his left eye. He released the bat and pawed at me instead. His claws grazed my wings, but the bat and a swarm of beetles came and helped me attack the bear's head from all sides. He leapt out of the nearby window in frustration. We flew back in to continue warding off the enemy's army.

All the bears were now either unconscious or on the ground at the base of the building. The humans below were probably disturbed at this point, but we didn't have time to worry about that. They would have to deal with the situation.

Since all the bears were gone, that meant only crows were left. Even though we'd defeated so many, we were still outnumbered. I still hadn't seen Spike.

Nyoka was clawing at three crows, who were pecking at her tail. I rushed in and knocked one over. He fell into the one beside him, who fell into the third crow, and they all toppled onto the ground.

I found Hazel in the cooking room next to the great hall. She was chucking nuts at about ten nasty-looking crows. I used my power to keep them still for a moment so she could hit them more easily. When I released them, they fell to the ground, knocked out by nuts.

A group of crows were advancing on two small white mice. I snuck up behind them and banged the sides of their heads together as I flew past. Although it wasn't strong enough to hurt them, they all spun around quickly and bonked their heads together, and each fell to the ground. They would have serious headaches when they woke up.

I helped a couple of hummingbirds whose beaks had been stuck in the wall by some bully crows. I helped a few more squirrels, several mice and rats, sparrows, robin, foxes, raccoons, rabbits, beetles, bats, and others. I helped Rebekah, who was struggling against three of her own kin. At some point, I figured I must have helped every single member of the thirteenth floor at least once. Again and again, they thanked me; again and again, I left with no more than a nod.

As I looked around now, I could tell we were slowly but surely beginning to win the battle. Knocked out crows were strewn everywhere. Some larger animals were gathering the unconscious crows, taking them to the windows… and tossing them out. "Hey!" I shouted, charging over. "Don't do that! We aren't savages. We shouldn't cause more casualties than necessary."

"But Sheer," a badger responded, "you said to…"

"I said to put them outside if they were *injured,* not if they're unconscious. You can take them to a room on the outer edge instead. If they start waking up, then you can put them outside. I don't want them to hit the ground before they've gotten a chance to fly away. Do you understand?"

"Yes, sir," the badger replied. "I understand."

"Good."

Finally, I found Spike in the great hall, fighting a couple of squirrels. He flung one of them around by the tail with his good talons, knocked over the other one with her friend, then released the poor creature. The squirrel skidded on the enormous table and came to a halt just before falling off the edge.

Spike was moving in for another round of torture when I attacked him. I used all of my might to get him onto his back, out of breath and distracted. I was tempted to kill him, right then and there. He'd taken Barrie from me, and my mother and sister. But deep

123

inside, I knew it wasn't the right thing to do. What would Samuel have said? Instead, I got up and used my power to constrain the old crow within a spherical boundary just large enough for me to understand what he was saying through his body language.

When he stopped trying to escape, I knew it was time to attempt to sever his connection to the darkness that clung to him. I'd done it before with Nyoka; perhaps I could do it again.

"Spike, this is enough. Don't you see the devastation you've caused?" It was incredibly difficult to speak and hold him there at the same time. My power faltered, and he dropped a bit, but I corrected and held him up again.

Spike snarled. "Why should I listen to you, Sheer?" I tried to impose his accent in my mind, but it was too hard, especially when I was also trying to restrain him. Instead, I refocused on holding him still and interpreting what he was saying.

"I don't recall telling you my name."

"Nivek told me, and he knows everything. Besides, I have a spy on the thirteenth floor. You think Gander is loyal to you? You're a fool."

Despite my normal difficulty of picking up names out of context, this one popped into my mind almost unbidden.

Nivek?

I vaguely remembered hearing the name before. Samuel had told me the animals in my visions were the enemies, and after Spike, only one was left: the wolf. Nyoka had also mentioned being controlled by darkness...

The wolf must have used the darkness as a weapon to control the other two.

Spike spat, forcing me to pay attention to him again. "Well? Have you nothing to say?"

"You're the fool," I responded. "Gander *is* loyal to me. He told me when you were going to attack. And now hundreds of dead bodies are scattered all over the thirteenth floor. When will this be enough, Spike?"

"When Nivek says it's enough."

"And why are you following *Nivek's* orders?" I asked. "Don't you have a will of your own?"

"Nivek's will *is* my will."

XXIII

This was going to be harder than I'd thought. If Nivek really had been in control of Nyoka, he'd done a much better job with the crow. Spike's mindset was refusing to budge.

Maybe talking about the damage isn't enough. I focused on the invisible barrier I'd created around Spike, and it started to move. I brought him out of the great hall, through one of its many arches, to where I'd seen the most destruction. The animals who were collecting crows hadn't arrived in this area yet, so the floor was littered with bodies from both sides of the battle.

"Do you see this, Spike?" I pressed, allowing my focus on his barrier to relax slightly now that we were still. "Not only have you brought destruction to the thirteenth floor, but also to your own army. How many of these crows were related to you? You even fought against your own niece. Would you still be standing with pride if you had killed her in battle?"

"I…" A glimmer of remorse flickered in his eyes, then vanished. "What's done is done. If many must die to accomplish Nivek's goal, then so be it."

Now that I'd glimpsed the good heart inside this ancient crow, I knew there was hope. I pressed harder, trying to exploit this sensitive issue to bring him back the same way I'd saved Nyoka. "Sure, Nivek's goal would be fulfilled. But what was yours? What was your goal in all of this? To kill me? To destroy all of us? To murder half of your own army… your own species? Rebekah fought valiantly against you, against the darkness that has its hold on you. Fight back with her."

"No, I… I didn't plan on killing so many. That was not my goal at all."

Finally, I had his attention. "So when you die," I continued, "how do you want to be remembered? As a merciless, hateful commander who sent his troops to their deaths and murdered his own niece?"

Spike turned away from the carnage, no longer able to look at the bodies. I released my focus on his barrier and flew closer to him. "Don't you see, Spike? Nivek has been controlling you. He has been telling you what to do, and you've been obeying without question. He used dark magic to hold on to you, to keep you from thinking for yourself. But his magic can't control your soul. Reach deep inside and find that sense of right and wrong. Use your soul — your heart — not your mind, to decide. Will you be on our side, or his?"

Spike's brow furrowed. He shook his head from side to side; his pupils dilated and contracted. His talons flexed, and it seemed his entire body was struggling against some invisible force. After wrestling with himself for several minutes, he suddenly stopped, panting. Slowly, he stood, then looked directly into my eyes. His own were strong, clear, and defiant. "I choose your side," he said.

At that moment, the entire building shook. A hairline crack ripped across the floor and up the wall. Early morning light shone brightly through the walls, and dust rained down from the ceiling. The animals left alive on the thirteenth floor ran around in panic. I turned to Spike. "Are there more bears?"

"No. I've never heard anything like this before. It almost sounds like…"

Before he got a chance to finish, a black metal sphere the size of the archway crashed through the walls. Shards of metal, wood, and stone flew in every direction.

"We have to get out of here!" I shouted.

Spike and I flew as quickly as we could, stopping to help slow or injured animals that couldn't run fast enough on their own to escape the wrecking ball. I dove out of the window at the end of the hallway, planted my feet on the ground, and spun around. Some animals were trying to make their way down the stairs on the side of the building, but many were falling. Channeling all of the energy I could muster, I used my power to slow some of the falling animals. I couldn't help them all.

When everyone was out of the building, we fled to the forest. I took one last look at the building as it crumbled at the hands of an ungodly metal machine. The humans controlling it looked like mice in comparison to its size. Our home was lost.

Everywhere I looked, evicted animals of the thirteenth floor with their shreds of blue were huddled in clusters among remaining hummingbirds, beetles, and crows. Anna was passing from one patch to another, offering what comfort she could despite having lost the stash of medical supplies she'd accumulated over the years. She turned and looked towards me — no, beside me. I followed her gaze to see Amery speaking to the crowd.

"We need to bind together," she was saying. "Now, more than ever. With Samuel gone, and our home destroyed, we need a new leader to bring us through this tough time." She looked at me, and I immediately knew what she was implying.

"No, I don't want to lead," I said. "What about Anna? She's been an established member of the thirteenth floor all her life. Or even Nyoka or Spike. They've mended their ways and have much more experience than me."

A tiny white rabbit kit bounded up to me and put her paw on my wing. "I want *you* to be our leader," he said.

"But I…" I tried to protest, but other animals began to stand and voice their approval. Out of respect for my disability, they took turns giving me their reasons. Bewildered, I watched their expressions, full of respect and adoration I didn't feel I deserved.

"You helped all of us in battle."

"Yes, and you were with Samuel more than any of us."

"And you have already led us."

"You're the best fit for the job."

"You're the smartest…"

"…and the most courageous."

They all whispered a phrase I couldn't quite grasp, but the exact words didn't matter. It was a sort of name, respectful and admiring. I looked to Amery for a final opinion, hoping she'd changed her mind. I didn't want this power.

"I think you can do it," she said simply.

"Do all of you really want me to be the next guardian?" I asked, turning back to the crowd.

Many said, "Yes." Others just nodded their heads, but all were in support of the decision.

"It's unanimous, Sheer," Amery told me as I turned back to her. "Everyone really does believe in you."

I gazed into her eyes, trying to tell her I didn't want it. Her own eyes softened as she said gently, "I know you don't want power, Sheer. That's why you're the best one to receive it."

I stood quietly for a moment, then addressed them all. "I guess you have decided, then. I'll be — I am — the new guardian of…" I hesitated, not sure what to call our group at first. *The thirteenth floor* certainly wasn't fitting anymore. But then again, there was only one name good enough for this. Paying tribute to my mentor and the previous guardian, I finished: "…of Samuel's family."

Wolf

XXIV

I cleared my throat and hopped onto a large rock to address the crowd once more. "Well, the first order of business should be... order. All the former members of the thirteenth floor have pieces of blue fabric that have helped identify us from other animals and keep us safe. That is more important than ever, now that we are no longer sheltered by the safety of the building and its wards." I shivered, recalling the other way Samuel's wards were keeping me safe. I'd traveled outside the thirteenth floor in confidence before, but I'd never stayed in one place for more than a night without him beside me. Now that we were permanently moved outside of its walls, and without the constant presence of the wise lynx himself, would his protective spell on me hold true?

"Everyone who fought beside us in the battle is welcome to join Samuel's family, if they so choose. Please ask your neighbor to share a piece of their fabric. We should have a few expeditions into the city to try to collect more. Does anyone volunteer?"

Nyoka was the first to raise her paw, and several other rats joined her. "Excellent," I continued. "You should blend in with the city dwellers enough to go unnoticed, but travel at night just to be safe. As for any other newcomers who might wish to join our family, I'll need to make sure they are safe first. Without Samuel's wards to protect us, we don't know who we can trust out here, so make sure to introduce me to all new creatures so I can scan them for signs of darkness."

Many animals nodded in agreement, and some were already exchanging pieces of blue fabric with those who'd fought alongside us. When I had their attention again, I continued. "Now, the other thing we all need to keep in mind is that we are encroaching on established territory. I need as many of you as possible to spread throughout the forest and talk to its current residents. We need to make sure they are willing to relocate, willing to coexist with us, or

133

even better, interested in joining the family. Our total territory needs to be large enough to house all of us peacefully. Who is able to help with this important step?"

I was exhilarated to see over half of the animals step forward as one. Of those who didn't volunteer, almost all of them were injured. "Thank you!" I cried. "Thank you all for your willingness to help rebuild our society. Before we disperse, I'll let Anna talk about specific herbs and roots we need to treat the injured right now. Please look for them while you're out and about, and bring back as much as you can. But always make sure to leave enough of the plant intact that it can grow back, or else we won't be able to sustain our supply." With that, I stepped down from the rock, letting Anna take my place.

"That was good, Sheer," Amery said to me as I walked towards her. "See? I told you that you'd make a good leader."

I simply shrugged, then turned to watch Anna. Even though I knew just as much about the plants needed for medical treatment, it was nice not to be the center of attention for a while.

When Anna had finished speaking, everyone who was well enough to scout the forest dispersed into the woods, following my instructions. Amery and I went together to get a more detailed scope of the land and look for landmarks we could use to mark the boundaries of our territory if all went well. With the wolf still on the prowl, Samuel's army needed a defined border to defend in case of another war.

Amery and I traveled deep into the forest until we reached a brook that flowed gently as far as we could see in either direction. If we could convince everyone between the brook and city to relinquish their land to us, this would make a clear edge of our territory. Moving northwest along the edge of the brook, we stopped at an enormous pine that had fallen over a long time ago. Five of its branches had taken root and become their own self-sustaining trunks, stretching high into the sky in parallel lines. From the top of one of these, we could see the roof of the last tall building on this side of the city. To the west, I noticed a long ridge of dark, barren cliffs. It contrasted starkly with the tree-covered mountains in the east.

Has that ridge always been so dark?

It didn't matter now; they were far beyond any territory we could possibly fill. Amery and I looped around to the other side of our potential territory and found a large clearing cutting into the forest on the opposite end of the city, then a sandpit next to the stream.

Having determined the four corners and outer edge ideal for sealing off our territory, we returned to the center of it all, where everyone had begun to gather in another clearing. We'd been too busy fighting a battle to have breakfast, and a few animals had gathered some supplies to prepare our first meal outside of the thirteenth floor. Clusters had formed based on diet. I realized I'd never learned where Samuel had procured all of the fish, grains, fruit, and vegetables all of the members had subsided on for decades. As much as it pained me that we'd lost so many lives in the battle, we could no longer afford to feed many more mouths than those who'd survived. I shivered when I saw a group of hawks huddled around the body of a vole, and hoped everyone would continue to respect the other family members, even when meals were tight.

Just as I was about to step into the clearing, something underneath a huckleberry bush caught my eye. I lighted down next to the soft ground, curious.

As soon as I stepped under the overhanging branches of the wild bush, I stopped short in horror. I could only stare, not wanting to look at it but unable to look away.

When Amery joined me, she asked, "What is it, Sheer? What's wrong?"

"Don't you see that?"

"What, the stem of the bush? It seems normal enough to me."

"No, no… the claw." A shiver ran down my entire body. "The bloody claw." I continued to stare at the grotesque wolf's claw, glistening with fresh, red blood.

"No, Sheer. I don't see it. I'm sorry."

A vision.

It had come too soon. I wasn't ready for this — none of us was. I'd seen Nivek's claw in my visions before, but it had always been clean and white. The change could only mean he'd shed blood and was gaining power. We would have to act quickly if we wanted to stop him.

I sighed. "The war isn't over. It has only just begun."

Amery looked at me, fear in her eyes. I wanted to protect her from what she was afraid of, but I felt powerless to do so. The only thing I could do was fight and hope no one else got hurt in the process.

"I hate this!" I cried, suddenly overcome with frustration and anger. "Why can't we just live our lives? I haven't had a single break since I woke up in that stupid fire. Every time I found a place that was safe, something terrible happened."

"I'm sure it's not as bad as you think," Amery started to say, but I couldn't let her finish.

"Not that bad? When I lived with the squirrels, fire struck wherever I stayed for more than a night. When I found the thirteenth floor, I was roped into this whole thing about fighting evil, or something. Of course Spike found out where I was and poisoned me. When that was over, I went out to try to do something good — to rescue my father and save the animals from the cave of smoke — but guess what happened then?"

"Sheer, you don't have to…"

"No, listen to me! I lost everyone, okay? I lost my sister and my mother. I lost my best friend. And when I came back, Samuel was gone! I didn't even get to say goodbye to him. He was just… gone. And now our home is gone, too. Everything I've ever gained, everyone I ever cared about, I've lost."

Amery's eyes wavered. "Everyone?"

136

Anger festering inside me, I spit out my answer without thinking. "Yes, Amery. If Samuel hadn't risked his life for you, his leg would never have gotten infected and he wouldn't have died. It's your fault he's dead. I wish he had never tried to save you."

"Fine, Sheer. Thanks for telling me how you really feel." Amery turned and flew past me to sit beside Anna, and I realized that some of the animals nearest to us were watching me. When our eyes met, they looked away.

"I just want my mentor back," I mumbled, but my anger was fading, and I felt bad for hurting Amery. I grabbed a peck of seeds from the pile in the center of the clearing and sat by myself to eat, facing away from all the other animals.

XXV

When I was halfway through my pile of seeds, I felt a light tap on my wing. I turned around to see Amery standing next to me. I opened my beak in an attempt to apologize, but she averted her gaze and simply gestured behind me, where a badger was standing with a chickadee held softly but firmly in his mouth. As soon as I looked back at Amery, she was already walking away.

I'll talk to her later, I decided, then addressed the badger. "What is it?"

The badger wrote his name in the ground with his claw. "My name's Ryan," he said, releasing the chickadee from his mouth. The tiny bird was sopping wet and trembling. "Everyone who was in the expedition to talk to the current residents of this part of the forest came back with good news, sir," the badger continued, eyeing the bird. "But this is a newcomer. I thought you'd want to see him."

"Why'd you treat him so harshly?" I asked, examining the new bird. He was about my age, I supposed, perhaps a little younger, but it was hard to tell.

Ryan responded without taking his eyes off the chickadee. "He was struggling, sir. He wouldn't allow me to escort him to you, and he didn't want to wait until you had returned from scouting or until you had finished eating. He was too eager to see you, sir, and he wanted to find you on his own. I was afraid he might have intended you harm."

"This little guy? He seems harmless enough. Thanks for your concern, Ryan, but I'll take it from here."

"Thank you," he replied, then bowed and uttered another word or phrase I didn't recognize. Perhaps he had called me something other than "sir" or "Sheer" or "sparrow." It seemed respectful,

138

anyway, so I didn't worry too much about it. Instead, I turned to the newcomer.

"I'm sorry for your trouble," I told him. "Everyone's a bit on edge since we're still new to the forest. Why were you so eager to see me?"

"I've heard a great deal about you, sir," he said with wide eyes, shaking out his feathers. "Your name is well known where I'm from. I wanted to see you myself; to see if you were real."

I chuckled, then stopped. No matter how long I'd endured this ailment, it was still awkward to feel the rumbling in my throat and tickle in my sides, but to hear nothing. It was far worse than not hearing my own voice, which I'd mostly gotten used to by now. I cleared my throat. "What's your name, chickadee?"

He spoke his name, and I blinked. I'd gotten so used to reading body language, I'd forgotten I had no way to learn details like names. I glanced at Ryan, thankful he was still present. "Could you write it down, please?" Realization crept into the chickadee's eyes, then a flash of pity — a look I'd seen many times before, whenever someone learned I was deaf.

"Kevin," the badger wrote.

"Nice to meet you, Kevin." I could feel Amery watching me from across the clearing, as if her eyes were burning into the back of my head. It was time to adhere to my earlier claim and scan the first new member of the family for any sign of the darkness that had pushed Nyoka and Spike to become villains. It felt silly to scan this tiny chickadee; he was so innocent and frail, like a child. But I had a duty to fulfill, so I would humor her.

"Stay where you are for a moment," I instructed Kevin. When his composure shifted to fear, I comforted him. "Don't worry; this won't hurt, and it will only last a second. I just need to look at you... from a different perspective." He seemed to relax a bit but was still tense. He'd never been reviewed by me and wasn't a member of Samuel's family, so he'd never seen me procure a vision before. He

139

had no idea what I was going to do, and I didn't know how to explain it any further, so I decided to act swiftly and get it over with.

I closed my eyes and willed the image to appear. To my dismay, the bloody claw from earlier snapped into view and overtook my thoughts. The darkness around the claw was dense and seemed... *alive.* It reached for me, trying to smother me, strangle me. I tried to shove it down, to bring the vision back to a perspective of my current surroundings, but the darkness only grew bolder and stronger. Finally, just as it reached me, I had no choice but to release it. When it cleared, I gasped for air. For a moment, it had felt as if the darkness really was constricting my throat. I shook my head, trying to clear my mind and compose myself.

"You're fine," I told him once I'd caught my breath. There was no use worrying about a harmless chickadee when there were much bigger concerns looming in the future. The deadly claw was a sign I couldn't ignore, and we would need to prepare for another battle — perhaps one worse than the first. "So, do you want to join Samuel's family? We need everyone we can get to help fight Nivek. That wolf is dangerous. I'm not sure exactly how, but I just know."

"Yes, actually," the little bird responded. "That's why I came to see you."

I could still feel Amery's eyes boring into my skull, though when I shot her a glance, she looked away. It was making me uncomfortable. "Really? Why don't you tell me about it? Let's find a cozy spot to chat. I'd love to hear about your journey and where you come from."

XXVI

Kevin and I flew a little further off, to a bush near the border stream. "I live with my family over there, where the forest edge meets the mountains," he said, pointing to the east. It was very easy for me to read his body language, even though I hadn't met many chickadees, because it was so similar to my own and full of extra flourishes — though he could have been adding those intentionally on account of my disability. Either way, I was grateful. I relaxed in his company, not burdened with trying so hard to understand what he was saying.

"Nivek and his wolves have invaded those lands," he continued. "The mountains are no longer safe. The wolves have traveled from the far north and are making their way west now that they have come near the forest. They have already taken over all the barren land up there. From what I've heard, Nivek has gathered together more than a hundred packs of wolves, and there may even be a worse creature with him."

"What sort of creature?"

"I've never seen it, but I've heard rumors. It's a creature of legend supposedly hovering over the dark western cliffs, where the wolves are headed. it's a dark animal, evil beyond all evil, and answers only to Nivek. Some say it's the spy and servant of the devil himself." As soon as he said this, I recalled the myth Samuel had described to me.

Malvador. Could it be real?

Samuel had thought that perhaps, if it was real, it had something to do with the fires that had haunted me when I lived with the squirrels. I shivered, imagining this shadow vulture lurking in the darkest places.

"No one who ventures near the dark cliffs ever returns alive," Kevin continued, "so no one really knows for certain whether Malvador truly exists. But it's said that it can traverse miles with a single swift beat of its wings, and that every place it passes over is consumed by fire and turned to ash. I don't know whether all this is true or not, but one thing I do know: Nivek has been terrifying both animals and humans into submitting to him. He burns any village or region that resists. On top of that, the numbers behind Nivek have been staggering ever since the wolf murdered his father just a couple days ago."

"Wh…He did *what?*"

"You haven't heard? Their pack was one of the strongest in this part of the country. He murdered his father, the original pack leader. He was second in command and next in line, but he couldn't wait. Nivek's lust for power was just too great. And his desire for power wasn't satiated when he became pack leader. Oh, no. Now he wants to rule *everything.*"

Kevin's last statement was so fierce, I was suddenly very afraid. I thought for a moment, realizing this enemy was far more evil than either of his predecessors. I could see the fear reflected in Kevin's eyes and knew he'd come to me because he worried his community was next in line. Anger towards Nivek brewed inside me.

How could he do this? Why would anyone want that much power?

"I'm shocked to hear this," I told him. "But why come to me? What could I possibly do to stop such a monster?"

Kevin's countenance sank. "What do you mean? I've heard of your great strength in war, of your vast army. If anyone could defeat the wolf, it would have to be you. I've even heard rumors of your… special abilities."

I was flattered, but at the same time confused. I hadn't told anyone about my powers, not even my closest friends. Samuel would've been the first to know, if I hadn't been afraid to let it show.

I'd only used it openly in the heat of a battle, when everyone was distracted. How could anyone have known?

Spike, I realized, my eyes widening. *He would know. I never told him not to share the information… there was no time. It hasn't even been a full day since the battle.*

"Who told you of my powers?" I asked.

Kevin hesitated. "I don't know. I just heard talk of all the things you've done. You didn't think actions that great would go completely unnoticed, did you?"

I thought for a moment. I supposed if Spike had started to talk about my powers, others may have attributed them to my assistance in the battle. After that, it wasn't really that surprising to think the news would've spread like wildfire.

I wish someone had confronted me about it, though.

"What exactly do you know?"

"Only that you can control an object's movement without touching it, that's all. I don't know how you do it, but I sure wish I did. It's really cool."

"You're not afraid of me because of it?"

"No! Of course not, why would I be? I'm on your side, right? And you're on mine. So, I'm glad to have your abilities in support of me."

I had never thought of it that way, and it made me smile. After all, once I gained control of it, I had only used my power for good. Maybe it wasn't something to be afraid of anymore. "Well, thanks. I don't really know what to say, Kevin. It's nice to have someone I can talk to about it."

Kevin smiled. "Of course! So… do you think you can defeat Nivek?"

I shook my head. Even though I'd won over the snake and crow, this was an entirely different situation. "I know you think highly of

143

me, and that you think I can accomplish anything, but how could I possibly fight him? We lost over half of our army fighting against Spike's bears and crows. Forget Malvador; if Nivek really has hundreds of packs of wolves behind him, what can a few woodland creatures do against him? We'll be obliterated."

"I don't know... maybe you don't need to fight him. Maybe you could strike a deal with him so he won't destroy the forest. But if you don't do anything at all, the entire place will be nothing more than burned tree stumps, ashes, and millions of creatures without homes — if they survive." He looked at me with big, pleading eyes. "Can't you help?"

I sighed. "Why me? What could I have to offer him? I'm just a little sparrow with weird eyes and no hearing and some sort of matter manipulation ability I barely understand. Surely, there's someone more powerful than me that could strike a deal with him."

"Not really. You're the only one who poses a threat to him, Sheer. The only thing he's afraid of... the prophecy. *The only hope against the scourge, the hero shall restore the light*," he paraphrased. "Only you have something to offer that he might be interested in."

"What would that be?" I asked. *Does everyone know about this prophecy?*

"Not to be a threat anymore."

"Oh." I thought about that for a moment. I had spent all of this time chasing phantoms from my visions to defeat the darkness and evil, to fulfill the prophecy like Samuel would've wanted. What meaning would my life have if I just let everything go? Would Nivek terrorize another region, even if I made a pact with him for this one? But would *not* making a deal with him be worse? Maybe making a deal would reduce some of the damage...

"How would he even find me to strike an agreement?" I asked. "Why would he even want to make an agreement instead of just leveling us all right now?"

"The way I see it, if he made an agreement with you and you were honor bound to keep it, he's reducing the risk that you could

144

somehow stop him from taking over everything else. He doesn't have to know you aren't actually strong enough to stop him. But don't worry... he'll find you. He always finds what he's looking for. It's scary, almost."

I looked over to where Kevin had said his home was. Somewhere out there, Nivek was murdering and plundering human villages and swaths of forest and grassland.

How long before he finds us here?

In the distance, dark clouds that mirrored my thoughts were quickly forming. The air grew dense with coming rain. "Speaking of scary," I said to myself.

"What's that you said?" Kevin asked as I turned back to him.

"Nothing. Let's get to a more sheltered place before it starts raining."

"All right. I saw a tree hollow nearer to the center of the camp. We can go there."

Together, we flew to the indicated tree. The hollow was an old squirrel nest, and it reminded me of my days before the thirteenth floor. It was homey but brought back memories of fleeing from hiding place to hiding place, never safe for long.

It wasn't long before the sky unleashed a torrent of water. I shivered, watching the many silvery droplets plummet outside the hollow. Kevin looked at me with knowing eyes. "Afraid of rain?"

I nodded slowly, hesitantly. I trusted him, but I'd never voiced this fear before. Samuel had known, I was sure, but I'd never acknowledged it openly. "Don't tell anyone."

"I won't."

Kevin and I sat quietly, watching the rain for some time. Even though I was afraid of it, I was glad I had something to distract my mind from the horrible, bloody claw. After a while, Kevin shifted on

145

his feet. "I hope you don't mind," he said, "but I do have to leave in the morning."

"What? Why?" I didn't want to lose this friend I'd only just found.

"I need to tell my family that there is hope… that you will protect them from Nivek."

"Couldn't you have brought them here?"

"No," he replied. "My mother is too sick to make the journey. All the smoke isn't good for her. I wish I could, though."

"Oh. I'm sorry to hear that."

"Yeah. I don't really want to go. I'd rather stay here, with you, but I promised them I'd return. They need some good news. There's been far too much bad news lately."

"I understand. Family comes first. At least you have a family to go back to. You should cherish that."

"You don't?"

I sighed. "No. I watched my mother and sister die, and my father has probably been at the bottom of the Cave of Smoke for a long time." Thinking about them made my heart wrench with a sadness I'd kept inside me for far too long. The sadness lingered, then morphed into guilt. There were so many things I could have done that might have prevented their deaths. Maybe if I'd given them the coffee first instead of indulging myself…

"Not the Bottomless Pit!" Kevin cried. "How terrible! How did your mother and sister die? If you don't mind me asking."

"The same way. Along with my best friend." I tried to suppress the deep guilt rising in my gut as I remembered Barrie, but couldn't.

"I'm so sorry. I had no idea. So you have no one, then? Is there no one else you can call a friend?"

"I had a mentor, Samuel... but he's gone now, too. He lost his life to an infection after saving Amery. She's still here, but... yeah. It's hard to look at her and not wish Samuel were here instead."

"So you have no one? Not a friend in the world?" Kevin's eyes were full of sympathy.

I choked. "No one."

"That's so sad."

"You're telling me." I wanted to look away, to forget everything again, but I had to keep my eyes focused on Kevin to understand him.

"Can I say one more thing?"

"Go ahead."

"I don't think it's your fault your family and friends are no longer with you."

"What... what do you mean?"

"Who was the one who created the Bottomless Pit in the first place?"

"Spike."

"Well, yes, through Nivek. He was influenced by the darkness, remember? Pushed far beyond where he would ever go on his own."

I nodded, starting to realize where Kevin was going with this. "He... he probably wouldn't have been able to revive the extinct Beasts from the blood of birds without some external influence either. One of those monsters ate my sister."

"Right! Don't you see? How can it be your fault they're dead, if it was the wolf who instigated it all in the first place?"

"And if the snake hadn't been influenced by Nivek, she would never have created that world or captured Amery, and Samuel wouldn't have had to risk his life."

147

"Exactly! It's not your fault at all. It's Nivek you should be angry at. And now his full power is being unleashed on the entire world, not just through a few measly puppets."

"You're right!" I said, my guilt quickly fading and churning into anger. "You're right, it's all his fault! That does make me feel better... I just need to find a way to destroy him. To stop him from hurting anyone else. Thank you, Kevin."

Kevin beamed. "At your service."

XXVII

"You're special, Sheer," Kevin said. "I just know it."

"What makes you say that?"

"Can't you see? You've lost so much, yet here you are, a leader and a friend. You're deaf, but you're talking to me as if that didn't hinder you at all. And you have special powers that, as far as I know, no one else has ever possessed. I wish I had been there when you used them. It must have been amazing!"

A hint of pride blossomed inside me. Everything he had said was true... maybe I *was* special. "Thanks, Kevin. You know... I could show you. If you want."

Kevin's eyes widened with excitement. "Would you really?"

"Just give me a moment to think of something." Kevin's expectations were high, and I wanted to exceed them. After his encouragement, I was full of confidence and felt sure I could accomplish anything. I wanted to try something new. I'd manipulated matter in the past, from rocks to bears to even my own body. But what about *air* itself?

I stared at the rain outside the hollow, concentrating, and steeled myself against the fear. My instinct was to close my eyes and draw back from the water, but I wanted to see my creation.

As I watched and focused, a small sphere devoid of rain formed among the downpour. I allowed it to grow to twice my size, then held it steady. Rain fell on and around it, curving around its shape until it was a shimmering, watery orb. Finally, I released it. The sphere fell apart, and the drizzle filled its place as if nothing had happened.

"Wow," Kevin said when I turned back to face him. "That was beautiful, Sheer."

We watched the rain fall for a while, then drifted off to sleep. When I woke in the morning, the rain had stopped. Kevin was gone.

He left to go back to his family without saying goodbye?

I didn't have much time to sink into my disappointment, because Amery suddenly popped her head into the hollow.

"There you are! I've been looking all over for you. Breakfast is starting."

"Oh… okay." She turned to go back to center camp, but I stopped her. "Amery, wait. About earlier… I'm sorry. I miss Samuel, but I shouldn't have said that I wished you had died instead."

Amery turned back to face me and sighed. "It really hurt me, Sheer. But I forgive you."

We flew back together in silence. When we got there, I stopped in surprise. Kevin was there, eating breakfast.

"Amery, why didn't you tell me that Kevin was still here?"

"Why am I supposed to keep track of him for you? Is he leaving?"

"Just, I don't know, be more informative next time. We were together all of yesterday, and suddenly he's gone, and you were just here, so you must have known. He's leaving this morning, and I didn't get a chance to see him off."

"Well, now you know. Why's he leaving, anyway?"

"Does it matter?"

"Yes, Sheer… why would someone come here, join Samuel's family, and then leave the next day? Don't you think that's suspicious?"

"He's going to see his family, if you must know. Don't jump to conclusions like that. It's rude."

Amery fluttered her wings. Finally, she had no more to say against my new friend. I flew past her and joined Kevin for breakfast.

"Hey," he said when I landed next to him. "Is everything okay? I didn't want to leave without saying goodbye, so I decided to wait until you woke up. But then I smelled food being prepared and got hungry, so I came out here. I hope you weren't too worried."

"No, it's okay," I told him. "I'm glad you didn't leave." I sighed, pushing away my anger towards Amery. I didn't want my bitterness to seep into my conversation with Kevin. I could see her watching me out of the corner of my eye. I sighed. There was nothing I could do to convince her to like Kevin, too.

"I'm going to need to leave soon, though," Kevin said. "I'll head out after breakfast is over, if that's okay with you."

"Of course."

When we'd finished, we said our goodbyes and Kevin took off towards the mountains. Poison and her beetle clan, and Rebekah's hummingbirds, also left to return to their proper homes. Spike's crows took their leave, but Spike remained. After that, the day continued into what I guessed would quickly become routine. I patrolled our borders, and a few other newcomers joined Samuel's family. I tried to scan them for darkness, but the claw still overpowered any vision I tried to conjure. This time, I didn't let it continue far enough for the darkness to reach me. Instead, I cut it short as soon as I saw the claw and the darkness started to move in my direction.

It was a very long day, and by the time the sun began to set, I was exhausted. Most of Samuel's family was going to sleep, but many others were nocturnal, just waking up. I perched on the highest branch of a pine tree and took a deep breath, savoring the scent of pine sap and crisp evening air. It would be autumn soon. I looked out at the clear sky, where a few stars were coming out and the full moon glowed brightly. I knew the frogs, crickets, and other night creatures would be stirring and joining their melodies together, like I'd heard in my first visions back when I lived with the squirrels. Amery had described the sounds to me multiple times as well; she loved to listen to them as she went to sleep. I wondered if the wolves were close enough that she could hear them howling. I considered asking her but changed my mind. She wouldn't want to talk to me anyway.

I turned my thoughts from things I couldn't hear to things I *could* see. The sunset was beautiful tonight. The perfect mixture of orange and pink just along the horizon contrasted the deep, dark blue of the coming night. The sun made it look like the edge of the forest was on fire. The wind shifted, blowing from the east instead of the west, and I froze. I smelled smoke.

I spun around, nearly losing my grasp on the branch, and saw the source: where the forest met the mountains. Kevin's home.

XXVIII

I flew to center camp, where many of Samuel's family had already gathered, waking in panic. Kevin's home was nearly a day's journey away, but the wind from the east carried with it the scent and threat of fire. It could spread to us quickly if we didn't do anything. Everyone looked to me for answers, but I had none to give. We couldn't possibly quench the fire in time. It was too far away, too large, and growing. We could try to keep it from spreading, but we'd run out of resources long before we got it under control.

I looked again at the sky. Why did it have to be clear *tonight*, of all nights? If only rain would come and quench the fire, or if the wind would change again and send the fire back towards the mountains and the wolves. I remembered back to my first days on the thirteenth floor, when I'd dreamed of deterring an evil wind. I didn't know how to sing that language, but I could try. I whispered to the wind, not sure what else to do. "Please," I said. "Please change directions. Please save us from this fire... and Kevin, too." I felt stupid talking to the wind, and nothing happened.

Please help us, I called out in my mind, trying to channel my focus into a nonverbal shout. *Please help us, please help us, please help us!* The wind only blew stronger, still from the east. "Well, that did a lot," I mumbled.

There was nothing else we could do. This was not under my control. "We're going to have to escape through the city," I addressed the crowd. "Before the fire..."

"Wait!" Amery exclaimed, flying over to me and pointing the tip of her wing to the east. "Look!"

I turned back around, facing the ever-strengthening wind. The fire was slowly spreading towards us, but clouds were coming swifter still, carried by the wind. They were dark and heavy — full of rain. The mighty rushing of air slowed to a gentle breeze as the clouds gathered over the distant valley, and rain began to pour. Smoke billowed into the air, followed by steam, and the flames flickered in the night. The sky emptied the last of its moisture as the fire died out, and soon everything was as calm and clear as it had been before. The breeze was even coming from the west now.

Was that a huge coincidence, or did the wind really respond to me?

Either way, we were safe now. I just hoped Kevin was, too.

The moon waned to nothing, then waxed to full, and I still hadn't seen Kevin. My heart fell each and every day without him, and I worried he'd died in the fire and I'd never see him again. If that wasn't bad enough, I saw the bloody claw everywhere now. Along the bank of the river, in the middle of the clearing at center camp, around every twist and turn in the forest. Amery kept her distance from me, but I caught her out of the corner of my eye, watching me with worry. I didn't know why she was staying away, but I was glad she wasn't constantly nagging me about the visions.

I knew the wolf was dangerous, but the bloody claw wasn't giving me any new information anymore. It was just always there, always haunting me, keeping me awake at night and on my toes during the day. I hadn't tried to summon a vision in a long time, but maybe it was time to try again. As much as I was afraid of the darkness trying to strangle me, I needed to know what the wolf was up to. I needed to know how much time we had before he would strike.

Taking a deep breath, I cleared my mind and narrowed my focus on the wolf. Only when my mind was filled with nothing but the idea of the dark wolf did I call upon the vision, in the hope that the focus would bypass the apparition of the claw.

It worked. Soon, I saw Nivek, but at first I didn't recognize him. The wolf was as black as shadow, much darker than before. The murky, evil darkness surrounded him and permeated his entire body,

154

as if it was a part of him. His figure was crisp and clear, so I knew he was nearby.

When he spoke, I realized Nivek also had an accent I wouldn't have recognized outside of a vision. "Ya," he was saying. "I understahnd."

"Good," a deep voice resounded, echoing through the vision. I spun my head as if to locate the speaker, but saw nothing. "It must be tonight," the voice continued, "for he has seen what we can do. The untimely rain ruined our initial plan. We must act before he grows any stronger, Finsternis."

Finsternis? I wondered. *Why would this speaker use a different name for Nivek?*

"I vill do as you 'ave asked," the wolf declared, his lips curling up in a sneer and revealing serrated teeth stained with blood.

XXIX

Just as I cleared the vision from my mind, I saw Amery flying swiftly towards me. Her eyes were wide with fear, and she was shaking uncontrollably. She spoke so quickly and made so many wild motions, I had to ask her to slow down so I could understand her. I couldn't read her movements if they were so erratic. She paused and gathered her wits together. Even when she spoke slightly slower, I was still only able to catch bits and pieces of what she was trying to say.

"Sheer, the wolves... camp is surrounded... howling... everyone afraid. What do we do?"

She stopped to catch her breath, and the terrifying reality suddenly crashed on me. They'd come. I racked my mind, trying to come up with a plan on the spot. Spike, Nyoka, and I had come up with some plans, but none of us had anticipated them coming from out of nowhere like this. We were completely unprepared.

And then, suddenly, Kevin flew beside me. I couldn't tell where he'd come from, but was overcome with relief that he was alive and here to help. "Sheer," he said, slowly and calmly so I could understand, "Nivek is coming to speak with you. I heard him myself."

Kevin's calm mannerisms helped me relax, but I had no time to react. As if on cue, the scarred wolf and two others lunged through the bushes behind the chickadee. Now that I was face-to-face with him, Nivek was even more terrifying. The formidable glare in his yellow eyes, the ragged scar across his face, the razor sharp teeth in his maw, the pitch black fur standing up from his back, his immense size... and his long, sharp, blood-stained claws evoked the deepest fear I'd ever felt. His gray-coated companions seemed like pale, harmless puppies in comparison. I was no longer astonished that he'd be capable of murdering his own father.

Kevin and Amery stood perched behind me, shaking with fear. The sky seemed to darken with the wolf's very presence, and I could feel the dead silence, even though I couldn't hear it. It felt as if the world were holding its breath. I sensed a deep, rumbling tremor as Nivek began to speak. I tried to pretend I was brave, brave for Samuel's family and Kevin and Amery.

"I have heard of you, Sheer," he snarled, "though we have never officially met. I am Finsternis. Your worst nightmare." I barely had time to register that the wolf had used his longer name before a high-pitched ringing blasted through my head, flooding it with pain. The sound dimmed for a moment, and I heard a voice in my head, just like Samuel's so long ago. This voice was different — higher pitched and tinny, but a welcome relief when compared to the ringing resounding in my mind.

"He's trying to control you, Sheer. Don't let him in, and don't let him fool you. The name Finsternis is only a cover, to conceal his true identity. You know his true name, but he doesn't know that and wants to keep it secret. Names have power; knowing a name can make the bearer vulnerable. Trust me, and I can pull you through this."

I forced my eyes open through the pain, and through my bleary surroundings, spotted Kevin's eyes boring through me.

So it's him.

I was surprised at Kevin's ability to speak in my head like Samuel had, but I was too distracted to care. I bent over, cringing in pain at the sound in my mind as it amplified again. Kevin could apparently hear my thoughts as well, for he responded, *"I didn't want you to be afraid of me, but I figured you needed some help right now. With me by your side, you can evade Nivek's mind games."*

As soon as he said that, the pain and ringing faded away. I had collapsed on the ground, and I noticed Amery was watching me with concern from a distance, not wanting to be too close to the menacing wolf. As I stood, I felt the hot breath of the wolf next to my head and stumbled backwards. I had no idea I'd fallen so close to him.

Why didn't he just kill me?

"I know who you are, Nivek," I proclaimed. "And your tricks won't work on me."

He only smirked. "We'll have to see about that."

"What do you want?" I asked, confidence and strength blooming inside me now that I had Kevin's help. "If you want my friends, forget it. You will never have power over them. I will fight to keep them."

"Feisty, aren't you? But you see, I have no interest in fighting you, puny one. I could destroy you in a heartbeat if I wanted to. However, I believe I could make good use of you, with a little… adjustment. So, I'll make you a deal. Surrender yourself to me, or I'll make you watch all your little friends die, slowly and painfully, one by one, until you do turn to me. Starting with this pretty little one," he said, turning a claw towards Amery.

My heart pounded. Deliver myself, or deliver my friends? That wasn't a choice I wanted to make. Samuel's family depended on me, as their leader, to defeat Nivek. How could I give up on the quest and the prophecy now, when I was so close? I looked at Amery, and the expression in her eyes tugged on my heartstrings. Even though we'd been fighting lately, perhaps especially so, I couldn't leave her. Not now. Not like this.

I had only one choice. "I will never surrender," I declared. "*And* I will not let any of these innocent creatures die. We will fight together, and you will be defeated." My thirst for vengeance and justice surged with my declaration. I needed to kill him. He was the reason all of my family and best friends, and so many others, were dead. He wouldn't get any more of them.

Nivek growled, sending vibrations through the air. Amery flinched, just within my peripheral vision. The scarred wolf looked ready to kill, but so did I. "You have until next full moon to surrender yourself," he snarled, pointing a curved, shining claw to the sky. He lowered his paw and dug two channels into the dirt, then poked a hole into the intersection. "You will meet me where two streams merge into the one that borders your territory. If you haven't showed up by then, you and your entire settlement will be nothing but blood and ash when I'm finished." Without another word, he and his two companions turned and stormed out of the clearing.

I hung my head with a sigh as soon as they were out of sight, my mustered courage withering away. What could I do? I had promised a fight, but we were nowhere near ready to face the terrible wolves. "You did the right thing, Sheer," Amery said to me with soft and gentle eyes. But when I looked to Kevin, he remained silent, and I wasn't comforted.

More animals streamed into the clearing now that the wolves had left. Something needed to be done. I couldn't surrender. I couldn't just let them all die, and I still had anger and vengeance burning inside of me. We would have to fight, and somehow we had to win. "You've done it twice before," Amery said. "Maybe you can defeat Finsternis, too."

"Nivek," I corrected. "Finsternis isn't his real name."

"Well, Sheer?" Kevin asked, landing on the ground beside me. "What will you do?"

"We will fight," I said softly.

"We will fight!" Amery exclaimed, and I could feel the roar of assent from Samuel's family. I flapped my wings with conviction.

"We will fight," Kevin agreed, his eyes narrowing with determination.

Since everyone appeared to be in the clearing already, I decided to start battle plans immediately. There was no time to waste.

"Commanders!" I called out. "Come forward. Nyoka." The rat scurried up to my side. "You're in command of small mammals, reptiles, and amphibians." She nodded.

"Spike, birds of prey." He flew to my side.

"Ryan, all large mammals." The loyal badger leapt forward and nearly trampled Nyoka in his eagerness and excitement of being included.

"Amery," I asked, turning to her, "would you take command of the other birds?" She nodded solemnly.

I called other elders and loyal creatures to serve as lieutenants under the chosen commanders. I found Swift among the crowd, the peregrine falcon who'd helped find recruitments for the battle of the thirteenth floor. He and a fish eagle joined Spike; a fox and beaver walked up to Ryan. A weasel, garden snake, and toad stood next to Nyoka. Finally, I asked a robin, duck, and woodpecker to join Amery.

"I need scouts," I declared, "to find Poison and her beetles again, and Rebekah's hummingbirds, plus any others who might join us. I'll take Spike's place while he goes to fetch his crows. Does anyone volunteer to go out and look for allies?"

I was amazed at the sheer number of animals that immediately came forward. Only a few took a step back. I went among them and picked out a few that seemed the fastest or most fit that would be able to endure the journey and come back quickly. Most of them had joined after we came to the forest and had no injuries from the battle, but some were from the thirteenth floor. The hawk, squirrel, wild dog, bald eagle, kingfisher, and mole left right away.

"Anna, could you come forward? Is there anyone else experienced with medical herbs?" Samuel's granddaughter approached me, along with three others: a field mouse, an otter, and a lizard. I had all of them set up a medical facility adjacent to center camp, with the help of a pair of beavers.

"Patrols will be triple what they were before," I announced, "to watch in case Nivek breaks the agreement and ambushes us earlier. I'd like one animal each from Spike's group and Ryan's, and two each from Amery's and Nyoka's command, to check the camp border during each shift. We'll switch shifts at dawn, noon, sunset, and midnight, when the moon is the highest. The commanders can

160

choose who goes on each shift. Does everyone understand?" I felt and saw the mass consent expressed by the crowd.

Finally, there were no more positions to be wanted. "We only have one cycle of the moon to prepare," I warned. "So we must begin training immediately. Commanders and lieutenants, make sure that no one in your group falls behind. We are only as strong as our weakest member, and all should reach their maximum potential. This is Nivek we're dealing with this time. Who knows what he's capable of doing." I then dismissed them to their tasks and watched the animals hustle off to various potential training grounds. At that moment, I felt a tap on my back. I turned around to face Kevin.

"What should I do?" he asked.

"I need a friend," I replied.

"I can do that."

XXX

No more than half a day later, I sent Spike off to get his crows. As I'd promised, I took his place as commander over the birds of prey. The group had grown since we left the thirteenth floor and now consisted of over a hundred birds. In fact, all groups of loyal warriors had increased in number, just from newcomers to Samuel's family since we'd moved to the forest. There wasn't enough room for all the additional members in our territory, so many animals of all kinds continued to live in their previous homes but came to our part of the forest for news and training. Thankfully, the initial expeditions for more blue fabric had been successful, and we had an abundance of blue scraps to mark all the new members. I sensed some were joining just for the protection against predators, who were now sending hunting parties far from the territory borders to bring back large game to feed multiple animals. At this point, though, we needed all the help we could get. I didn't care what their motivations were, as long as they were willing to fight alongside us.

I'd lost count of the number of new devotees that had come to seek my approval for entry into the army. Ever since Kevin came, the others didn't seem as important. I was still unable to procure any vision other than the bloody claw or, if I concentrated hard enough, the wolf himself. Kevin's presence helped me forget about the apparition momentarily, but it always came back. I was tired of seeing it and afraid of what it could mean. I knew Nivek had murdered his father, but was another even more dreadful act being foreshadowed? Something that might affect me or Kevin or Amery? Chills slid down my spine every time I contemplated it.

I shook myself and tried to focus on the task at hand. It was the first day of training, and many of the hawks, eagles, and other birds in Spike's group were incredibly inexperienced when it came to fighting. Only those few that had been original members of the thirteenth floor had any experience at all. I'd have to start from the beginning, with the basics. I realized that this would be harder than

I'd thought, and waited impatiently for Spike to return so I wouldn't have to do all his work for him.

I thought about what a bird of prey would need to be proficient in to fight well: mainly flying, diving, and scratching or grabbing with talons. For each of these movements, the birds would need the strength to carry heavy objects or fly to great heights, and good endurance to last throughout the fight.

With this in mind, I decided flying strength would be a good place to start. I gathered the hundred or so birds of prey before me, standing by the river bordering our territory, and began to instruct them for their first training exercise.

"I want each of you to fly as high as you can into the sky, while holding the largest riverside rock you can carry. When you get tired, hold on a little longer, then make your way back down. Then you may rest, take a swift drink from the stream, and begin again. Start now, warriors."

I stayed on the ground while they lifted into the air as I'd ordered. I wouldn't participate, of course. Sparrows simply weren't made to fly as high as these birds, nor did we have claws large or strong enough to grip stones.

As I squinted into the sun, watching the birds under my command, I slowly saw some beginning to come back down. Four came around the same time. Three sipped from the stream, flapped their wings, then struggled into the air once more. The other, a fish eagle, glanced at me... then switched his rock for a smaller one.

"Hey! What are you doing?" I called out to him.

He answered me without meeting my eyes. "My other stone was too heavy, sir. I won't be able to fly back up while carrying it."

"That's the point," I retorted. "To push yourself, in order to become stronger. I want you to use the same stone as before."

He hesitated, testing my patience. "I've lost it now, sir. I don't know where I left it. May I use this one instead?"

"No! It's right behind you. Quit fooling around."

After spinning briefly, he argued back. "I don't see it."

I thought about using my power to lift the rock and drop it on his wise head. Instead, I sighed and flew over to the side of the river, landing on the stone he seemed unable to find.

"This one. Now get back up there."

"Yes sir," he said, nodding unwillingly.

Incompetent bird, I thought to myself as I flew back to my previous spot. Without warning, my head suddenly seared with pain, accompanied by the excruciating ringing sound. Even though Nivek was further away, he was still somehow reaching me. *Help me, Kevin!* I cried with my mind.

"I am with you," I heard in my head, and the pain diminished to a dull throb. I wasn't sure how he did it, but I was glad he was able to assuage the attack. *"Just wait it out,"* Kevin said. *"And soon the pain will be gone entirely. Just wait."*

I did, and slowly the ringing and pain faded into nothing. Back to normal, I looked up at the soaring birds to make sure none of them had noticed. I saw the fish eagle, climbing in the sky. He stopped short of where the rest of the birds were circling, then began to descend again. This time, he didn't try to switch his stone. He obeyed the command and continued to work after a quick drink of water, which made me glad. He wasn't as strong as the others yet, but soon he'd be able to fly as high as the rest of them, heavy stone or not.

When the sky began to change colors and the birds seemed exhausted, I allowed them to stay on the ground after drinking from the stream. Once they'd all returned, I dismissed them to their nests.

"Good work today, warriors."

XXXI

Yawning, I snuggled into the nest I'd built a few days ago, in my favorite bush beside the stream. I was thankful for Samuel's wards keeping me safe — I'd been out in the forest for over a month now, and nothing bad had happened yet. Besides the wolf, of course, but I figured even the most powerful of Samuel's wards wouldn't have been able to keep him out.

Kevin lighted down onto the branch next to me, still wide awake. "You asleep yet?"

"No," I replied, stifling another yawn. "Do you want to talk?"

He nodded. "That'd be nice. I enjoy talking to you, Sheer."

"Yeah, same. What's up?" I perched myself up to see him better. It was always so easy to talk to Kevin that I rather enjoyed our conversations, too.

"How was your day with the predators?"

"Oh, it was okay. One of them didn't want to put up with the task I gave him. He tried to dumb his way out of it."

Kevin was aghast. "He back-talked you?"

"Not exactly, but I guess you could put it that way."

"How can you tolerate that? It must be terribly aggravating. Animals should obey their commander, no questions asked."

"I suppose you're right," I said. "But he behaved after I talked to him, so I think he'll be okay."

"I still don't think you deserve to be treated that way," Kevin replied, shaking his head. "You're the leader of the army and the possessor of many great powers. You're practically a celebrity, and you deserve more respect from the rest of the animals here."

"Thanks."

"What exercise did you have them do?" Kevin asked.

"They flew up as high as they could, carrying heavy stones."

"While you stayed on the ground?"

"Well, yeah. I couldn't see any way around it. I wish I could be more involved, so they trust me more, you know? Like, fly with them. But I could never do that."

"That's probably true in this case, but… if you're ever going to have them fly long distances, you definitely want to be with them. They could develop bad flying techniques, and you wouldn't be able to correct them. I think some of these birds don't even know how to catch a good draft, even though they've been flying all their lives."

"I was going to have them do something for endurance training. What should I do? I can't keep up with them or fly as high."

"What if you rode on one of their backs? Maybe that weakling you mentioned. Even though you don't weigh much, it would still help train him for strength at the same time."

"That's brilliant! I think I'll do just that. I'm glad to have you here; you have great ideas. And before I forget… thank you. For keeping me safe from Nivek again today."

"That's what I'm here for," Kevin replied. I yawned involuntarily, though I tried to hide it. "Well, I'll leave you to your sleep," Kevin said. "Goodnight, Sheer. See you in the morning."

"Goodnight, Kevin." My friend lifted off, sending the gentlest breeze through the leaves, just enough to move them softly. I wondered if they made a sound, and what it was like. But I shook the sadness from my head. I had a friend again, and I was happy.

Ever since Barrie had died, I hadn't had someone to talk to, really. Amery's conversation was often awkward, and lately we'd been disagreeing more than I'd have liked. I was glad she was there, but Kevin was what I really needed in a friend. I wanted to keep him close so I wouldn't lose him like I had the hawk. If Kevin died, I wouldn't know what to do. It would be like losing Barrie all over again, and my sister and mother, and most of all, Samuel.

I felt and heard the ringing in my head again, but it went down almost immediately. I knew Kevin was protecting me. A fleeting thought crossed my mind.

I wish I hadn't named our group "Samuel's family." It's a nice tribute to Samuel, and I miss him more than anything, but it's also weak. The name "Sheer's Army" is much more appealing. I shook my head, as if arguing with myself. *Changing it now would confuse everyone and make me seem selfish.*

My eyes were getting heavy, but I had so much on my mind, deep sleep still wouldn't come. Why was I cursed with so much responsibility? I wished again that Samuel hadn't died. If he was still here, I wouldn't have had to take on the leadership role. Then, for the first time, I thought again. If Samuel was still alive, if he'd never launched himself from that tree, Amery wouldn't be here. Even though her friendship barely compared to my mentor's, she was still a good friend. She was there when I needed her, even when I hadn't been kind. Realizing I hadn't spoken to her today, I felt sad.

I should value her more.

The pain and ringing from Nivek's attack surged again, but it felt more like an annoyance thanks to Kevin's assistance. The attacks were more frequent now, but much less severe, and I was grateful.

I breathed deeply, closed my eyes, and imagined hearing the sounds of the night again. Amery had described them to me back when we were in the city; different sounds than what I'd heard in visions while spending time with the squirrels. A sweet melody would arise, beginning with the hum of mosquitoes, then the chirping of crickets, and then the other bugs would chime in. Night frogs would come out, some peeping, some bellowing deeply. They usually sang the loudest in the spring, but if you were lucky, you could sometimes hear them now, in the fall. If we were close to the streets, the mechanical rushing of cars would add a new tone to the symphony, and everything would be in perfect harmony.

For Amery, though, the most magical sound was that of rain. A gentle drizzle, she'd told me, was the most perfect music to her ears. I didn't think I'd like it much if I ever got the chance to hear it. It held too many haunted memories of my past, and I still hadn't gotten over my fear of water.

As I continued to imagine the magical orchestra of nighttime sounds, I opened my eyes and watched the stars begin to dance along with the music in my head. They swirled in circles around each other, performing beautiful twists and turns in the dark night sky. The moon, too, joined the chorus. It was the first good dream I'd experienced in a long while. I couldn't remember ever having a dream like this before, and I savored it in solemn, grateful reflection.

I watched the slender, graceful movements in the heavens, failing to notice that the moon was growing. I finally saw it once it had engulfed half of the sky, and the sweet chords came to a screeching halt. The long, lonely howl of a wolf echoed through the open air, reverberating against the silent mountains. It was an eerie sound. I wondered if this was what a real wolf sounded like, outside of a dream. In my visions, I'd only heard Nivek's growls.

As the howl faded, so did everything else. Soon, all I saw and heard was dark, cold silence. Finally, I drifted off into uneasy slumber.

XXXII

Morning came, and the sun shone down brightly on my head through the browning leaves. I blinked and squinted in the light. Had I overslept? Worried, I flew as fast as I could to the clearing at center camp. I saw a few animals still there, but it looked as if they'd already eaten the communal breakfast.

How come no one woke me up?

I couldn't miss out on tradition like this! I immediately wondered where Kevin was. He would have come to get me, even if no one else was willing to.

Where has he gone off to?

I was about to go searching for him, but then I remembered my duty to the predator birds. I sighed. Looking for Kevin would have to wait.

Pumping my wings to pick up speed, I made my way to the river where I'd called the predators the day before. To my delight, I saw them already in the air, carrying their rocks from the previous day. Upon seeing me, they glided back down to the ground.

"Good morning!" The fish eagle, who had given me trouble the previous day, landed closest to me. Again, there was something more to the phrase; something I'd need written down to understand. I recognized it, though, as the same respectful phrase Ryan had uttered previously. I decided to ask either Amery or Kevin about it later, if I could remember.

"Did you enjoy your extra sleep today, sir?" the eagle continued, seeming oddly pleased with himself.

"Well… yes," I responded, still confused. All the birds of prey looked at each other, as if they were sharing some sort of secret.

"Okay, what's going on here?" I demanded.

"Today marks a full year since you joined the thirteenth floor," the eagle explained, gesturing with his wings and talons. "It was Amery's idea. She said you needed a break and hadn't really fully rested since you recovered from the poisoning. All of Samuel's family thought that today was a great day to cut you some slack."

"Oh, that was very sweet of her," I replied, taken aback. *Has it really been a year?* "I'll make sure to thank her later. But in the meantime, you all need to get back to work. We don't have much time to prepare, so we shouldn't waste it chatting."

"Right away, sir! Do you want us to continue the same exercise as yesterday?"

"I have a different plan today," I replied, recalling my talk with Kevin. "You need strength in war, but also endurance. You must be able to fly in the air for a long time, and you need to be capable of flying long distances in pursuit of the enemy. This battle will be very different from the one on the thirteenth floor. We will be in the vast forest, not confined to a building. The wolves are fast and strong and will easily outrun you if you aren't prepared to pick up speed and maintain it for a long time. So today, you'll fly around camp for as long as you possibly can. I'd fly alongside you to make sure you're using proper technique, but of course I don't have the same capabilities as a sparrow."

"What would you do, then?"

"One of you will carry me on your back," I stated simply.

They all looked at each other sheepishly, then the fish eagle stepped forward with a grimace. He was clearly trying to make up for his ill behavior the previous day.

About time.

He turned his back to me so I could hop on. I did so and caught myself as I slipped, grabbing his shoulder bones. I found I could wedge myself there, holding on to his shoulders with my claws to keep from falling off.

170

I instructed the predators to lift into the air, and soon we were soaring above the forest. It was a much different view from so high up, and I gazed at the dying autumn foliage. A cool breeze was stripping trees of their leaves. This high above the ground, the wind was much stronger than it was in the underbrush. I directed the birds to fly headfirst into the wind and watched their feathers ruffle as they pushed against the current. I held on dearly. I tried to imagine the sound of the wind through their feathers but couldn't think of what it would be like. Maybe I'd never know.

It was a depressing thought, that of being deaf forever, so I searched for another way to pass the time. All the predators seemed to be flying perfectly, except for one small hawk below me. Watching her struggle gave me an idea. It had been a while since I'd practiced my powers, and I might need them for the battle, so I experimented. I controlled the air around the struggling hawk, relieving the resistance for a short while. The hawk made a subtle movement as she caught herself, surprised she was no longer being resisted by the headlong wind. Slowly, I returned the air around her to normal, giving her a more gradual increase in resistance. When I was no longer helping her, she was flying better than before. I felt my chest puff with pride; I'd improved her flying skills, all by myself.

Now that I'd experienced a taste of power again, I liked it. I wedged myself more firmly between the fish eagle's shoulder blades and looked around for anything else I could play with. I pushed the trees to sway more strongly and watched the leaves swirl upward in beautiful spirals. A falcon ahead of me caught a tail current, and I pushed him back into the headlong wind. I was thoroughly enjoying this.

At that moment, I felt Nivek's attack again. But this time it was so faint, I paid no attention to it. Thanks to Kevin, the attacks were becoming more futile. Ignoring the sound, I morphed a nearby cloud into the shape of an *S* for *Sheer*. I pushed it along beside us for a while before letting it disperse.

Several of the predators looked tired, and the sun was now beginning to set, so I called out to let them know it was okay to return to the riverside and end the day's training.

When we landed, I hopped off the fish eagle's back. It felt strange using my own legs and wings again. It felt so uncomfortable, in fact, I decided I didn't want to fly back to my nest. After everyone had dispersed, I looked around to make sure no one was watching. Then I closed my eyes and used my power on my own body to transport myself back to my nest. When I opened my eyes to see the familiar bush surrounding me, excitement and pride welled up inside me so strongly, I forgot about being uncomfortable. I wanted to share the growth in my power, so I flew to center camp to tell Kevin about my day.

Amery was there, but Kevin wasn't. Excitement still bubbled in my veins, and I desperately wanted to share what had happened, so I told her everything. She didn't take the news as well as I thought she would.

"You did *what?*"

I fluttered my wings, disappointed at her reaction. "I just experimented with my powers, Amery. You know, to see what I'm really capable of."

"Sheer, I don't think you were given those abilities to use them that way."

The faint ringing in my head surfaced temporarily, but I ignored it. Kevin was taking care of me, after all. "How can you claim why I received my powers? I seem to have always had them, at least after I woke up after being nearly killed by a storm, and have had no shortage of challenges ever since. Maybe I deserve to do with them as I please because of everything I've been through just to be alive."

"I'm just saying that you should be careful with your gifts," Amery replied. "I don't know where or how you got them, but maybe it's outside your control. Maybe if you abuse them, they will go away."

I could tell by her expression that she was serious. Still, I couldn't help laughing. "Ha! Out of my control? Amery, this is a *part* of me. The more I use them, the more in control I feel. Not just of the abilities themselves, but of my life, my destiny… not to mention, everything that is a part of this world."

"What would Samuel say if he heard you speaking that way? Sheer, your lust for power is turning you into the very enemies you have been trying to defeat! If you keep going down this path, what makes you different from Nyoka or Spike before they changed sides?"

"I'm not turning evil, Amery! I'm not enslaving the minds of trapped animals in some imaginary world just to be their ruler. I'm not committing mass genocide, reviving beasts with blood magic, or poisoning random birds whose lives are already hard enough. Everyone *chose* me to be the leader of this army. *You* chose me. As the leader, why shouldn't I be more powerful? If we want to defeat Nivek, we will need all the strength we can get."

"Manipulating the bodies of your army and teleporting yourself because you're too lazy don't exude strength, Sheer. That is selfish, and the opposite of what a leader should be. You're setting an awful example."

"You just don't get it! Why is this such a bad thing?" Anger and annoyance boiled their way to the surface, and I wished Kevin were here to back me up. "You don't understand anything about this."

Not like Kevin does.

Kevin's voice echoed in my head. *"I'm coming as soon as I can."*

But to my surprise, Amery sighed with defeat. "I can tell you're not listening, Sheer. Just, if something does happen, don't say I didn't warn you." With that, she turned and left me standing in shock. I remained perched on the branch in silence as it swayed gently in the breeze.

"It's over, Kevin," I said when the chickadee came into view. "Amery gave up her argument."

"Oh, good! What was she trying to say, anyway?"

"Just some ridiculous claim that my powers aren't my own and I should be careful how I use them… or something."

"Why make that claim all of a sudden? What did you do to upset her?"

Knowing his response would be different, I gladly told Kevin the entire story. The excitement had long since fizzled away, though, and repeating it made me feel empty inside.

"Oh, that's all?" Kevin asked when I'd finished. "That doesn't seem so bad to me. You barely even influenced anyone, and it sounds like when you did, it was for their own good."

"Yeah, exactly. I don't know what her problem was."

"You have an amazing ability, Sheer, and are fully deserving of it after all you've been through. Why shouldn't you be able to use it as you wish?"

His words were reassuring, but something about what Amery had said still bugged me. "Do you… think she's right, though? That if I'm not careful, my powers could be taken from me?"

"Absolutely not," Kevin replied. "I mean, any more than your soul, or your heart. It's a part of you, isn't it?"

"Yeah," I said, nodding. "Yeah, you're right. Thanks. I knew you'd understand."

"That's what I'm here for," he said. He nudged me gently. "You should probably rest, though. There's another big day ahead."

"Right. Of course. Goodnight, Kevin."

"G'night."

I headed back to my nest, still mulling over the two opinions. Even though my friend had agreed with me, I still was troubled by Amery's opinion.

Why can't she just be on my side, like Kevin?

174

The moon hung high in the sky, large and bright, but already beginning to wane again. Suddenly, all thoughts about the correct usage of my powers were washed away and replaced with a feeling of dread. Time was running out, and I was afraid we'd never be ready to face the wolf's attack. Did we have any chance of surviving at all? Could I even trust him to honor the agreement and wait until the next full moon?

I closed my eyes in an attempt to see the wolf, but I struggled to clear my mind. Instead of the black wolf, all I saw was darkness, devoid of life and light.

XXXIII

The air felt completely still the next morning as I flew to the riverside for yet another day of training. There was not even a hint of a breeze; it was like the Earth had frozen in place. The stillness made me restless. I hoped Spike would return soon and take the duty away from me. I wanted the freedom to practice my powers, to become more powerful than Nivek himself. With this little time, it was my only hope. There was no way the army alone could defeat him, even if it was several times larger than the army we'd amassed on the thirteenth floor. Nivek was a totally different challenge, and we needed something — or someone — powerful enough to face him.

A shadow passed overhead, and I looked up to see massive, dark clouds looming in the sky. The sun shone faintly as it rose in the east, where the forest met the mountains, but its rays did little to warm the chill air. The earth seemed to be holding its breath, waiting for something to happen. I took a deep breath, taking in the brisk air as I rounded the bend and arrived at the riverside. Many of the predators were already at the bank, waiting.

"Today, warriors, I want you to practice diving," I announced as soon as I thought I was within earshot. "This will combine with the exercise from two days ago. You will take a stone, fly as high as you can with it, then dive back down. Just before you touch the ground, I want you to turn around and fly straight back up. Soaring will be your rest, but dive as often as you're able. Now go! Get started!"

I watched as the large birds in my command followed my order. I wondered what the other units were doing for training and was tempted to sneak away to find out but decided against it. I had a duty here, at least until Spike returned with his crows.

At that moment, I felt a breeze ruffle my feathers. Thinking the wind had returned, I turned my head to look at the forest behind me. Instead of swaying branches and tossing leaves, I saw the old crow.

His form was slumped with exhaustion, and his battalion filled the trees behind him.

"I'm here," he said wearily.

"Welcome back! How was your journey?"

"Everything went according to plan." He swayed, too weary to hold himself up steadily. My heart softened for his exhaustion. I knew he was willing to take over responsibility, and I would be happy to give it up, but...

Maybe I can wait one more day.

"Good," I responded. "Your command unit has performed well. They have awaited your return, but I'll continue their training today. You should get some rest. Will you be able to retake command of the combined units tomorrow?"

"I'll do my best, sir. Thank you."

As he turned to leave, I scanned the number of crows he'd brought with him. I'd forgotten how many there were. "One more thing, predator commander," I said. "The forest within our jurisdiction is rather full of animals. The army has grown since we arrived. You should be able to find a spot to stay, but... your crows may need to live beyond the border."

"Yes, sir."

"You're dismissed. Take your leave, and get some rest."

"Thank you, sir."

The old crow bowed and led his companions across the river, where they dispersed. I turned my gaze to the hawks and other predators above me. They seemed to be faring better than during their first training exercise. The long hours of strenuous work were finally beginning to pay off.

No birds were giving me any trouble, and boredom sank in. To amuse myself, I played with a pebble near me, lifting it and spinning it in the air with my mind. After a while, I felt a sudden tap on my back and dropped the stone in surprise.

What is it now? I spun angrily to face a young hawk, who cowered before me.

"Sir?"

"What?" I snapped.

He looked at the sky, then back at me. "It's getting late, sir."

I looked to the west, along the river. Sure enough, the setting sun was stretching dark bands of red and orange across the sky. "Oh, well, I suppose you're dismissed."

The hawk pushed himself back into the air to let the others know, and I marveled at how quickly time had passed.

Everyone else must be finishing up soon, too, I thought. Maybe there was still time to check on the other units.

I made my way to center camp as a starting point and was surprised to see Nyoka there. *Shouldn't she still be training the smaller animals?* "Good evening, crawler commander."

"Good evening, Sheer, sir."

"How has training been going?"

She said something with such exaggerated motions, I had to assume it was sarcasm. "*Fantastic.* In another year or two, they might be ready to fight a small army."

"There's no time to joke around, Nyoka. We don't have a year or two, nor is Nivek's army a small one. Why aren't you still in training? Work them from dawn to dusk if you need to, and if they still won't progress, work them at night. I don't care how you get it done, but they need to be ready by full moon."

The rat looked taken aback, but I didn't regret the severity of my words. We had no time to lose. "Yes, sir," she replied with a bow. "I'll go gather them for more training right away."

178

As she scurried off, I looked around for Amery or Ryan. The setting sun was draping the forest in shadow, and I couldn't see very far through the trees anymore. I flew up to the treetops and scanned the forest for any signs of the small birds or large mammals. If I squinted, I could make out a cleared oblong path in the distance. Only the larger animals in the army — probably with help from the beavers — would be able to make such an effect on the terrain.

Even in the darkness, I could make out the ominous cliffs far beyond their training grounds. Something about them made me shiver, and I redirected my attention to the east. From this vantage point, I could see a cloud of small birds hovering just above the treetops, and a few gulls gliding above them. That would be Amery's group. I only had time to visit one before night had truly fallen, so I decided on the badger's command.

The large mammals began trudging back towards center camp when I still had a ways to go to meet them. I landed on a tree branch and waited for them to come to me. I decided to nickname them "runners" for simplicity's sake, like I'd started to call Spike's command the "predators" and Nyoka's the "crawlers." Tomorrow, I'd come up with a name for Amery's command. The runners dragged their paws, clearly sore and exhausted.

Good, I thought. *The training needs to be tough, to get everyone to their best in time.*

"Greetings, runner commander," I called out when Ryan was within hearing distance.

He seemed confused for a moment but acknowledged me when he spotted my resting spot. "Good evening sir," he responded. I noticed he was once again using the phrase I struggled to grasp. I kept forgetting to ask Kevin or Amery what it was.

"Has training been going well?"

"Yes indeed, sir. They're faring much better than they were at first."

"Excellent. What exercises are you using?"

179

"Running, distance and speed, and various strength training exercises."

"What about fighting?" I asked. "Have you begun any training on battle techniques?"

Ryan sighed. "Not yet, sir. I'll begin that momentarily... when they are ready. It's only been three days, sir."

"Of course," I replied, but I couldn't help feeling slightly disappointed. The large mammals were already so fast and strong — why not start with proper combat? I held my tongue. "Very well," I said instead. "On your way, then."

While the runners continued to lumber past, I looked up at the darkening sky. There were dense clouds above us, but nothing moved at all. The moon shone dimly through a crack, and I sighed. I wondered if the sounds of the crickets and frogs would be prevalent on such a still night, or if the whole world was engulfed by the dead silence that clung to me for all my waking hours. Without the distraction of a cool breeze or the scents it carried, my senses felt dull and heavy. I returned to my nest, weary and aching for a change.

XXXIV

Now that Spike had returned, I no longer needed to tend to his battalion. Instead of going to the river in the morning, I headed east to check on Amery and her command unit. Peckers and gliders, I decided to call them. As I went, I looked anxiously at the sky. It was so dark now, day could almost be mistaken for night, but there was still no wind and no hint of rain.

I found Amery's troops and sat watching them for a while from the shadows. Sparrows, cardinals, and other peckers flew for distance training among the dry, barren trees; gulls, geese, and other gliders soared high above them. Amery was fully participating in the activities of the peckers, while supervising the gliders at the same time. She could multitask far better than I could.

While I watched the flurry and frenzy, I felt Kevin come up beside me. After some time watching them together, he nudged me to get my attention.

"Isn't it beautiful?" he asked when I turned to face him.

"What is?"

"The way the gliders are effortlessly suspended in air," he replied. "It's as if they are held there by strings."

I glanced upward, then looked back at him. "Yeah, I guess so."

"I wonder what would happen if one of them fell back from the others. Do you think the rest would go help him, or just move on? And would their commander notice, or is she too busy with the peckers?"

I shrugged. "I dunno."

Kevin looked into my eyes for a little longer, and I couldn't tell what emotion they held. His inner thoughts were a mystery to me, and their depths held me captivated until he looked away. What he'd said tugged at my curiosity, and the urge to answer his question sunk in. I puffed my chest. Maybe if I could show Amery what I was really capable of, she'd understand. Maybe then she'd approve of how I wanted to use my powers and grow my abilities so I could fight Nivek.

After a quick glance in her direction — she was still preoccupied fluttering between a maze of branches — I concentrated on a young goose who was flying along with the crowd above us. I held her in the air, then cut her off from the draft and watched her fall. She flapped her wings desperately and opened her beak to squawk in surprise, and I laughed. This time, the laughter felt natural, like it was coming from deep inside me, and I didn't shirk away from it.

In response to the goose's plight, nearly all the gliders changed course and rushed to her aid. I concentrated harder, pushing all of them so she was just beyond their reach as she flailed about. Elation filled every fiber of my being. I wanted this; I wanted *more*. And then I saw Amery, looking straight at me. The expression on her face quenched my joy like the cold grip of a winter wind. She wasn't angry... just... sad.

A twinge of guilt threatened to strangle me, but anger rose to fight it. "What?" I snapped at her. Why should I feel ashamed for what I was able to do? Why did she have the right to decide how I should use my gift?

"You know what," she said softly, turning away with obvious disappointment. I released the goose, the fun long gone.

"Well, that's ruined," I mumbled to Kevin.

"Come on, don't worry about her," he replied. "She's just a stuck-up grouch who doesn't want to see you succeed. *I* thought it was hilarious."

I tried to appreciate his words, but Amery's disapproval still stung. *Why can't she be as supportive as Kevin?* With nothing left for me among the peckers and gliders, I decided to leave her be and head west along the river.

When I came across the training ground of the predators, I saw that they were all on the ground, practicing one-on-one combat. Spike was flying high above to observe. "How's it going up there?" I called. Upon hearing me, the old, mangled crow came down from his post.

"Good afternoon, sir. You have trained them well."

"Thank you, predator commander."

"Not at all, sir," he replied. "My unit explained the exercises you used, and I thought they were excellent. I'll continue to use them, while adding my own concepts to the mix. One, you can see now."

"Wonderful," I said. "Do you think these birds will be ready in time for the next full moon?"

"I sure hope so. I've seen significant improvement, even in one day, but... I don't know if any of us will ever truly be prepared to fight him, sir."

"I appreciate your honesty," I said, "but we need to do our best to be ready. Nivek's army may be larger and fiercer, but fighting is our only option. Keep up the good work, and maybe we'll get close enough."

"Of course, sir. Thank you, sir."

I turned and left him to train the predators. Besides, I wanted to see what the runners were up to. By the time Kevin and I neared the western edge of the territory, I could feel the vibrations of their many heavy paws pounding on the ground and shaking the trees. As the name I'd given them suggested, they were running; hard and fast.

Already, they'd tramped a dirt trail through the woods. It led to the river, where they must have crossed, dipped into the woods again, and come back around. Rocks and boulders were piled up in some places; enormous logs in others would force the runners to duck or jump to avoid them. I recalled the oblong track visible from the treetops. They'd created a massive obstacle course.

Brilliant! I thought. *A perfect training exercise.*

I felt them coming 'round the bend and held on to the branch for dear life as they rushed past in front of us. I closed my eyes and felt the rumbling ebb and fade as the mighty warriors ran. When they came 'round to pass us again, I called out to Ryan.

"Ho there, runner commander!"

He drew the company to a halt, giving them a well-deserved break, then approached me, panting. "Good afternoon, sir," he said, followed by the same mysterious phrase I kept forgetting about.

"How goes the training?" I asked.

"Wonderful, sir. My unit has made a lot of progress. But I worry about what the wolves are planning. I don't know whether we'll be ready to face them… the wolves are fast, strong, and many. We can train as much as we can, but do you think it will be enough?"

"I know, Commander," I replied. "We're all worried, but we just have to do our best. You and your warriors seem to be more prepared than any other unit; I'm proud of you."

"Thank you, sir." Ryan looked down at his paws. "We should get back to training," he said.

"Of course. I'll leave you to it."

"Farewell, and good luck, sir," the badger said as I prepared to move on. I yawned. Checking up on all the command units was starting to feel like a chore, but at least I had Kevin for company as I traveled between them. As much as I was pleased by the runners' progress, I wasn't looking forward to seeing Nyoka again. If the rat hadn't pulled her battalion together yet, we'd never be able to fight the wolves. We were only as strong as our weakest members, and they were definitely on that list.

Still, I had an obligation as the leader to visit all the commanders, so I sighed and made my way back towards center camp. If the peckers and gliders were to the east, the runners were to the west, and the predators were on the northern edge by the river, the only area remaining with enough space for training was the southern border, facing the city.

When Kevin and I arrived at center camp, the sky had darkened even more. It was hard to tell what time of day it was. The air was just completely still, as it had been for the last few days — no leaves were swaying in the nonexistent wind.

It must be high up in the sky, I thought, *if there is any wind at all.*

"Can you hear the other command unit?" I asked Kevin. He listened closely, then nodded and led me through the trees ahead and to the right. Soon, I could see several small animals running about in what seemed to be utter chaos.

"Is there any organization here?" I wondered aloud, not expecting a response.

"Sir! I didn't realize you were near," Nyoka responded, popping into view from some sort of hole underground. I nearly jumped in surprise.

"Wh… where did you come from?"

"Did I startle you, sir?" She slunk back and adopted a sly, secretive look.

I narrowed my eyes. "Yes, you startled me… is this some sort of battle strategy? What are you doing?"

"Of course, sir," she replied, returning to a more professional composure and performing a small bow. "I'm sorry you thought otherwise. It may not look like much, but I do have a training session organized here. You see, my group is divided in two, and they take turns on opposite sides." She pointed in the direction of animals in each group as she explained what they were doing. "One group digs tunnels underground and attempts to catch the opposition off guard.

185

The second group is running through the forest and trying to catch the ones under the ground, pinning them down before they can surface."

I looked back at the scrambling rodents, lizards, and frogs. Now that I knew what was going on, I could see mounds from the tunnels, and it did look more organized — or at least, intentional — than it had at first glance. I remembered my conversation with her the other day, and how she'd expressed her frustration at their lack of progress. "Clever. Is this a new strategy, or have you been using this method for the last few days?"

"I just started this regimen today, sir."

"Good. How do you think it's going now?"

"Very well, sir. They've improved significantly since the first day of training. I think I finally have this all under control. It's… different to need to communicate what I want done, rather than force it on all of my subordinates to follow blindly. It's harder, but more rewarding."

"Excellent. I still want you to work them extra hard, to make up for three days of wasted training."

"Of course, sir. I apologize for not meeting your standards the first time."

"Get back to work, then," I said. "I don't want to hold back your training any longer. You've got a lot to do."

"Yes, sir. Thank you, sir."

XXXV

As we made our way back to center camp, the air started to thicken. The clouds above were finally getting too heavy to stay in the air, and I knew it was going to storm… worse than it ever had before. I shivered. "Kevin," I said, "let's get under cover before it starts to rain."

He didn't even have time to respond before the air shook with one mighty rumble of thunder and the downpour began. I was soaking wet in seconds, paralyzed with fear. I'd made progress since my state when I arrived at the thirteenth floor, but this storm brought everything back. Terror threatened to strangle me from the inside out. *"Be calm,"* Kevin's voice soothed inside my head. *"I am with you. Concentrate, and you can conquer this. Use your powers. You can shield yourself from the rain."*

I took several deep, shaky breaths. I landed on a tree branch and closed my eyes. It was harder to clear my mind of the fear, but after a moment I felt the rain stop falling. As soon as I opened my eyes to see the bubble of dry air I'd created, I lost my concentration and got wet all over again. It was even colder the second time.

"Close your eyes, Sheer, and focus. I'll lead you to a dry hollow."

I followed his advice and flew shakily behind him, following the gentle breeze of his wings. I trusted him to lead me, and soon I heard the magical words: *"You're safe now. You can relax and open your eyes."* When I did, I was sheltered in the hollow tree where we had lodged on our first night together. It had rained then, too, but only a light drizzle. Now, the torrential downpour had already turned the ground to a slurry.

Breathing deeply, I told myself I was safe. Soon the rain would pass and I could live normally again. I thought briefly of the many animals currently out in training and wondered if they'd also sought shelter.

No, I countered. *They shouldn't be sheltered.* The rain was good for training. They would need to be able to fight regardless of inclement weather. They didn't have a reason to be afraid, like I did.

"I'll check on the others for you," Kevin said in my head, since I was still transfixed by the water streaming from the sky outside. *"You just rest. Don't worry about your duties. You deserve a good, long sleep."*

I yawned, exhausted. "Thank you, Kevin," I said softly. Then I drifted into sleep.

"Ze moon is half gone! Vill 'e come or not?" The voice of the scarred wolf rang out, and I opened my eyes to see him. The heavy smoke wrapped tightly around him; it was like he was wearing it as a second coat. I wasn't sure whether this was a vision or merely a dream, but I knew it wasn't real because I could hear. The black wolf was looking at something to his right and didn't see me.

"All in good time," a voice responded. I recognized it as the same one Nivek had spoken to in my previous vision. It was a strange voice, deep and echoing.

"How long must I wait?"

"Before the next full moon, he will surely offer himself up. I assure you."

"But *when?*"

"Not much longer. He'll soon notice that something is amiss. Just wait, you'll see. He will surrender. But if you're impatient, perhaps you should try something more… drastic."

"Vat do you suggest?"

I tried to continue listening, but the voices became muffled. At the same time, a distant voice called my name.

Sheer!

"…some of his friends…"

Sheer, wake up!

"…that will make him…"

Sheer!

"…of course, Your Majesty. I vill do as you 'ave commanded."

Sheer! Come on, wake up!

I groaned and opened my eyes, returning to the silent world I'd become accustomed to. "Amery, I was dreaming." My brain felt heavy and dull, but I vaguely wondered why I was able to hear her in the dream.

"I could tell. You were shaking terribly. Come on, it's morning."

I looked out of the hollow. It was still raining, and the sky was so darkened by clouds, it was impossible to tell the time. "How do you know?"

"If you paid attention, you'd see it's a bit brighter than it was before. Come on, the communal breakfast is starting."

"But… it's raining!"

"So? That's part of life in the forest, Sheer." When I didn't respond, she cocked her head. Her eyes widened with understanding. "Oh right, you're afraid of rain, aren't you?"

I nodded.

"Sorry, Sheer, but… there's nothing to be afraid of. It's good for the earth. Water makes things grow, you know. Without it, we'd have nothing."

Thunder crashed. Its vibrations shook the entire tree, and me with it. Even Amery flinched, but she continued to look at me firmly.

"I'll pass, thanks," I said. "I want to stay here, where it's dry."

"Sheer, you're the leader of this family," Amery scolded. "You can't show this kind of petty fear. There are too many animals depending on you to be brave when they can't be. Come on, join us."

My fear isn't petty. "No."

She sighed. "You're hopeless, Sheer. I know you're stronger than this. Act like it." She turned and left for center camp to join the others. I didn't care what my duties were. I wasn't about to fly in the dreadful, wet world outside the cozy hollow.

I thought about the dream I'd had before Amery woke me up so rudely. I still didn't know who the other voice belonged to. My visions showed nothing but darkness. And what were they planning to do to my friends? I certainly didn't have many left... I hoped they weren't planning to hurt Kevin.

"SURRENDER," I heard in my head. I nearly fell over with shock.

It was the deep voice from my dream, but even more menacing. The voice echoed, as if multiple creatures were saying the same thing at once. The voice had a lower pitch than was natural for any creature.

Will I have to fight against the owner of this voice? I wondered.

If so... I didn't think I'd ever survive. The voice sounded like it wielded unspeakable power. I was suddenly afraid, even more afraid than I was of rain. A battle with this enemy would surely mean death for the entire army, no matter how much we trained. Would fewer animals have to die if I...

"SURRENDER," I heard again.

But what would happen if I turned myself in? Would the wolf and mysterious speaker honor their agreement, or would they destroy everyone out of spite?

I was at a complete loss. I was afraid and had no idea what to do. I wanted to break down and weep. I wished it were all over already. Why did *I* have to bear this load? Why couldn't someone else be the subject of the prophecy? Was that silly poem really the only thing that gave me this responsibility? Did they think they could force me to work for them, or did they just want me out of the way?

I had so many questions but no answers.

Why, of all things, does it have to be pouring? I wondered, looking mournfully out at the rain. If only the sun were shining, then I'd be able to think straight and come to a decision.

"Surrender," I heard in my voice again, but this time it was faint. Just as I wondered whether Kevin was helping me again, I heard his gentle voice echo in my mind. It was so different from the deep, powerful voices that wanted to me surrender, I was immediately at ease again.

"Just go back to sleep, Sheer," he said. *"Everything will be alright. Sleep as long as you need to. I'll take care of you."*

XXXVI

Dreams came and went, but fitful sleep kept its hold on me. Most of the dreams were soon gone, forgotten, as if they'd never existed. There were times when they seemed so real. I dreamed that I awoke, and that Kevin and Amery gave me rain-soaked seeds to eat, or a washed-out worm. I wasn't sure whether I really ever woke at all. Everything was a haze, and the rumbling of rain and thunder echoed through my body like a pulse. I lived and breathed in the monotony.

My head ached, but I wasn't sure if the pain was real, a figment of my imagination, or a faint memory from the distant past. Days could've passed, weeks, even. I lost track of time in the never-ending rain. I couldn't tell dream from reality, or day from night.

"Ze veather vill get 'im, for sure."

"Yes. Just wait; he'll come soon."

I saw a flock of butterflies, flitting about in the rain. One in particular caught my eye: it was a beautiful crystal blue, with black tips on its wings. As I watched, the black spread across the membrane, forming deep veins that connected its body to its wingtips.

I heard Amery's voice. "Sheer, get up and do something. I know you're afraid of the rain, but it's time to face your fear."

"Let him be," Kevin replied. "Let him sleep. He deserves his rest, small one."

192

"Who are you calling *small*?"

"Have all plans been made?"

"Ya, Your Greatness, und carried out."

"Excellent."

The black continued to spread on the butterfly's wings, engulfing it completely. No hint of color was left. Now that butterfly flew among hundreds of others, and as it passed them, each also lost its color.

"It's been so long… food is becoming scarce. Sheer, what do we do?"

"We need to store food."

"I wasn't asking you, Kevin. I was consulting Sheer's advice. He's the leader of this family, not you."

"I *am* Sheer's advice."

"Do whatever Kevin says," I mumbled.

The entire flock of butterflies was pitch black now. Then, in an instant, they were no longer butterflies. They were black bats, swarming, eager to feed.

"Ze third quarter moon 'as come and gone, und still ze sparrow 'as not showed."

"He will come, in time. This is all part of the plan. Be patient, dark one."

"Sheer, get up and do something. Your army, your family, is counting on you."

"Leave him be."

"What have you done to him? Why is he still sleeping?"

"I haven't done anything. Just leave him alone."

The horde of bats came closer, closer. They wanted flesh… they wanted me. I tried to move, but my wings and legs were stuck in mud. I tried to scream, but my voice was broken. I was silent, ever silent, and no one would hear me die.

The rain poured on, never ceasing, the torture never-ending.

"Sheer, this isn't good for you. Get up, you need to get up!"

"Let him be, small one. Let him be."

"No, I won't! He's hurting, can't you see that? He's been still for too long. What have you done? Sheer! Sheer, wake up!"

The bats… I could feel them, tearing apart my flesh. I couldn't move. I couldn't scream.

"Sheer!" It was just a whisper. "Sheer, help me!"

Suddenly, I wasn't the one who'd been under attack. It was Amery, and there was nothing left of her. She was gone, far gone, and I'd done nothing to save her. Now the bats were turning to me again, to make a meal out of me as well. Her flesh hadn't satisfied them.

I woke up with a start. It was still raining.

"Amery!" I cried out. "Oh, Amery! What have I done? She's gone!"

Amery popped her head into the hollow, water dripping from her beak. "Sheer! Are you okay?"

"You're... alive?"

"Yes, of course. Why wouldn't I be?"

"I thought you were... but the bats!"

"There are no bats, Sheer. You were dreaming. But I'm glad you're awake now..."

I looked out of the hollow, trying to see the moon, but it was still obscured by black clouds and the never-ending sheets of rain. "How long have I been asleep?"

"Fast asleep, just a few moments... but you've been in and out of it for the past several days. You were in a sort of stupor. I wasn't sure if you were *really* here, even if your eyes were open. Even if you spoke. I think it's been six days that you've been like that."

I stretched my wings. Had I really been out that long? The moon must be completely dark by now. "What happened while I was out?"

"Well, it's been raining the whole time. The river has flooded, and food is short. There's standing water up to my beak everywhere, because the ground just can't soak it in anymore. Kevin said to store food, and you agreed with him. Then you decided to start rationing food, in case there wasn't enough for everyone."

"I did?"

"Yes. You don't remember? Everyone's been living on less lately."

My stomach told me she was telling the truth. "What about training?"

"It's continued, as best as it can. Things are progressing much more slowly, especially for the birds. Flying is just so difficult in this weather."

"I know," I said. I paused, not sure what to do anymore. How could we be ready to fight against the wolf if this rain didn't stop? "Amery... should I surrender to Nivek?"

"What? No! Why would you even think that? If you give up, none of us will have any hope left. We have to fight. We have no choice! If we fight, we at least have a chance. If we lose, at least we will have kept our honor."

"Well, look who's out of the dumps!" Kevin exclaimed, bounding into the hollow and shaking droplets of rain from his feathers. "Amery, don't you have troops to train or something?"

She gave me one last look, then flew back out into the endless downpour.

"So, how was your nap?" Kevin asked when she was gone.

"I had no idea I was knocked out for so long."

"Hey, don't worry. I'm here for you."

"Kevin, what do *you* think I should do? Should I surrender?"

"You want my opinion?"

"Desperately."

Kevin's chest moved as he exhaled a sigh, and I felt the gentle warm air brush my feathers. "There's no way around it, Sheer," he said. "I think you'll have to give yourself up. If you do, you can at least hope that the scarred wolf will keep his word. If you don't, you'll have to dread that his word *will* be kept."

"Yeah, I know, but… it's just so hard."

"I'll go with you, if you want."

"I know that. I just need more time."

"Time is running out. You realize that, right?"

I was silent. How could I choose? Both arguments were valid. I trusted Kevin, and he made a good point that if we refused, the wolf would just kill us all anyway. But I trusted Amery, too, and her perspective of hope was strong as well. On top of that, I had my own motives. Surrendering myself wouldn't provide the sweet revenge I secretly wanted against the one who'd caused the deaths of everyone I cared about. It wouldn't be justice for all the other harm that had been done either. But which was better in the long run? Whom should I follow? Whom should I believe?

XXXVII

In the past, I'd have sought Samuel's advice. Or maybe Barrie's. But neither of them was here, and it was Nivek's fault. Trying to bury my grief as it resurfaced, I did my best to think about what they might have said. It had been so long since they'd been with me, though, I just couldn't picture it. I looked out at the dreadful rain. Why did all of this have to happen to me? Why not someone else?

My stomach rumbling, I asked Kevin where the food was being stored. I kept myself dry with a protective bubble, so much easier now than it had been when this all began.

Did my skill improve as I slept?

I wondered about this as Kevin led me to the five trees that had grown from branches of a fallen pine, marking one corner of our territory. One of them was hollow and filled to the brim with food.

"Wow!" I exclaimed. "There's so much here!"

"We have many mouths to feed, and winter is drawing near."

"Right, of course. I know that."

"Still," Kevin said, "you're the most important of them all. If you didn't get enough to eat, we'd all suffer. Besides, you're the one who made the ration rule in the first place. I don't see any harm in taking extra for yourself."

"Good, because I'm starving."

I peered inside and found a pile of grass leaves resting on a large leaf so they wouldn't fall down into the hollow. I ate until I could no more.

"I've been inactive for a while," I told Kevin when I'd finished. "I want to see how the others are faring."

"Of course. I'll go with you. Some have chosen different practicing areas, since the old grounds are flooded."

I followed Kevin, protected from the rain by my conjuration. I could feel the power pulsing through my veins as I maintained it effortlessly. We found the runners first. I could tell just by looking at them that they'd been hit hard by the flooding. Many of them were thin and weak, and others looked sick as well. They trudged slowly through the muck, pushing themselves harder than ever, but moving so slowly.

"Come on, warriors, keep it up!" Ryan called as he moved in front of me. He came closer in greeting, and he looked worse than any of the others. His skin was sagging around his visible ribs, his eyes were bloodshot, and his fur was coated in mud. Still, a glimmer came to his eyes as he approached. "Sheer, sir. I haven't seen you in a while."

"How are you faring, Commander? You look... terrible."

"I'll be all right," he said, but didn't look it. "It's this nasty weather, that's all. Several members have stopped showing up, but I don't blame them. I think they may have just given up entirely and left the region for somewhere drier."

"Really? That's unfortunate." Ryan nodded, and looked like he couldn't stand still much longer. "I'll let you get back to it, then," I said, wishing I could do something to help.

Kevin led me to the crawlers next. They were in a little better shape than the runners, but not much. They were scrambling across tree branches. Every once in a while, one would fall off into the deep muck; the larger of them would go down and rescue him. I sat there for a while, sheltered by tree leaves, and helped. I kept the small animals from falling too deep into the mud and gave the larger ones footholds to get to them more quickly.

After a while, we left the crawlers and headed to see Spike and his predators. When we got there, it was a truly devastating sight.

Some were trying to fly despite rain-soaked wings, and many were sick and weak. The weather had really taken its toll on all of them. Spike, especially due to his old age, looked especially beaten. He shouldn't have been out in the dreary conditions. He looked tired and worn, but pushed on despite the obvious pain he was in. I could see it in his eyes; the desperate plea for an end to the madness. Focused on his troops, he didn't notice me watching from the bushes. I couldn't do much to help, and I didn't want to distract them, so we moved on to Amery's group.

The peckers seemed okay, sheltered slightly by the branches, but the gliders were faring no better than the predators. Everyone was sick, wet, and tired. We'd never be ready in time. At a loss, I looked to Kevin, but the glance he gave me reminded me of his proposed solution. I wasn't ready for that yet. The deep down thirst for justice and revenge kept me from moving forward with surrender.

The next morning was even more dreary. The thunder was much more frequent, and with it came many sudden bolts of lightning. The sky rumbled on like a constant earthquake. Still, the training continued. No matter how bad the storm, we had to go on. We had to be ready.

A wind whipped up; the first wind we'd had in a week. Almost all the trees stripped of their soggy, dead leaves. Branches swayed, and trees leaned heavily with the burden of rain and wind. I tried to imagine the sounds but couldn't. All I knew was that they would have been frightening — even more so than the sound of rain alone.

I was heading to the food storage near midday, when suddenly the bellowing clouds that filled the sky flashed a shade of green. One cloud dipped down to the earth as if some massive creature had stuck its talon through it. A tornado was coming.

The long black finger twisted as it came nearer to the ground, and the wind thrashed the trees harder than I'd ever seen before. Leaves and sticks swept up into the air and gathered around the cyclone, dancing some kind of insane duet with the cloud. It picked up dust, mud, rocks, even some unlucky animals and dashed them against trees and boulders. Finally, a flash of lightning exploded as the cloud struck the ground, and I fell over with the mighty quake of uprooted trees and stones. In a split second, the devastating twister had left a trail of ruin, then it was gone. The rain was back to a mere drizzle, and the wind died down to a gentle breeze.

I got up from the ground, dazed, wet, and covered with mud. My left wing stung with a sharp pain, and I inspected it. One of my primary feathers was bent. I grimaced and turned to look instead at the damage caused by the raging storm's sudden outburst. I'd been approaching the five trees at the corner of our territory, but now they were nothing but splinters. Most of the food looked to be gone or ruined. Along the ragged trail, animals were sprawled about — some were deathly still. This would be a major setback for our plans.

A large number of animals were making their way to center camp, where Anna and the other members of the medical team were stationed. There were so many injured from the storm, adding to the dozens who were ill, and several who seemed to be seeking help for a dying friend. Everything had piled up all at once.

Kevin came up beside me again, and I was glad of his presence. "Are you hurt?" I asked.

"No," he replied. "You?"

"Yes, a little. My wing—"

Before I could say anything more in explanation, Kevin was dragging me through the crowd, clutching the forward edge of my wings in his claws. I could feel him shouting something, probably similar to "Make way! Sheer is injured!" — but I couldn't tell, since I couldn't look straight at him as we moved past all the other animals.

The tiny chickadee pushed to the front of the line, dragging me behind him with incredible strength. "What do you need?" he asked me when we got there. "Is it pain? Do you have a headache, nausea?"

201

"Pain," I mumbled, slightly embarrassed. Most of the other animals here needed help more than I did. Then again, I was different.

"Sheer, what are you doing?" Anna started to say. "You, more than anyone else…"

"Deserve to be treated first," Kevin interrupted, jumping on the rock she was standing behind, blocking my view of her. "You're our leader." He scanned the measly stores behind Anna and darted in to grab a leaf for pain relief from under her paws. She swiped at him, but he dodged elegantly. "Here, Sheer. Take this."

I was flattered by how far he was willing to go to look out for me and didn't feel bad for jumping ahead anymore. In fact, I felt entitled. Kevin was right. I did deserve better. I was special. I was the leader. Without me, the army would be lost and unable to continue. I grabbed the leaf in my mouth and stepped aside to eat it, making way for the others to come forward.

When everything had cleared up, Amery found me. I could tell right away she was unhappy. "Sheer, the medical team is all out of supplies. There's nothing left. They are turning away everyone except those with the greatest need. Anna told me you came by for aid, but you look fine. Why did you go to them for help?"

I thought about lying to her, telling her I'd broken something or was dying of some terrible illness, but I couldn't bring myself to do it.

Then again, why should I care? I deserve to be treated first, no matter what.

I showed her my bent feather.

"What? That's it? Sheer, someone in this camp has a broken leg and can't be treated for pain because you took the treatment for your bent feather? What's gotten into you? You used to be so…" She turned her back to me, both furious and sad at the same time. I struggled to understand why she felt that way. I could see how her perspective would cause her to be angry, but the sadness was unexpected.

I shrugged it off. "Sorry, Amery, I..."

"Forget it, Sheer," she said, turning back around to face me. "Your case is lost. We're all lost." Her eyes softened with... *grief*? "You don't even know her name, do you? The fox whose leg is broken?"

I shook my head slowly, and Amery turned around again, hopping slowly away from one bush to the next. I went back towards my lonely nest, rain pounding on my back, not bothering to make a protective bubble. My confusion over the situation was stronger even than the fear I felt with each drop. Kevin had made such a good case for me, and I felt good when I was with him. Why did I feel so bad when I was with Amery?

No dreams came to me that night. After spending so long sleeping and dreaming of terrible things, it was nice to have a night of relatively peaceful rest, even though puzzling over my situation kept me awake long into the night.

When I woke again, it was still raining. I hated it. I hated the weakness, the depression, the hopelessness of the situation. We were lost, dreadfully lost. We needed help. We needed the skies to clear and the clouds to go away.

I sat on a branch, looking up at the sky through the leaf-barren branches, and felt a breeze ruffle my feathers. Was it just me, or had the raindrops become more like mist? I looked again, and sure enough, there was a tiny spot of light in the clouds. A beautiful, slender sunbeam pushed its way through. The clouds lightened as the sunbeam grew, and the colors of the rainbow refracted among the droplets. The storm was finally ending. Finally, there was hope!

XXXVIII

A slender crescent moon hung high in the clear sky that night. I had to look closely to see it at all. We'd already lost nearly half of our time. On the other hand, we still had until the moon waxed to its fullest to prepare. I stayed awake all night long, looking absently up at the moon. I feared so much, worried about so much. My head felt as if it were ready to explode.

Still, there was hope. At least, I hoped there was hope. The rain had stopped, and that was good. The clouds had blown away. But how would we ever be ready in time to face Nivek and his massive army? Could we ever be ready?

I must have fallen asleep at some point, for I woke when it was morning. I blinked in the sun; it seemed like ages since I'd last seen it. The chill air foretold the coming of winter. Food was already scare. How would we survive, even if we *did* defeat the wolves?

I made my way towards center camp, still deep in thought and misery, but stopped short while I was still in the shadows of the forest. Kevin and Amery were perched on the same branch of a tree ahead of me, and I could feel the tension even from my hiding spot. I could almost see sparks of anger between them. I was at the perfect angle to see both of them speaking, so I tried to watch and see what they were arguing about. Kevin paused in his speech and glanced into the forest, near where I was perched. Had he seen me?

"Ever since you arrived, Sheer has been getting worse," Amery said, taking advantage of Kevin's short hesitation. "I'm not sure what you're telling him, but it has got to stop."

"Sheer's fine," Kevin replied, turning back to face her. "Stop worrying about him. Don't you have a group to train?"

"Sheer is most certainly not fine! He's been taking extra rations and putting himself ahead of truly injured animals to get aid for a simple bent feather. He's been strutting around like he rules the world, and what have you done? You encouraged it!"

"Of course I did, small one. Sheer is special, in case you haven't noticed. And unlike you, I care for his well-being above my own. Above everyone else's here."

"What? Is that what you're saying? You have no idea what I've gone through to make sure Sheer is all right. But you... you have poisoned his mind."

"I have not. You're the one hurting him! You say he must take the same measly rations as everyone else, and if he has pain, too bad. He has to hold his beak shut. What good would it do if he died of hunger or couldn't fly alongside his army? He's a leader, and leaders must be strong. You don't seem to understand this, small one. You say you want him to leave more food for others, to care more for others, but you really mean yourself. You don't care about him at all."

"Stop calling me that. You're a chickadee... nothing more than a 'small one,' yourself. And I do understand, and I do care, more than you know. But what you don't get is that leaders have to care for those underneath them, too. Leaders should be role models for everyone else."

"You don't get it, do you? Do you even know what he's capable of? He's a living wonder, small one."

"Stop calling me that!"

"I call you that because you're small-minded. I may be small in size, but you have no idea what I hold inside. Really. You're just full of mush, and that's not what wins the war."

"If enough animals had empathy, which is what I assume you mean by 'mush,' there wouldn't *be* any wars."

"But they don't, do they?"

"Apparently not. But they can learn," Amery said, giving Kevin a meaningful look.

"Some animals will never learn."

Amery steeled herself. "Then those animals should not be in any position of power, nor near anyone with power."

Kevin puffed up with anger. "How dare you!"

"Who said I was talking about you? But now that you mention it, I think I was."

"You make no sense at all."

"You're just saying that because you want to avoid the truth."

"No, I know the truth," Kevin said, with a strange look in his eye.

"Which is?"

"That Sheer will never like you as much as he likes me. I'll always be his better friend. Nothing you can do will change that, and the harder you fight for him, the more you will find that you have been fighting against him."

Amery took a step back. "What does that have to do with anything?"

"Everything, small one. See, you didn't even know, did you, that Sheer has been listening this whole time?"

I caught my breath.

He knew?

Amery jerked her head around, scanning the forest, but didn't see me. "You're lying," she said, her eyes narrowing, but she was shaking.

"I am not. I'm closer to Sheer than you think. Closer than you can even imagine. You're trying too hard, small one, and you're pushing yourself away from him. You're losing him. If you find reason to agree with me, you may be able to find him again. All you've been trying to teach him has done nothing but make him feel terrible and distract him from what needs to be done. We need a leader with confidence. Your time is up, small one. Face the facts. You're not wanted anymore."

Kevin took a step towards Amery, who stumbled backwards and nearly lost her grip on the delicate branch. I didn't know who to believe. I thought I trusted them both, but how could I, when they were so against one another?

At the moment, Kevin's argument did seem more convincing. He *had* been closer to me, protecting me in ways Amery couldn't. Had Amery known when I was struggling with Nivek's attacks on my mind? Was it true? Did she just want me to feel bad about myself?

"Come on, Sheer," Kevin called in my head, turning to look straight at me. *"You have hidden long enough. You need to see the wreck Amery has made of herself, to avoid falling down that path yourself."*

I slowly slunk out of the shadows, into the light. I looked at Amery, huddled in sorrow at the edge of the branch. "Is this what you were looking for?" Kevin asked her. "Ask him yourself. Ask him if he cares."

She looked at me imploringly, and my heart felt as if it were torn in two. Whom should I follow? I knew they both awaited an answer, but nothing would come. I opened my beak to say something, but no words came to mind, after all I'd seen.

Instinctively, I turned to Kevin for help. "You see?" he said immediately, his face lighting up in triumph. "Just as I told you. Come on, Sheer. Let's leave this miserable creature be."

I slowly turned to follow him, my head hung low, not sure what else to do. I had to choose. But as I left, I looked back. Amery's head was turned, and our eyes didn't meet. I went on, through the forest, wondering whether I'd made the right choice.

XXXIX

Evening came, and I still hadn't spoken a word since witnessing the argument between Kevin and Amery.

"You did the right thing," Kevin reminded me again. "Amery was holding you back from your true self."

Each time he said those words, I felt like I was lifted a little higher, and I began to disregard Amery and her comments. Still, my mind refused to stick to one side or the other. My head was telling me going with Kevin was the right choice — this, I knew for sure. But my heart was a different story. Sometimes it whispered to follow Amery, sometimes Kevin.

It felt as if there were two persons within me: one that *was* me, or my conscience at least, and one that wasn't. It was impossible to tell which was which, but my head seemed to be the steadier one, so I followed it.

"Sheer," Kevin said suddenly, nudging me with his wing, "there's someone here to see you."

I turned to face the direction his beak was indicating, still deep in thought, and nearly jumped out of my skin. Before me stood a single gray wolf.

"What are you doing here?" I asked, on guard against attack, already tapping into my powers in case I needed them.

The wolf glanced nervously behind him. "I snuck away, sir. I can't do this anymore… please, don't hurt me. It was hard enough to get away from Finsternis." It took me a brief moment to recognize the name in his motions, since I was used to referring to him as Nivek.

"What do you mean?" I asked, still wary of an attack.

"I couldn't... someone had to tell you. It just isn't right."

"What is wrong?"

"He's been taking them," the wolf blurted out. He spoke so quickly, I could barely grasp the words. "It was him."

"Taking who? Who's been taken?"

"Members of your army. He's been taking them hostage. It's not right. The moon isn't yet full. I had to tell you... someone had to."

"What? How... how many has he taken? How has this been getting past the patrols?" I glanced at Kevin, and he looked just as shocked as I felt.

"He has taken about ten now," the wolf explained, pausing at my request to imprint a toe mark in the mud for each stolen warrior. "He's been taking one or two every night. He has some sort of power that enables him to become one with the shadows, I think. He sneaks into the camp at night, taking them away quietly while they're sleeping."

I was furious. How could I not have known? My need for justice boiled inside me, but fear rose quickly to counter it. What if I failed? If Nivek really was this powerful, enough to snatch members of my army right from under my beak... what would happen to the prisoners when we attacked?

"What is he doing with them?" I asked.

"I'm not sure," the wolf replied, shaking his head. "I think he's just trying to draw your attention, but if you don't show, he might start using them to find out what your battle plans are." He looked up at me with sad eyes. I was distraught. It now seemed my only option was to give in... the prisoners wouldn't even have a chance to fight back. My heart sank. I wanted to avenge the death of my family and friends, and now the capture of my army, but how could I? How could I, when the blood of innocent creatures could be spilled at a moment's notice?

"What does he want from me?" I asked, though I knew the answer.

"I don't know."

I was quiet for some time, not sure what to make of all of this. The wolf seemed to be waiting for some sort of response, so I said, "Thank you for your information."

"It had to be done. I must be getting back now, or Finsternis will notice, and that'll be the end of me."

"Wait. Why go back? Join us!"

"I can't. He'll know, and that would just endanger both of us. I have to take this risk."

"How would he notice one wolf among a hundred, my friend?"

"I'm his brother," he said simply.

"Oh." I thought for a bit. "Well, don't risk your life again to bring us news, unless it's very important, like a plan to attack before the moon is full. That information would be invaluable."

"Of course." With that, the wolf turned and disappeared into the dense forest in a single bound.

"Amazing," I said to myself when he was gone. "I had no idea." I shook my head sadly.

"That the scarred wolf has a brother, or that your warriors were being stolen?" Kevin asked.

"Both. Did you know he had a brother?"

"No, I didn't."

I glanced at the sky. The stars were shining brightly, but there was a dark black hole where the moon usually hung. Time was half-up.

XL

As soon as I drifted off to sleep that night, my dreams were punctuated by a frantic whine. It was closely followed by a growl, then a yelp. I saw the friendly gray wolf, slammed against a boulder. He struggled to lift himself but slumped back to the ground. A dark shadow passed over him, and the perspective shifted slightly to reveal a scarred face.

Nivek.

He growled again.

"Vy?" Only a moan answered him. "Tell me vy!" he barked again.

"Nivek… told me… to tell…" the helpless, matted gray wolf gasped in reply.

The answer didn't make any sense to me, and it clearly didn't satisfy Nivek either. The massive scarred wolf was as black as a dead, starless night, and his malice couldn't be contained. He paced back and forth twice before lurching forward with a giant paw, claws outstretched, towards the neck of his brother.

I woke, terrified, the image of the scarred wolf soaked in his brother's blood imprinted on my mind. I stared about me, but all was calm in the night. The stars above twinkled, and a cool breeze tossed dead leaves across the forest floor. Before long, I drifted into sleep again.

This time, I dreamed of a great shadow, like a vulture, standing in a pool of blood and picking at his prey. Remembering then what Kevin had said when he first arrived, I immediately knew this was Malvador. I shivered at the name, and even more so, at the mortifying scene. Nivek had left his own brother outside to be pecked to pieces by the most horrifying of creatures.

211

My head was still swimming with the awful images when I woke the next morning. I sat staring at my uneaten breakfast, Kevin beside me. "What do you think Nivek wants with me, anyway?" I asked him, shuddering. "Will he kill me?"

"I don't know," Kevin replied solemnly. "He'll probably try to get you to join him, and you'd be safest doing that. He would give you more power than you have now, that's for sure. If you don't join him, he might kill you, or he might just ask you to stay out of his way. He's afraid of your abilities, and of what might happen if you fulfilled the prophecy. He might even let you return here, unharmed, if you strike the right kind of deal."

"You really think so?" It was a relief to think there might be hope if I surrendered. Some outcome other than the death and destruction that was sure to come if we tried to fight this monster.

"Why would I lie to you? What good would it do me to lie to my best friend? I'm on your side, Sheer. You know that."

"I know." I thought for a long while. I *knew* this was the right thing to do. The *only* thing to do. Why was it still so hard?

"I can go with you," Kevin said. "If you want."

"No, no… I wouldn't want you to put yourself in danger. I just need more time, that's all."

"What about the hostages?"

I sighed. "I know. It's… I'll go eventually. I'm sure he'll let them go if I surrender. *When* I surrender. I just can't bring myself to do it. Not right now. Not yet. I'm not ready. But sometime, sometime soon."

"Maybe he'd give you more time if you called off the training. After all… if you surrender, you wouldn't need to go to war."

"No, I don't want to do that. I want them to be able to defend themselves, in case he attacks anyway. Or in case he kills me and they need to defend themselves someday." I shuddered at the thought of not being here the next time my army needed to fight. It wouldn't be my army anymore, I supposed.

"That makes sense."

"I'm scared, Kevin."

"I know."

"I'm not ready to die. Not like this. I'll die fighting for what I believe in, but... it's hard to just give up."

"Sometimes the best choices are the hardest ones, Sheer. It's natural to feel afraid."

"Why does he want me? Why not someone else, someone more..." I trailed off in thought.

"Because you're special, Sheer. There's the prophecy, for one. Besides, the ones with power and privilege are the ones who have to make the most difficult choices. It's not every day that someone like you comes along, someone with your extraordinary abilities. You can control matter with your *mind*. That's not exactly normal."

I picked at the mud with my claw. "Do you think I need to prepare myself to fight him, just in case? If he tries to kill me, I don't think I could just *let* him. It'd be worse than torture, to stand there and wait for him to strike."

Kevin shrugged. "Whatever you feel is necessary," he said.

A frantic urge to use my powers rose to the top of my mind, and I let it flow freely out, lifting Kevin into the air.

"Hey!"

Already feeling a bit better, I laughed. "Did I surprise you?"

"Yes… but, if you'd like to practice your powers, I know a better place. One full of rocks, branches, and unsuspecting animals galore."

My heart skipped a beat, and excitement rose in my gizzard. "The runner's obstacle course! That's perfect!"

I transported Kevin and myself there but was surprised when the effort left me weary. I was going too fast; I was too excited. I stopped and took a breath, waiting for my energy to return.

"Carry on," I said when the runner commander saw me and slowed down in anticipation of a greeting. He continued on his way, and I prepared for my next action. The obstacle nearest to us was about to get a bit more challenging for the larger mammals.

I lifted and rearranged the rock pile to be taller, gathering some stones from where they were scattered on the forest floor. Now, even the largest animals would have to climb over it instead of jumping. When the runners came back around, I nearly burst out laughing. Most of them skidded to a halt with confusion. Hardly any of them saw me, and of those, most wouldn't know I had powers. Only a few had been on the thirteenth floor before it was destroyed. They all looked around in bewilderment, then continued on.

When they'd all passed by, I did my best to return the pile of stones to what it was before. This time around, none of the runners stopped, but most slowed and shook their heads vigorously. They probably thought they'd imagined the change. Kevin and I snickered softly.

I moved from one obstacle to the next, making various changes to each one in turn. Sometimes I made a minor alteration, like lowering or turning a log; other times, I dug out a mud puddle or shifted the entire obstacle, like I had with the rock pile. When I was done with the runners, I moved on to the crawlers, then the predatory birds, then the peckers and gliders. Each time, Kevin and I stayed in the shadows while I made training day confusing for everyone — except the two of us, of course. The rest of the day passed so quickly from the fun I was having that it was soon dark, and I couldn't see well enough to continue. Exhausted but exhilarated, I slept soundly that night and almost entirely forgot about the wolf.

XLI

Over the next few days, I continued to practice my powers during the warriors' training. Despite the clear skies, I also decided to increase storage and rationing again. After all, winter was coming, and many animals were sharing the territory. I didn't ration my own portions, of course. I'd probably be dead in a few days, and eating freely helped me cope with my anxiety.

I could see Amery watching me when I sat with Kevin, enjoying my oversized portion at the communal breakfast. She clearly didn't approve, but that just made me all the more compelled to continue. She didn't have the right to tell me what to do. Kevin supported everything I did, with great enthusiasm. The more time I spent with him, the more I felt he was the only one who understood me. Amery just wanted me to feel miserable.

I started to stay near Amery's training grounds and laugh at her as she tried to lead her troops despite my meddling. She ignored us, but we continued to make sport of her anyway. It was a delightful distraction from the inevitable. I'd decided that I'd turn myself in to the wolf when the moon was half-full. The first quarter moon... and it was approaching fast.

The day before my demise, the sun was shining brightly, as if to mock me. I struggled to keep my spirits high, and to help, Kevin suggested I use my power on Amery. Thus far, I'd never touched her — only her troops and surroundings. I tried to use my power to force Amery to stay on the ground, but... it didn't work. Shocked, I watched as she went up in flight without restraint. It didn't even look like she'd noticed anything different. I tried again, this time, to force her back down. Nothing happened.

I began to panic. I tried to lift a pebble, something that had seemed too easy only one day before. It remained stubbornly on the ground. I must have cried out, for Kevin prodded me and asked me what was wrong. "I can't do it, Kevin!"

His beak dropped open, but he quickly shut it again. "What? What's wrong? Are you afraid all of a sudden? I told you, I can go with you..."

"No, it's not that..." Suddenly, I wondered what Kevin would think if he knew I'd lost my powers. He stuck loyally to me, more so than any other animal I knew, but he valued my abilities so highly. He was always telling me how special I was, how powerful I was.

"Well, I guess," I corrected, choosing my words carefully. "I'm afraid to go on with it. You know... tomorrow."

"Oh. You can't change your mind now, though. It's too late for that."

"I know," I replied. *More than you know.* Now that I had no powers, I was no use to my army anymore — not alive, anyway.

"Do you want me to go with you?"

"I suppose that would be good," I said. *Now that I can't even defend myself.* I was overwhelmed with hopelessness, with helplessness, and wept. "I don't know what to do," I cried.

"It'll be okay," Kevin said in my head since my eyes were closed. *"I'll go with you. I'll protect you, if you need me. I promise."*

"I need you, Kevin," I whispered sadly. "I need you desperately." I was suddenly overcome with incredible fatigue.

Kevin must have arranged for some animals to carry me back to my nest, for I woke when it was completely dark. I could hardly see and wasn't sure whether it was late night or early morning. My mouth felt dry, and my eyes felt sore.

Why do I feel so awful?

The shadows formed frightening shapes, and all of a sudden I was more afraid than I'd ever been before.

Without my powers, I felt completely helpless. How could I defend myself? I imagined the night sounds in my head, trying to calm myself, but was distracted by the shadows. For a moment, I was glad I couldn't hear. I was sure if I could, every sound would seem like something coming to hurt me.

"Kevin, where are you?" I called out, a wave of fear spreading over me in the dark.

"I'm near." Kevin's voice comforted me a little, and I strained to see him through the darkness. A shadowy form hopped onto the branch beside me, and I was pretty sure it was him. Kevin's voice in my head confirmed it: *"It's me. I'll watch over you. Get some sleep, Sheer. Tomorrow is a big day."*

Right, I thought. *Tomorrow.* I was dreading it more than ever.

XLII

The next morning, the ground was soft with dew as I looked everywhere for Amery. Even though I'd given her grief for the past several days, even though we'd barely spoken and I was sure she was still angry with me, even though Kevin didn't get along with her... I still wanted to talk to her. One last time. But everywhere I looked, there was no sign of her. I sighed and looked at the sunrise, trying to prepare myself for what was to come. It was probably the last one I'd ever see. I closed my eyes, dreading every second that passed. Then I felt a breath on my back.

I jumped, turning quickly, and saw the friendly gray wolf who'd previously helped by bringing me news of missing warriors. Something about this seemed wrong, but I couldn't place it.

"What is it?" I asked. "What's wrong?"

The wolf stamped his paw in the ground seven times, then added one more toeprint. Twenty-nine in total. "That's the prisoner count now, sir," he replied. "Finsternis was especially pleased with the most recent one. He said the bird was important, somehow. She wouldn't give her name, not like the others. Not at first. He nearly killed her to get it out of her. She finally admitted that her name was..."

I didn't need to be able to hear to know the answer. My heart pounded in its cage. *Amery.*

"No!" I shouted. "No, not her!" Despite all the arguments and everything we'd been through, she was still the closest thing I had to family besides Kevin. And now that I had no powers, losing her somehow felt even worse.

Pure hatred simmered inside me and threatened to spill out. Nivek had taken from me everyone I'd ever cared about. My sister, my mother, my best friend, my mentor... and now, Amery. I

219

couldn't let him win. I couldn't let him take another. I had to save her.

I looked back towards the wolf, but he was gone, without a trace. He hadn't even left another footprint. It was then I realized it had all been a vision. The wolf was dead. Nivek had killed him, the night of the darkest moon.

How could I not have noticed it wasn't real?

Yet I knew it was true. I was full of conviction, full of anxiety, but most of all, full of determination.

When I told Kevin about my vision, he shook his head sadly. "You're still planning to surrender, though, right?"

"No. My mind has changed."

"But you can't change it now. It's too late!"

"It's never too late. I have to go after her."

"You hate her!"

Even though I'd felt as much sometimes, I couldn't bring myself to agree with Kevin this time. I shook my head. "I can't leave her to the wolf's mercy. I don't know what he would do to her, or what he's already done."

"What about your promise? We were going to go, together."

"Kevin, I'm sorry. I've made up my mind, and I'm going after her."

"Forget her, Sheer. What about the rest of your army? You know they have no chance. You're practically handing them over to the black wolf if you do this."

"That's a risk I'll have to take. I can't leave her, Kevin."

Kevin stamped his foot. "Just how do you plan to do this, then? You had no hope before. You were planning to surrender, Sheer! How can you change your mind so suddenly?"

"Well, we'll fight. Soon. The day after tomorrow," I said, deciding the plan on the spot. "I've got to save her. Whether we win or die, at least we would have tried."

"You're breaking the pact!"

"No, I'm not. I never said I'd wait until full moon. Only Nivek said that. Our time is almost up, anyway. I don't think we would be any more prepared if we wait than we are now."

"Do you have a clear head?" Kevin demanded. "You're crazy! You can't do this! You will all die!"

"It's clearer than it's ever been," I insisted. "I'm going after Amery, and that's my final decision. We'll wage war the day after tomorrow. Besides, even if we are lacking in number and strength, we'll have the advantage of surprise."

"I can't convince you, can I?"

"No," I replied, fluttering my wings and looking towards the river. "There's so much that needs to be done!"

I took off and left to speak to Spike. When I got there, the predators were soaring high in the sky, practicing in-flight combat. They had no idea their time had just been cut incredibly short.

"Spike!" I called out as soon as I saw him, forgetting all formalities. I had no more time for such petty things. "I need to speak with you, right away!"

The old crow made his way down and landed in front of me. "What is it, Sheer, sir?"

"Our warriors have been captured by the wolf. And they have Amery. I've decided we need to change plans… and attack the day after tomorrow."

His eyes grew wide. "I thought our ranks were thinning because we were drilling them too hard! That's awful! I'll try to have my troops ready by then, sir, but I cannot promise that we'll be ready to

221

conquer the wolves. It was a slim chance already, even if we waited till the full moon."

"We can at least create a diversion," I said, ideas flowing through me faster than the river behind him. "That will allow us to rescue the prisoners at least. After that, if there's no hope of winning the battle, maybe we can try to run away. I don't know where we could go, with Nivek's terror spreading so quickly, but surely there is still a place that is safe."

Spike nodded. "All right, sir. I'll tell my warriors now, and we'll hasten training immediately."

"Thank you, Spike."

I flew as fast as I could to where Amery's group was gathered. In the absence of their leader, her lieutenants were doing their best to keep up the work. That made me proud.

"You three," I called, "come here. I need to speak with you."

"Greetings, Sheer, sir," the robin said as they approached.

"I see you've heard the news, sir." The duck shook his head in sorrow.

The third, a woodpecker, then asked, "What are we going to do, Sheer, sir?"

"I need you to work extra hard. We will launch a surprise attack on the wolves in two days."

"Two days!"

"Yes. I can't let this snatching continue. It must be stopped, and soon. The battle will be a distraction while I free Amery and the others."

"We'll do our best, sir."

I told the same to Ryan and Nyoka and got the same reaction from both. We would fight in two days. Time really was running out now, far faster than before.

XLIII

That day and the next were the busiest I'd seen in my life. I was constantly going back and forth between the different groups, doing everything I could to help. I helped Anna for a while, trying to get as many of our sick and injured warriors back to normal as possible, now that we were on a tight schedule. I slept very little, and the time not spent in training was occupied by meetings among all the commanders and lieutenants — except Amery, of course. We discussed battle plans and strategies and tried to think of every possible outcome. I talked to scouts, who searched for the best location to approach the wolves. We knew they were at the point where two rivers merged into the one that bordered our territory, but I needed more specifics. I had no time for light conversation with Kevin. As soon as the day was up, I was so exhausted, I fell asleep immediately.

The scarred wolf haunted my dreams that night. I saw the battle and woke up feeling like I'd flown a great distance, either in his pursuit or in pursuit of him. I wasn't sure whether these were visions, dreams, or nightmares.

It seemed like the two days of rushed training and final night traveling closer to where the wolves were camped passed in the blink of an eye. All of a sudden, it was time. I was anxious to rescue Amery and the others, and nervous about the inevitable confrontation with Nivek.

The sky lightened before I could see the sun. We were so close to the mountains, the great masses blocked out the flaming ball of light. But soon, the forest behind us was bathed in gentle light, while the foothills where the wolves were stationed remained in darkness. It was time. This was the moment when we would attack.

I gave the word, and each command unit split among the lieutenants and headed off to surround the camp as much as possible. Not a figure stirred.

The scouts had reported glinting metal at the far side of camp, and I guessed that was where the prisoners were being held, in human-made cages like the one the crows had stuffed me into. I'd begin my search there, assisted by a few members of my army: a slender weasel, a chipmunk, an owl, and a blue jay.

We snuck around to the other side of camp, and I knew we were in the right place. I could see about thirty cages, each with an animal locked inside. I asked those with me to begin releasing the prisoners while I searched for Amery. I passed many cages and animals. I saw a raccoon, goose, and groundhog; a squirrel, eagle, and two ferrets; a crow, wood mouse, and the fox with the broken leg. Finally, I saw a sparrow, all alone and forlorn. Amery.

Now, I could feel the battle raging around us. The ground was shaking with attacks and counter-attacks. I looked around and saw blood beginning to spread. We were losing, and fast. We were far outranked by the massive packs of wolves. As quickly as I could, I rushed to the cage that held my friend and undid the latch with my beak. It was only a small cage, and the slits weren't even wide enough for a juvenile bird to slip through.

Amery looked up at me with wide eyes as she realized she was free from her cramped quarters. She looked terrible. Her feathers were ripped and broken, and a dark line of blood stained the corner of her mouth.

"I'm sorry," I told her. "I'm sorry about everything. I'm here now."

We turned to exit the narrow compartment, but a shadow darkened the exit. Before me, the black wolf suddenly materialized out of the shadows… somehow looking even darker and meaner than ever. How had he known I'd be here?

I felt the rumbling in the air as Nivek growled. I was terrified, but I refused to let him get Amery. I wouldn't let him hurt her anymore. I faced my fear and stepped in front of her.

"It's me you want," I said. "Take me. But leave her alone."

The wolf growled again, the hair on his back spiking. I felt the rush of air on my feathers as he bared his teeth and snarled, but I still refused to back away. "Leave her alone," I repeated. "Take me. You don't need her anymore."

Nivek seemed to growl again, but there was no vibration. Nothing came out. He seemed slightly confused, as if he was fighting something from within. "I've never seen..." he muttered, the rumblings of his voice thinner, weaker. He shook himself and regained his threatening posture. It was too late, though. I'd seen him crack.

Could he really be saved from the evil inside him, just like Spike and Nyoka?

"Why are you doing this, Nivek?" I prodded. He growled and reset his stance.

Perhaps, I thought, *Nivek is the name he adopted after the darkness took over. Maybe if I used his other name, this would be easier.*

"Finsternis, I know you're in there somewhere. Don't let the darkness control you. Don't become Nivek for all of eternity."

The wolf seemed troubled, so I pushed forward. "Why did you murder your father? Your brother?"

He shook himself again, as if trying to toss away the thought. I was going in the right direction. "Why did you, Finsternis? For power? Is that really worth their lives?"

"Enough!" he shouted. Suddenly, he tensed up and made to strike.

Afraid for Amery — not myself, for the first time — I instinctively spread my wings to shield her from his attack.

In an instant, the scarred wolf's composure changed. His open maw clamped shut, he sheathed his claw and slowly lowered his paw to the ground.

"You… you think of her, when you're about to die. I… I was weak."

I was stunned by what had just happened, but regained my composure. I couldn't let this opportunity go. "Is that why you killed them?"

"I was weak. I didn't stand up to him. I gave in to what I wanted."

"There's still time to change, Finsternis. You can pull yourself from the hold of darkness."

"It's too late," he said, shaking his head. "I can't save them now."

"You can honor them by changing."

"Do you think… do you think they would forgive me?"

"Of course."

"Do you? Do you forgive me?"

I hesitated, then nodded. "Yes, I do." In that moment, I knew Finsternis had been saved from the darkness. I didn't understand how it had happened. Nothing I had said had helped; nothing I'd done had convinced him. Was it just because I'd attempted to shield Amery from further harm, without regard for my own safety?

The vibrating ground jolted me back to my senses. Finsternis may have stopped fighting, but the battle still raged on. "Please," I addressed the wolf, "we need to stop the fighting, and quickly!"

Without a word, the black wolf turned and rushed out to spread the news that he no longer wished to continue the fight. He was no longer under the influence of the darkness that had held so firmly onto not only him, but Spike and Nyoka as well.

Soon, the battle ended. We buried the dead, mostly members of my army, and treated the wounded. I made sure Amery was well taken care of. Then I stayed with Anna until the last of the animals had been cared for. It was a nice feeling, to be helping again. When everyone had dispersed, it was evening, and I decided to speak with Finsternis. His figure was still menacing and sent shivers of fear down my spine. The scar across the left side of his face and his dark, shadowy composure would never fade, but I knew he was no longer a threat. I had some questions without answers, and I hoped he'd be able to help.

I found him by the river, looking up forlornly at the waxing moon. "The moon, she is so lonely, don't you think?" he asked when I came near.

"Yeah." We sat there for quite some time, looking silently up at the sky. After a while, I cleared my throat. "Can I ask you a question?"

"Of course."

"I've had visions, dreams, of you with someone else. He had a strange, deep voice, but I was never able to identify the speaker or even see him. Who is he? What is he?"

"Oh." The wolf paused. "That… would be Nivek."

I stared, confused. "What? I thought *you* were Nivek."

"No, you were mistaken, Sheer." He drew circles in the air with his paw. "Nivek is… well, he doesn't have a form. He's not really a *he,* either. It's this horrible mass of dark spirits that compelled me to do things that were far beyond how I'd normally act. Sure, I was jealous of my father and wanted his position of power, but I would never have killed him on my own. And my brother… that was all Nivek's work. I'd never have gone that far."

"Oh," was all I could say.

The wolf looked down at his paws. "Were there others? You know, like me? Others that Nivek controlled?"

"Yes, two. Nyoka — she's a rat, but he… it… made her transform herself into a snake and enslave dozens of animals in an unnatural form. The darkness gave her powers, but more than she ever wanted. Spike, the old crow, was affected, too. He was driven to

227

mania. He slaughtered birds and used their blood to revive terrible Beasts, and unleashed crows and bears to attack the thirteenth floor. At least in that battle, we were a little better matched than against your packs…"

"Yeah," the wolf replied. "Sorry about that."

"They've both joined our side now, you know. In fact, I trust them to be commanders. Nyoka trained and led the reptiles, amphibians, and small mammals. Spike commanded the predator birds."

"That's good," Finsternis said, looking up at the sky again.

After a moment, one more burning question forced its way out. "What's it like?" I asked. "To be controlled by the evil spirits?"

"Terrible," he replied. "Terrible, and cold."

Shroud

XLIV

After the battle in the valley, only the darkness remained in my dreams. The shroud was no longer mysterious; thanks to Finsternis, I knew it was Nivek. I shivered when I thought of the formless mass of dark spirits that had possessed the rat-snake, crow, and wolf. Worse, Malvador was out there somewhere... and if Kevin was right, the shadow vulture and evil spirits were working together.

Where is Kevin, anyway?

I turned to Amery. After rescuing her, I'd told her everything. She knew I'd lost my powers; she knew about the plant I'd abused. She knew I'd eaten my fill even when everyone else was living on measly rations. But was there something *she* was hiding? "Amery," I asked her, "have you seen Kevin lately?"

"No," she replied. "I thought he was with you."

I thought for a bit, trying to remember exactly when I'd last talked to him, but I couldn't quite place it. "I haven't seen him in several days," I said, settling on something more vague.

Amery shrugged her wings. "I mean, I haven't either, but that's no surprise."

"How so?"

"I haven't seen either of you much lately, Sheer. You spent entire days with him, away from me. How would I know where he went? He's *your* friend." Her response spiked anger in me; her answer wasn't satisfying. I *knew* she had something to do with this. I didn't know how, but I knew. "Why'd you chase him off?"

"What?"

"I know you did. Why else would he have left?" Why was she arguing with me?

Amery shook her head. "I didn't…"

I gripped the branch tightly in my claws. "You're lying."

"I'm not lying, Sheer! Maybe I was jealous you were spending time with him, maybe I didn't like the influence he had on you, but I'd never send him away. He's your friend. Besides, even if I'd wanted to, do you really think he would've listened to me? Do you even remember what happened last time I tried to stand up to him? You were there. You saw how he attacked me."

My anger and frustration grew so intense, dark thoughts flitted through my mind. I imagined lashing out at her, hurting her so she could feel the same pain I felt as I missed my friend. But then I remembered how the wolf had hurt her, and I turned away. I didn't want to argue with her, after all she'd been through, but I knew she was wrong. There was no other explanation.

Suddenly, my head surged with too-familiar pain. *"You're mine,"* a deep voice resonated in my head. Now I knew it as Nivek's. It was the same voice that had spoken to the wolf in my nightmares. *"You'll never escape or conquer me,"* it said. *"I'm in your very mind, and you can never shake me from it."* My head seared, and I wondered vaguely where Kevin was as I fell to the ground.

I needed his help, but it didn't come. Instead, the pain only intensified. *"You have one more chance to surrender,"* the voice echoed. It was like multiple voices were speaking all at once. *"If you fail again, you will suffer."* I arched my back in pain, unable to move, unable to resist. Nivek was trying to control me. So far, he was succeeding. Everything went dark.

When I woke, I smelled smoke. I sat up.

The pain in my head had dulled, but I was sure Nivek was still there.

How had he taken over so easily? Where is Kevin, now that I need him more than ever?

I looked around and examined my surroundings. I was in my familiar nest near the river. Amery was nowhere to be found.

My eyes stung, and the thick odor of smoke made me cough. It reminded me of my first memory, of the first time I woke up in this world. How could I have forgotten the strange, magical fire that had nearly ended my life in the beginning? And now, I realized, Nivek had made true to his word. The forest was being burned… or had been burned, at least. I saw no open flames, which was odd. How had I slept through all of this?

The closer I got to center camp, the greater the devastation. All around me, slain animals lay dead on the forest floor. I choked on the smoke.

I closed my eyes, trying to shut out the stinging, but my vision didn't fade. *Is this a dream?* A gentle wind blew past me, whisking away the horrid scents of fire and death. It *whispered* to me. Not with words, nor with any sound at all. I didn't know how to describe it, but somehow I could understand it. I remembered the dream I'd had so long ago, back on the thirteenth floor. The dream where I'd sung to the wind.

"If you seek calm and freedom from your bondage," it whispered in my head, *"follow us."* As soon as it was finished, the wind carried me away at incredible speed. Landscapes rushed past me; the forest below was no more than a dark green blur. The dark western cliffs rose swiftly as I approached. *"Here,"* it said. *"Here is your destiny. Here is your peace."*

The wind took me swiftly through the steep crags, and ahead I could see a dark cave. Darker, even, than the cave of smoke to the north, where I'd lost nearly all of my friends. It slowed as I approached the entrance. Deep inside, I thought I could see a pair of eyes glinting in the pulsing darkness. It seemed like the shroud from my visions was condensed here, looming in the depths of the cave.

Once more, I heard the deep voice in my head. *"Surrender now, or you will suffer."* Then the image was gone. I woke up, panting, and was back in my nest. I blinked in the light of dawn, and sunlight sparkled off the first frost. When I sniffed the air, there was no sign of smoke. It had all been a dream.

I didn't know what to make of the dream. Was the wind truly trying to help me, or was it a ploy of Nivek's? His voice had interjected with the whispers of the breeze. Had he sent the vision? One thing I knew for sure: I needed to go to the dark cliffs. Perhaps there, I'd be able to defeat Nivek once and for all and restore peace to the land. Perhaps there, I'd find my true calling… if Kevin was right, and surrendering myself was the option that had the greatest possible return. Either way, Nivek was waiting. I could sort out truth from lie along the way.

Amery popped into view, her eyes full of concern. "Are you alright?"

I knew she meant my physical health, as I'd collapsed from pain before, but how could I explain what was really happening? The dull ache in my head reminded me that Nivek had forced himself in, and I had no idea how to push him out again. I'd divulged all my secrets to her, but this one was different. Would she still trust me if she knew?

Rage and hatred for Nivek boiled inside me. I hated him for destroying everyone I loved. I hated him for infiltrating my mind, giving me these headaches, and incapacitating me with his threats. I closed my eyes.

Once I kill him, then everything will go back to normal.

I could almost taste the sweet satisfaction of justice and victory. I latched on to my hatred, knowing Nivek would never fuel this kind of desire. He wanted me to surrender, and instigating my lust for his destruction had the opposite effect.

Determined to be off, I turned to Amery. To my surprise, a shadow crossed over her face. She started to speak, but my vision suddenly blurred. It only resolved once she'd finished speaking. For some reason, Nivek must not have wanted me to know what she was saying. It made me curious, but I dismissed it. I needed to focus on my task.

"I'm leaving," I said plainly. "It's not safe for you, or anyone else here, if I stay. I had a dream that called me to the western cliffs, and that's where I'm going to go."

Amery blinked, then stood up straight and looked me in the eyes. "I'm coming with you."

"What? No. It's too dangerous. You should leave me, and leave this place. Go where Nivek can't find you anymore. If you come with me... he will know."

"I don't care if I'm safe," she replied. "You need me."

I stared. Did I need her? Whether I did or not, the determination in her eyes told me I had no chance of convincing her otherwise. "Fine," I said. "But we need to go soon, before Nivek attacks again. I'll tell the commanders we're leaving and make sure they disperse the camp. I don't know where they'll go, but with Finsternis, Spike, and Nyoka to guide them, and Anna to care for them, I'm sure they will be okay."

"No, I'll tell them. I just think it might be easier that way. Since, you know..."

I knew she meant my inability to hear, but it also occurred to me that the commanders might inquire of where they should go. I didn't want Nivek to have any idea where they went to, and anything I knew, he would know, too. "Okay. I'll wait for you on the western border of our territory, by the food stores. Don't take too long."

"I won't."

I watched as she left for center camp. By now, the communal breakfast would be ending. My stomach churned, and I remembered I hadn't had anything to eat yet. I flew off towards the western border, deeper into the woods. The shadows darkened, and so did my thoughts.

XLV

Amery and I set off toward the dark western cliffs when the sun was high in the sky, shining through the mist. We would be able to stay on track by following the river, at least for a while. I avoided looking at her. Each time I did, a muted feeling of anger pushed its way to the surface. Now, I was sure the feeling was caused by Nivek, if only because I didn't think I had a good reason to feel angry towards her, myself. It was nearly impossible to tell the difference between Nivek's thoughts and my own, which scared me. I didn't want to do something harmful to her, fueled by his anger.

What if I let my guard down? What if I attack her in my sleep or blurt out hurtful words?

I was stung, thinking of how many times I'd already done just that. Kevin and I had made fun of her, to the point of cruelty, and she'd just taken it without a word. I wondered how much I'd hurt her.

My head throbbed, and I knew Nivek wasn't pleased with my thoughts. My anger surged again, but this time, against him. How long would I have to put up with his presence in my mind? I wondered how strong Nivek really was, and what it would take to break this bond.

The pain in my head intensified, and I couldn't bear it anymore, so I tried to think of something else. Turning my attention to the cliffs far ahead, which were just barely visible above the tree canopies, I wondered how long it would take to get to our destination. It seemed like the forest went on forever before it even came close to that barren wasteland. Why had Nivek chosen such a desolate place? Nothing should be able to live out there, not even a powerful mass of evil spirits. Unless the land was only barren and dark because of his presence...

Suddenly overcome with fear, I tried to stop. Instead of obeying my wishes, my body propelled itself forward. Nivek *wanted* me to go on, and he used my mind to take control of my wings for a moment. Forced to fly much faster, I passed Amery; she hurried to catch up. When I stole a glance back at her, I felt Nivek's fury pulse in my blood. I was horrified. I steeled my mind, focusing all my energy on escaping his grasp... and was surprised when I succeeded. Now that my body was back under my control, I plummeted from the air. I hit the ground hard. My head and wings ached from the rough fall and struggle to regain control. I could feel my heartbeat in my temples. But this small victory, no matter how painful, proved I could still have some control over myself. Nivek hadn't won me over. Not yet. I could still fight him.

Amery landed next to me, her eyes wide with concern. "Are you okay?"

"I'm all right now," I murmured, picking myself back up stiffly. "I just..."

She nodded, full of understanding, and I wondered how much she really knew. She nudged my side, helping me get back up. Her kindness made me want to cry.

Why is she being so nice to me? What did I do to deserve this?

If that weren't enough, the skies decided it was time to rain. I shuddered and squinted up into the trees as my back was splattered with water. I wanted to hide, to get away from this terrible substance that caused me nothing but anxiety and gloom, but I knew I had to push on. This journey needed to be over as soon as possible, before I changed my mind. I wondered if Nivek had somehow made it rain, just to test me. If it was in his power, I wouldn't put it past him to utilize it.

As I stared straight ahead through the downpour, I struggled to keep myself sane. I wished I wasn't afraid of the rain. All I wanted to be was fearless and brave, like Samuel's family thought I was. All I felt was the exact opposite.

237

I could sense Amery's concerned gaze boring into the back of my head, but I refused to look back at her. When I could barely control my own paranoia, how could I possibly control Nivek's anger?

Samuel once told me to face my fears to escape their oppression. It had helped me get this far, at least, without memories of the storm incapacitating me every time I saw water. I stared defiantly at the droplets dripping from leaves as we passed by. Then a bolt of lightning shattered my resolve and I quaked in fear again.

I'll never be rid of this fear.

I needed to think of something else — anything other than the storm. I risked a glance at Amery. The anger came just as I'd predicted, but I tried to ignore it. This, at least, was something I knew was foreign. All the other thoughts in my mind were impossible to distinguish, but I knew she didn't deserve the hatred Nivek had for her.

To my surprise, Amery seemed to be enjoying herself despite the miserable, cold rain. *Why is she so happy?* As I watched her, a different emotion seeped through the cracks in Nivek's wrath. A different emotion; a stronger one. I had no idea what it was, and it scared me. Even more frightening, I couldn't tell whether the emotion was mine or Nivek's. I quickly looked away.

At that moment, something odd caught my eye. I stopped and landed on a low branch to get a closer look. Amery followed behind me, curious as well.

Below us was a chubby, soggy muskrat. He was half-buried under a tree, digging for roots. Every once in a while, a little pile of dirt and mud would scoot out from underneath him as he dug deeper. After a few moments, he paused and wiggled his way out tail-first. He turned around with a fat white root in his mouth, then stopped. He spotted Amery first, since she'd landed one branch below me.

"What?" he said, dropping the root. "What's wrong?" I couldn't help noticing a peak of untidy fur in the middle of his back, which seemed to be pointing the wrong way. Then his eyes drifted to me and he staggered backwards. "You!" he exclaimed. "Is it really you?"

"Me? What do you mean?" I asked.

"You... You're the..." he ended with the same quizzical phrase Ryan often used. I felt a pang in my heart for leaving behind my warriors, but frustration from not understanding his words quickly surpassed it. I looked to Amery for help, and she fluttered down next to us.

"The *Silent Warrior*," she wrote in the mud. I blinked rain from my eyes. *Is that what they're calling me?* She nodded to the muskrat, affirming I was who he thought I was.

"You're *the Sheer*, the Silent Warrior? The mighty one from the thirteenth floor who defeated the snake, the crow, and the wolf, all on his own?" The rodent nervously tried to straighten the ridge of hair on his back but only succeeded in making it messier.

Why does everyone seem to know this? "Well, it wasn't all by myself," I said, nodding to Amery. "I did have help."

"It's such an honor to meet you, sir!" The muskrat exclaimed, practically shivering with joy. "Tales of your deeds have spread far, even beyond the forest. There's no one from one mountain range to the dark cliffs who doesn't know the name of the Silent Warrior."

The way Amery looked at me as he said this tore at my heartstrings and carved guilt into my soul. I didn't deserve the awe and respect the name offered. I bowed my head in shame but lifted it again as the rodent continued to speak, this time with hesitation. "Are you really deaf?" he asked. "As the legend says?"

"Yes," I replied.

He nodded as if determining something. "My name is Al," he said, pausing to let Amery write it down in the mud where the previous words had already faded. "I don't know where you're going, but I want to come with you."

"Are… are you sure?" I asked. "We're going to the western cliffs. I really don't think you want to go there."

"No," he said, shaking his head. "You don't understand. I feel like I've waited my entire life for this moment. I don't care where, as long as it's alongside a hero like you."

I shook my head in amazement, but I couldn't persuade him. The three of us continued westward, Al sharing far too many facts about roots, until the sun began to set. By then, my head was throbbing, and it was time to rest for the night.

Between waves of pain, I watched the rain stop, the clouds roll away, and the moon rise to its highest point in the sky. I tried to sleep, but every time I nodded off, my pounding head jerked me awake again. Before long, the moon had fallen, and the sun began to peek over the horizon. Even then, I still wasn't free from my torment.

XLVI

Nivek. He was even angrier now, and I had no idea why. I shouted out, so accustomed to deafness and overcome with pain, I barely noticed my inability to hear my own cries of affliction. Icy blades reached out from my pounding head, through the bones in my wings, and I felt as if I might be shattered into pieces by the sheer force of the pain. The torture in my wings surged, and I could think of nothing else.

I blacked out for a moment, then suddenly found myself on my back. The ground was cold and hard beneath me. My breast was thrust in the air, my wings arched in agony; my claws were clenched tightly, as if I could squeeze out whatever was hurting me. It did no good, of course, for Nivek wasn't in my body. He was in my mind.

With a final shudder, the pain in my head softened, but my wings burned from the damage. I realized I'd been holding my breath, so I let it out in a mixture between a shout and a sigh.

My eyes were squeezed shut. When I opened them, the light blinded me. Another wave of convulsive throbs crashed into my head, so I shut it out again, still shuddering from my burning wings. I took several deep breaths, calming myself and attempting to release the tension in my muscles. My back was in spasms from arching it so long, and with so much force.

Nivek is getting the better of me, I thought miserably. *Amery must be worried... and Al must think I'm a raging lunatic.*

Once more, I opened my eyes. How much time had passed? The sun seemed higher in the sky. I tried to get up, but my back and wings immediately spasmed again, so I stopped. I sensed Amery's presence somewhere nearby, but not Al's.

I moaned, automatically trying to sit up so my wings weren't in pain, but movement made it worse. I craned my head to look at Amery, pleading for her help.

"Lay still, Sheer," she said when our eyes met. "We'll do all we can to ease your suffering."

"Where's Al?" I asked slowly, struggling to speak through the agonizing pulses in my wings.

"He went to collect something from the forest that will dull your pain. Just lie still, and we'll help you." She looked down at me with sympathy. I suddenly felt angry at her, furious even.

Why is she treating me like a child?

Then, as soon as it had come, the feeling passed. When I realized it hadn't been my own, I was afraid. It had felt so real!

Nivek, I thought. *He's getting stronger.*

I shuddered. What if he gained full possession of my mind? What if I gave in without even realizing it? What would he do with me? What would I become? Was I even strong enough to fight him?

I suddenly knew why he wanted me. *Because* I was strong. Because I was trying. Perhaps he hoped sometime soon I'd regain my powers... but not before he controlled me. With me in his power, so too would be my ability to move things with my mind.

His mind, I thought miserably. *At that point, no one would be able to stop him.*

I knew I had to keep fighting. No one else but me was able to keep him from seizing complete control of my own mind. Even if someone out there was also able to destroy him, there was no hope left if I gave in.

I felt Al's soft footsteps approaching and looked up at Amery again. "Al's coming with the roots," she said. "I'm going to see if I can find a dense bush nearby so you can have a safe place to rest without needing to fly." I nodded, and she took off with a gentle gust of wind.

"Thank you, Al," I said when I recognized the sharp scent of Valerian root.

He nodded, a strange look glistening in his eyes. "You're welcome."

I paused, suspicious. *If he tries to poison me, I swear...* "What was that look for?"

"What? I was just surprised that you knew my native language."

"I... what?" I craned my neck to look for Amery, but my back protested. Instead, I called for her.

"What is it, Sheer?" Amery asked, landing beside me a moment later. She looked at Al, who quickly explained. Then she tilted her head in confusion. "You know his language?"

"I don't know." I sighed, agitated. "I don't understand what's going on. I could use some help getting up, though. Trying to talk from my back is exhausting."

As Amery helped me up, I mulled over what Al had said.

Had I really spoken another language? One besides Montin and Kisalan?

It had been so long since I was in the sole company of animals other than birds and small forest creatures, I'd almost forgotten I could speak Samuel's language. The chance that this muskrat spoke the same language as foxes and lynxes, though, was slim.

"What is your language?" I asked him when I was settled in the shade of a nearby bush.

"Flussish," he said, sounding it out to Amery and beckoning her to write it down. "All the creatures that live most of their lives in and near water speak it, except for fish, of course." He looked up at me. "Many of the sounds share similarities to the bubbles of water," he explained, "though if you ask me, that was a poor decision.

243

Sometimes it's hard to tell when someone's talking and when it's just the creek. But when you're by yourself, you can pretend that the water is talking back." I chuckled, imagining the muskrat having a full conversation with a brook. He'd probably tell it all about the hundreds of varieties of roots.

The revelation that I could speak *three* languages rolled over in my mind as Al went back to foraging by the stream. How was I able to speak in these different tongues without even realizing it? It seemed I only spoke languages other than my native Kisalan when I was alone with speakers of Montin, or recently, Flussish. I wondered if I could hone in on this ability, as I had with my visions and the ability to move matter. And now that I was thinking about language, there was one other thing that I didn't understand: the wind that had whispered to me in several dreams.

"Amery," I piped up, turning towards where she was foraging for seeds. "Have you ever heard of a language spoken by the wind?"

She slowly shook her head. "No, but I was raised by Nyoka, remember? She never told me stories or myths. All I know is the little I picked up since you rescued both of us."

"Oh, right." *How could I have forgotten?*

"But," she continued, "Al might know. Plus, if you ask him, maybe he'll talk about something other than roots for once." She nodded towards the stream. When I looked over, Al popped his head up from where he'd been digging behind a rock, then bounded over to us.

"Did I hear my name?"

I chuckled. "Al, we were wondering if you've ever heard of a language spoken by wind."

He paused. After a moment, he gestured for Amery to fly down next to him. He sounded out a word, and she scratched it into the cold but soft ground. *Cielen*, I read when they were finished.

"I've only heard the name a handful of times," Al said, gesturing on my behalf and closing his eyes as if seeing something blissful. "Usually, it's simply referred to as the language of the wind. I heard that it's the most beautiful tongue, different from all the rest, and the purest source of all song and color. Then again, that could be an exaggeration. It's extremely rare for anyone to be able to understand it, so there aren't many first-hand accounts."

I wondered whether the language I'd heard, and even spoken, in my dreams was really Cíelen, or if it was just part of the dream. It had certainly seemed real, but I decided not to mention it.

XLVII

By that evening, the weather took another bleak turn. We still had made no progress towards the western cliffs because of my wings, and now it was raining again. Al was out and about digging for roots as always, and I pecked away at the Valerian root he'd fetched for me. Thanks to my medical training with Anna, I knew how much was safe for me to eat, and at what intervals.

While water streamed from the leaves above me and dripped onto my head, Amery was out in the midst of it. She danced and sang in the downpour, fluttering about happily. Nivek despised this, of course, and the intensity of my headache increased. I wished my powers hadn't sapped away. I wanted to move myself to an even drier spot, or at least shield myself from the wetness. I stared at a broken leaf in front of me, and tried to call on my powers to move it. Nothing. A desperate longing surged inside me. I missed the feeling of strength and invincibility I'd held when I'd been able to freely manipulate the world around me. Now, I felt useless and weak. I thought about Kevin's suggestion — if I joined Nivek, would he restore my powers? Would he increase my strength? Could we rule together? My mouth watered, thinking of the taste of power, the taste of strength. A tiny voice deep inside me squealed in resistance, but I couldn't understand it. My head rang with sharp pain, and I tried to think of something else. I focused on the rain.

I hated the rain. Sure, I knew it brought new life to the plants, but it could also bring death. It had almost caused my own; I recalled the flashbacks that had haunted me before I arrived on the thirteenth floor. I wished I understood why I was still so afraid of the rain. The flashbacks were gone, but the fear remained. Perhaps it was ingrained after that traumatic event; perhaps something had just gone wrong inside me. I wondered if Nivek was manipulating my mind to increase my fear, too.

When the shower's strength lessened and Amery finished her song, she landed happily beside me. "No!" I barked, suddenly filled with rage I knew was foreign. I struggled to contain it. "Please. You... can't trust me right now. Please go somewhere else."

Amery's expression fell. She was clearly disappointed, but she nodded. "Okay, Sheer. If that's what you want. I'll just be over in that tree next to Al," she said, pointing her beak to where the muskrat was curling up for the night.

"Right," I replied, refusing to meet her gaze. I didn't want to know what would happen when I was vulnerable to Nivek's influence on my mind, and she was within reach of my claws. The branch bounced when she took off, and the breeze felt cold in her absence.

Trying to think of anything other than Amery, I turned my mind back to the language of the wind. Did it always carry a message? As if in response, the breeze caressed me gently, ruffling my feathers. I closed my eyes, welcoming it, and did my best to clear my mind like I had when I wanted to procure a vision.

Although I couldn't hear it, I felt I could understand. The wind did have something to say, though not in the way one would normally expect something to be *said*. Rather than sound, the breeze carried scents and feelings, a tone — sad tidings from the west, of a portion of the forest wrought with suffering.

Suddenly, before me whipped a swift vision. I saw terrible things. A vast, dark cloud, darker than the smoky substance I'd seen in my visions before, crept along the ground. It spread, originating from the dark western cliffs. Everywhere it went, it consumed plants and animals and light. It left nothing but death and destruction. As animals were sucked into its grasp, they were subdued by its power and became one with it.

Some tried to resist, to fight, but they were far too weak to overcome its fearsome strength. How could they fight a cloud? I knew Nivek himself was behind this. Perhaps he *was* the smoke.

Then a shadow flitted across the image. I only saw it for a moment, but it struck horror into my soul. Half-bird and half-shadow, the massive vulture's red eyes were blazing fiercely, and a fiery grin ripped the darkness with flames.

Malvador.

With Nivek's spreading darkness, he had free reign over the lands. Two competing feelings rushed to fill me at the same time: fear, and excitement. The thrill of the beast's power made me want it. If I had control over this shadow vulture, I could do anything.

We need to keep going, I thought as soon as the vision faded.

I said it aloud, with more conviction. "We need to go!" Desperate to move, I spread my wings to take off. A wave of burning, searing pain pierced them. My head spinning, I grasped the perch tightly just before I fell off. Flying was out of the question.

"How can I go on like this?" I cried, to no one in particular. I felt helpless, hopeless. The reminder of powers I didn't have made my situation seem even worse. I strained to keep my grip on the branch. As I attempted to regain control, Al stretched and waddled over to where I was buried in the bush. He shook his rain-drenched fur, then dipped his head under the canopy, wincing at the twigs that poked his eyes.

"Sheer, sir, are you all right?"

"No," I said, grimacing. "I can hardly move my wings. The pain is unbearable. We have to keep going… but I don't know how."

The muskrat looked at me with pity, which stirred a feeling of anger inside me. I didn't want to be pitied! That was the last thing I needed. I was tired of being deaf, tired of having others look at me with sadness. I was frustrated with the world already, and I didn't need the pity of another random creature.

"Well," he said simply, ignoring my glare, "I'd offer for you to ride on my back, but I don't think I have the control to be still enough not to knock you off. But you could always just walk."

I blinked. The idea hadn't occurred to me, but why should it have? I'd always flown everywhere or hopped from place to place. I'd never traveled long distances without my wings. I looked over at Amery, where she dozed in a nearby tree. I'd be much slower if I moved without flying, but it would at least be faster than nothing at all. Would she grow tired of moving at a reduced pace? Would she be willing to join me on the ground, despite the humiliation of appearing like a bird without the ability to fly?

"I'm sure Amery would join you," Al said, tracking my gaze and catching on to my train of thought. "You should get some rest and think about it. Maybe we can try it for a while tomorrow."

I nodded. I wasn't sure why I was taking advice from a massive rodent we'd only just met, but his words rang true. "You're right," I said. "We'll try it tomorrow."

XLVIII

The next morning, we continued on towards the dark western cliffs, towards the danger I'd seen in my vision. We traipsed along the forest floor, Al waddling beside me and Amery as we hopped on the ground. Al was right about Amery's willingness to stay beside me — she hadn't even complained.

I constantly felt the urge to gaze around me. It was different, traveling on the ground despite the distance from our destination. The tops of the trees seemed so far away. Heartsick with longing for flight, I brought my gaze back to the ground. As we traveled, the brook beside us slowed to a trickle compared to its former self. The slow moving water was clouded with mud. At first I was glad not to be distracted by the fervent splashes of water, but after a while, the sticky feeling of thirst made me wish it had stayed.

We gradually came into an area where the trees and bushes were dry and dead, even the pines. The ground, though wet from the rain, wasn't muddy. None of the water seeped into the dirt; rather, it stood in vast puddles. I did my best to avoid them, but it was hard, and I tripped into more than one. I shivered, cold and wet and afraid, then shook off my feathers and forced myself to move on.

Al, on the other hand, was loving it. He jumped and frolicked in the puddles, drenching me with cold water. He looked at me apologetically for a moment, then went right back to what he was doing. Despite my frustration, I couldn't help laughing at his antics. The combination of his head, which seemed too large for his body, with the stubborn ridge of fur on his back, made him an interesting sight as he bounced around in the puddles.

We traveled like this for several days. The rain stopped, but the clouds above us became darker with each step towards the western cliffs. After my dream, I knew this darkness wasn't from the heavy load of an impending storm — it was from Nivek himself. The ground was cracked and dry; the forest around us was dying. Only the riverbed showed any sign of moisture. The stench of death hung heavy in the air, and the only things that seemed to be alive were the flies and mushrooms feasting on the devastation. Had Nivek really done all of this, and how? Did he control the weather? Even if Malvador was real and spreading fires throughout the land, that wouldn't cause this incredible drought... would it? Was this related to the horrible events I'd seen in my vision, where animals and plants that weren't destroyed by the shroud became a part of it and added to its power? I shuddered with fear and forced myself to hop onward. Hopefully, soon we'd be out of this terrible place.

Food became harder and harder to find. One morning, all Amery was able to find was a single bush with a few dried berries. I couldn't eat them. The memory of being poisoned still rang sharply in my mind, and I opted to go hungry instead.

That afternoon, we finally entered a shaded grove with conifers that were somehow still alive. The ground was softer here; I wondered if it had once been a marsh. Yet, though there was life, there was nothing to eat. Every bush and tree had been picked clean; even Al had trouble finding roots that weren't essential to the tree that had grown them. There was still no sign of animal life. My stomach rumbled. I wished I'd eaten some of those berries.

I turned to Amery and Al, perplexed. "You guys, where do you think all the food..."

Suddenly, a dirty rabbit hopped in front of us. I twitched my head from side to side, but I couldn't determine where he'd come from. He sniffed at us, then wrinkled his nose. "There's no food for strangers in this part of the forest," he said. "And we won't take chances. I don't know where you're going, but you'd best go 'round our grove." He tipped his ear to our right, where a log bridged the dried riverbed we'd been following. Perhaps once it had been used to cross the rapids. When I looked closer, I noticed a faint worn path leading off into the distance, away from the river, parallel to the western cliffs we were trying to reach. Taking that path would be a significant detour.

I shook my head and turned back to the rabbit, who seemed to be waiting for a response. "We can't do that," I said. "We have to follow the river. We're trying to get to the western cliffs, and this is the fastest path."

The rabbit wrinkled his nose again and narrowed his eyes. "Sorry, sir, but we cannot risk a misplaced step, a broken branch, or a stolen berry. We have many sick and hungry, old and young, to feed. Please..."

"But he's the Silent Warrior!" Al interrupted, ignoring my attempt to hush him. "We cannot lose our way."

At the mention of the honored name, the rabbit took a step back. "The Silent Warrior?"

I just looked at him, neither confirming nor denying the fact. He thought for a moment, looked me in the eyes, then turned and beckoned for us to follow him into the camp.

When we made it past the dense cluster of pines marking the outer border of their territory, I understood why they'd wanted no visitors. A number of animals rivaling the size of Samuel's family had gathered together in an attempt to survive the slow but steady devastation of the forest under Nivek's influence. As we passed by them, each turned their head to stare at me, and they whispered among themselves. They were all thin and gray, even the children.

Someone dropped the acorn they'd been carrying to one of several small community piles. It rolled towards me, and I instinctively grasped at it. A surge of want, of need, coursed through my veins. I struggled to control the desire to steal this food for myself, but the feeling was so overpowering, I began to shake. I gripped the nut so hard, my claw started to ache. Then I looked up at the squirrel who'd dropped it. She reminded me of Hazel, if Hazel had been younger and starving. Imagining my friend with a clearly outlined ribcage barely covered by loose skin and fur was enough to snap me back from Nivek's control.

I can't even eat this! What am I doing?

252

I let go of the acorn and pushed it back with my beak before the feeling could return. The squirrel delicately lifted it from the ground and nodded her thanks.

We entered a clearing, at the center of which was a single fallen tree. Many paws had turned the grass around the tree to dust, and the trunk was polished from frequent use.

Their version of our central hall on the thirteenth floor, I thought.

The rabbit led us to one side of the trunk which served as a table, then disappeared into the forest on the other side of the clearing.

After we'd waited several minutes, the rabbit returned with a few others: a falcon, beaver, robin, badger, and squirrel. I guessed these were the leaders of this community.

"Greetings, Silent Warrior," the beaver addressed me. "What brings you to these sad woods?"

"We're just passing through," I responded, glancing at Amery and Al beside me. "We are heading towards the dark cliffs."

All of them shuffled on their paws or talons, uneasy at this news. The falcon flapped his wings. "Why do you not fly there? Your journey would be much quicker that way. It's a quick flight for me from here, but the way you're going about it, you won't reach it till spring."

"I have… reasons of my own," I replied. I didn't want to share too much about my disability. "And besides, this muskrat is my friend, and I don't want to leave him behind." Beside me, Al grinned at my mention of *friend.*

Each of the animals at the other side of the table nodded. The badger backed away and left for a moment; when he returned, he was carrying a large piece of bark piled with food in his maw.

"Here," he said, setting the bark down on the trunk. He gestured at the seeds and roots it held. "Please, eat. You're welcome to rest the night here, as well. We wish you the best on your journey."

I stared at them, shocked. Other animals from the community had gathered at the outer edges of the clearing and were watching us. All of them desperately needed food, and the leaders before us were no better off. "We can't possibly eat this," I argued, snapping a glance at Al, who was already stretching his paw towards one of the roots. My head pounded in resistance, and the longing I'd felt earlier when holding the walnut returned. It took all my strength to subdue it, but I remained stubborn. We didn't deserve this.

The rabbit shook his head. "We insist. We know that whatever is causing this terrible devastation, it all seems to have stemmed from those awful cliffs. That's why you're going, isn't it?"

I nodded. The thrill of the possibility of power gained from joining Nivek seeped through my blood, and I let it. The rush felt good. I'd started out on this journey to defeat him, but though I was tempted to reconsider, finding Nivek was still technically the reason we were headed to the western cliffs. It wasn't a lie. The rabbit was saying something about hope in the Silent Warrior, but I didn't really care anymore. If they were insisting that we should eat their food and sleep in their hollows for the night, I wasn't going to complain.

"Thank you," I said when he was finished. "We appreciate your generosity."

We sat and ate while the community watched. I tried to ignore the envious looks of their youngest, but they still soured the meal with twinges of guilt. I repressed the feeling, choosing to savor instead the refreshing seeds that quenched my hunger.

XLIX

That night, I rested in the rabbit's burrow. He was kind enough not to ask questions about why I wouldn't choose a branch. I drifted off into an easy sleep, comforted by the full feeling in my belly.

I woke with a start. The earliest rays of morning sun were drifting into the burrow; the rabbit was still asleep. Something seemed odd, but I couldn't place it. I poked my head out of the hole. Everything seemed normal. Then I turned my head to see Amery, standing at the edge of the rabbit's burrow, speaking in harsh tones. Shaking my head to clear it, I stared at her and tried to discern what she was saying.

"Sheer, you're pathetic," she barked. "You gave up on your quest to destroy Nivek. Just look at yourself. I never complained before, but if there's an evil force in this world, it's you. You're selfish and full of yourself. Just yesterday, you let these poor animals stare at you eating while they starved. You're the one responsible for all these deaths — not Nivek. You abused your powers; no wonder you can no longer use them."

I shook my head in disbelief. *Where did this accusation come from?* I tried to protest, but she just continued with her rant.

"And yet you claim that because of your powers, because of what you've done in the past, you should be treated like a king? What about your actions in the more recent past? What about the present? This community may not realize what you've done since the battle of the thirteenth floor, but I do. I see your faults. They revere you for acts of good will and humility from the battle, and for how you ended the war against Finsternis. Where is that soldier now? He's certainly not in you. You allowed Kevin to influence you so much that he changed who you are. You have to snap out of it!"

I didn't know what to say. I was angered by her speech, but a creeping sense of guilt was there, too. I knew many of the things she

255

said were true. The guilt rose steadily until it overpowered the anger, and soon I was pleading before her. "Amery, I'm so sorry."

"Sorry is not enough, Sheer," she replied hotly. "You misused your gifts. You mistreated these animals... you mistreated me. Saying you're sorry isn't enough. You have to show it, too."

I closed my eyes, overpowered by the wave rushing through me. Though it hurt, it felt more like myself than anything else had lately. After a long pause, I opened my eyes, but I was confused to find myself back in the rabbit's burrow. I scrambled out of the tunnel, blinking in the morning light and searching for Amery.

Where did she go? She was just in front of me...

Finally, I spotted her. She was walking with Al, quite a ways away.

"Amery!" I called. "Where did you go?"

She looked towards me, then made her way to the burrow's entrance. "What's wrong? Al and I were just out in the woods, helping these animals to forage for food for their piles. You aren't normally up this early, so I didn't think to wake you. Should I have?"

"What... what do you mean? You were just here, speaking to me, a moment ago."

Amery cocked her head. "No, we've been gone since before sunrise, Sheer."

I was confused. Had I been dreaming? But it had seemed so real! It wasn't like any of my other dreams or visions. The time and place had been exactly the same as my actual setting, but that had happened before. Something else was different...

My heart stopped in realization. I'd heard no sounds. Unlike all my previous dreams and visions, I'd been unable to hear. That was what made it seem so real. Was this disability such a part of my life now that it extended into my dreams, too?

I realized Amery was watching me, waiting for a response. "Never mind," I told her. "It was just a dream."

We said goodbye to the rabbit and the rest of the community, but I still couldn't stop thinking about my dream. Even though it wasn't real, it had stirred up several things I'd let collect dust over the past weeks. Things I wasn't proud of. I struggled against an incredible desire to repress them. I didn't want to think about the things I'd done, or the negative impact they may have had on others. Yet this time, I allowed the tiny protesting voice inside me to speak up. Maybe the Amery from my dream was right.

Our journey continued for ten long days and nights. The entire time, I bore my sufferings in silence. My headaches rose and fell in intensity alongside my feelings of guilt and longing for power. Some days I strode onward through the pain, driven by the promise of power and strength that could come from joining Nivek. Other days, I felt so burdened by guilt and sadness, I could barely lift my feet from the ground. I grew accustomed to a certain pain in my stomach. It helped that it paled in comparison to the relentless aching in my skull. On days that were my lowest, though, I felt bad for Amery and Al. I knew they were hungry, too. They spent much of the journey talking to each other, since I was silent. I paid little attention, too busy with my own thoughts to decipher theirs.

One afternoon, on a day when I was feeling brighter and ready to meet Nivek, I barely felt any pain at all. I still couldn't fly, but that didn't matter as much anymore, especially since I had both Amery and Al beside me. Savoring the freedom, I actually allowed myself to enjoy the walk. I breathed in deeply, taking in the sweet, musky scents of the last days of autumn. All the leaves had fallen from the trees now, and the forest floor was blanketed in fading color. I tried to imagine what it would sound like as I hopped through the crisp, dry leaves, but I'd been without hearing for so long, I was unable to.

I couldn't remember any sounds at all. Even Amery's voice, which had been engraved in my memory ever since the single beautiful snippet I'd gotten so long ago in a vision of Nyoka, was fading. It made me sad. I'd been having a decent day, so I tried to turn my thoughts from the sorrow, but the more I tried to think of other things, the more my mind returned to her voice. I could almost

257

feel the memory slipping away. In a last effort to recall it, I tried with all my might to remember the vision. But the harder I focused, the faster it slipped away. I couldn't do it. I couldn't remember the beautiful voice that had echoed in my head so long ago, back when Amery was Nyoka's apprentice.

I realized with a start I'd stopped hopping forward and my traveling companions had turned to wait for me. Al seemed confused, which was a comical look on him, especially combined with his untamed peak of fur. I would've been delighted by the expression, but when I turned to Amery, my own emotions were reflected in her visage. I was sure she had no idea what exactly was going through my head, but she knew me well enough to know I was sad... and my sorrow made her sad, too. I wasn't sure what to think of this, so I hung my head and hurried to rejoin them.

Glancing to the side as we continued on, I noticed Amery and Al were no longer conversing. I wondered what they were thinking. Perhaps they wondered the same of me. I hadn't spoken a word since leaving the community of starving animals behind. Desperate to think of something — anything — else, I scanned our surroundings again. Ever since that community, we hadn't passed any more signs of life. It was nearing winter. The air was cold, and no more fruit would grow on the branches this season. Every bush was barren; every tree was devoid of fruit. There wasn't even anything remotely resembling food rotting on the forest floor. The only sustenance we could find to eat was the occasional spider or insect. Were there other settlements of animals out here, grouping together for mere survival?

I paused in thought for a moment, then quickened my pace again to catch up with Al and Amery. I suddenly thought of the headaches I'd been getting from Nivek. Why wasn't I being bothered by one now? What changed since the previous night? Was he holding back, waiting to strike? Though baffled and concerned, a new thought sprouted.

Why am I worrying so much about something that ends my suffering? I'm not in pain, so it isn't a problem.

Perhaps I was free, somehow, from Nivek's hold on my head!

A tiny voice in my head warned me not to dismiss my concern, but I pushed it away. *What good does worrying do?* Then another thought crossed my mind. *If I'm free of the headaches, what about my wings?*

I tentatively stretched them; my shoulders ached from carrying my wings so stiffly against my body, but besides that, there was nothing. None of the excruciating pain I'd come to expect. Elated, I immediately lifted up in flight and twirled happily in the air, ignoring the soreness in my wings. It was a good kind of sore — painful, but mine. I was free, finally free!

Amery and Al stopped walking and looked up at me with astonishment and joy. I'd never felt so happy in my entire life. I did a few more twirls in the air, then landed on a branch, full of glee. I was free to do my own thing now, not cumbered down by Nivek's unrelenting grasp. I closed my eyes with blissful happiness, then opened them with a start. I sensed something. Something wrong. Almost as if…

No, I thought immediately. *How could someone be watching us? We're in the middle of the woods, just trekking through. There's no way someone would be tracking us. What interest would we be to them?*

I shook the wariness from my mind. Amery had noticed the flicker of concern, though, and it was now reflected in her own eyes.

I have to stand up for us, I decided, *to be the strong one.*

I puffed out my chest with confidence. I would've looked away, but something in her eyes captivated me; it held me for a moment before I could break free.

As the rush of freedom settled, it reminded me of the longing I'd had for power. I missed the strength I'd had back on the thirteenth floor, and before I'd fought the wolf. I wondered if Nivek really would let me join him, even though he wanted me to surrender.

No, I thought suddenly. *He didn't want me to surrender. He always wanted me to join him, even from the beginning.*

But though I was intrigued by the feeling of power, did I really want to join him? He'd caused so many animals' deaths, their sorrow, their hunger. I twitched, recalling how my dream version of Amery had accused me of doing the same thing.

Am I really so different from him?

Besides, he'd done so much to hurt me. For the past few weeks, he'd tortured my mind and rid me of the ability to use my wings. *No... that's wrong. He never did torture me; that was all a dream, just like the dream of Amery being mad at me.* I was confused for a moment. Had I really forgotten it had all been a dream? How could I have been so wrong? And why would he want me to join him?

He's powerful, my thoughts resounded, as if responding to my own question. *He wants me to join him. That would make me, by default, almost as powerful as he is. He could help me regain the powers I've lost. He could enhance the ones I still have. I could utilize my abilities again — to speak in multiple tongues, and, if he returned my more famous capability, I'd be able to manipulate the world around me again. To control it, with nothing but my thoughts.*

The wave of desire blossomed, filling me with strength and urging me onward. "Come on!" I called to Amery and Al, who were still watching me from the ground. "Let's keep going! We've got places to be!"

L

We were finally able to pick up the pace now that I was flying again. As I hopped from branch to branch, Amery beside me and Al below, I tried to ignore my gnawing hunger. We'd traveled for twenty days now — almost a full moon's cycle — since leaving Samuel's family behind. Winter had set in, and so had the cold. I couldn't remember the last time it had rained, but if anything, it would be more likely to snow now. The riverbed we were following was nothing but an imprint in the dry, cracked earth.

The dark western cliffs were looming taller above us now, but they still seemed ages away. The stillness gave me more time to think. I kept flipping back between thirst for justice and thirst for power; the resistant voice inside me had all but faded away. I still wasn't sure whether I wanted to kill Nivek for taking so much away from me, or join him to refill my life with strength and pleasure. Either way, my mind was steeled on our destination. Every step we took gave me more determination and bitter resolve to finish this journey and achieve whichever goal was at the forefront of my mind at the time.

On top of this, a strange feeling that we were being followed persisted in the outer reaches of my thoughts. It always went away as quickly as it came, but it was starting to bother me.

It doesn't make any sense, of course, that someone would be following us.

But still. Though the feeling was fleeting, it was ominous. I looked at the sky, trying to make sense of everything, and noticed Nivek's shroud had thickened. The sun was obscured by black clouds now; still, there was no scent of coming rain, no moisture in the air at all. Heaven knew the forest could use it.

Perhaps the clouds weren't Nivek himself, but rather a symbol of his power. It was just like in my vision of the spreading darkness, which overtook the minds of helpless animals. Regardless of the extent to which the clouds resembled the mass of dark spirits we were traveling to meet, or confront, it was clear his power was spreading. I was overwhelmed by his power, the fear of fighting it, and the lust of sharing it. It made sense that his power had spread fires throughout the forest; it made sense that animals were coming together for mere survival because of what he'd done. I never thought it would come to this, to physically affecting the world, the clouds, and the weather itself. It was incredible.

Even though part of me wanted to revel in this power, to have some of it as my own, I was afraid. When would the destruction end?

Perhaps if I join him, he'll stop the destruction and be content, I thought.

Yet something deep inside me knew this was wrong. It was somehow extremely difficult for me to muster the thought, but I knew he would never stop. Not until he'd taken over all the animal kingdom; not until he ruled every species on the Earth. I shuddered to think what would happen if he managed to completely swallow the race of humans into the darkness. They may not be strong or mighty, but their reach, intelligence, weapons, and dominance would leave him unstoppable. With their power in his grasp, we would all perish.

Except for me, I thought. *If I joined him, I'd reign the world beside him.*

Suddenly, though the sky was dark, an even darker shadow flitted across the ground. I looked up and saw nothing. I stopped and called Amery and Al to me.

"Did you see that? Did you hear anything?"

Al nodded slowly, saying he'd seen a shadow, but Amery said nothing. Instead, she stared off into the distance, cocking her head, listening. Could she hear it, whatever it was?

She then quickly turned her head, and Al turned, too, having heard a sound. Again, a shadow passed over us. This time I saw something, though I wasn't sure exactly what it was. It resembled a large bird, but not a physical one. Rather, it seemed to be a sort of living shadow capable of flight.

My heart stopped. I stared at Amery and Al, and we all shared looks of terror. I'd seen it in my dream; they'd heard of it from myths. *Malvador.*

I knew Malvador was serving Nivek — whether by choice or by force, I had no way to tell. I wish I did. If Nivek could *control* this creature, that was even scarier than if it were just working alongside him by choice. But how could the shadow vulture make the mistake of being seen if it was a spy for Nivek? Unless… unless it was no mistake. Unless Nivek wanted us to know he was watching us. I shuddered with fear.

"What do we do?" I whispered. Amery just looked at me, her eyes wide with horror. But when I turned to Al, his eyes held a glint of hope.

Al motioned for us to follow him. He led us quickly through the woods, looking left and right and sniffing around many different roots. He was moving faster than ever before, and I struggled to keep up with him. The faint smell of burnt pine stung my nostrils and grew in intensity as I followed the muskrat.

Soon we arrived at a thick grove of trees, around which wound a dense thicket of vines bearing large, deadly thorns. We squeezed carefully through. On the other side was nothing, but the scent of burnt pine was overwhelming. It was dark inside the thicket; the trees, though they bore no leaves, were so closely packed together, hardly any sunlight made it through both the dense clouds and interlocking branches.

Al began to dig. Before Amery or I could make a move, he'd opened up a hole, dragged both of us underground into a tunnel, and closed off the hole again with stones. We were left adjusting our eyes to the darkness.

I couldn't see a thing, so I had no idea what Al was saying, but it was short. Then he led us deeper into the ground. Amery seemed to be having an even harder time seeing in the dark than I was, but at least she could follow the sound of Al's voice. Both of us stumbled in the dark, uneven tunnel.

We continued on, crawling deeper and deeper into the Earth as we went down the path. Small passageways opened to the right and left, but Al led us straight onward.

After a while, the slope of the tunnel leveled off, and the number of side tunnels decreased. The road forward became straight and long. Somewhere far ahead, something was glowing. It wasn't very bright, but in contrast to the darkness I'd already grown accustomed to, it nearly blinded me. Squinting as our eyes tried to adjust to the increasing brightness, we moved slowly forward.

Finally, the tunnel widened into a bulbous hollow. The rocky walls glowed in various shades of blue, green, and pink. Al stopped and grinned. "It's a kind of luminescent rock called Fluorite," he explained; Amery scratched the new words in the well-packed dirt so I could understand.

"What is this place?" Amery asked.

Al had a mysterious glimmer in his eyes when he responded. "Welcome, my friends, to the Rúnda, or more colloquially, the *Hidden Tunnel*." He paused while Amery wrote down the name for me, then continued. "It's a passageway that connects multiple thorny groves to the Caves of Mist, which reside in the dark western cliffs. It'll be much safer to travel this way than through the woods. Malvador can't follow us here."

I stared in wonder. "How did you know this existed?"

"Many myths and legends have arisen from the woods in these parts, and from the outskirts of the dark cliffs," he explained. "The tunnels and caves underground were formed by ancient residents as a form of travel and protection in times of war. They were rarely used for centuries until recently, when hard times came upon us once more. Now, it seems many refugees from Nivek's reign have retreated here for safety." He gestured behind us, and I turned to see the reflections of dozens of eyes watching us curiously. I guessed the side tunnels led to their homes. I felt sorry for the animals who had no choice but to seek refuge underground. I was hungry, but as some of the other animals came into the light to greet us, I felt a greater pity for them than for myself. They were even skinnier than the animals we'd seen in the forest. Still, the sting of hunger reminded me of the long journey ahead, of the sustenance we'd require to make it to the cliffs.

They're just staying here, I thought. *I deserve food more than they do. Who cares if they die? I should be fed.*

I shook my head, forcing the thoughts from my mind. How could I think such things?

I turned back to Al as he continued. "There are several thorny groves that mark the entrances to the cave system. They all have a peculiar smell of burnt pine. When I caught a whiff, I immediately remembered this place and decided to take you here. I've always wanted to come see the Rúnda," he admitted, "but I never had a reason to make the insane trip to the dark cliffs until now."

We rested there that night, in the home of a gracious ferret family. Their hollow was bare, but it was moderately dry and warm. Al nibbled on some roots around the tunnel, and the ferrets helped me and Amery find a couple insects to line our aching stomachs. It wasn't much, but it was better than nothing. More water was here, at least... I wondered how many animals had relocated for the groundwater alone. They'd built formal watering holes close to each cave of fluorite and posted guards to carefully control how much each animal drank from the limited supply.

When our thirst was quenched and we were well-rested — underground, we couldn't tell whether it was night or day — we continued on our way down the straight, narrow tunnel. As the light from the fluorite dimmed, I could faintly see the light from another similar cave farther down. We marched on, towards the one searching for us; the one who'd sent Malvador after us as a spy, the one who wanted me to join him or die. I still hadn't made up my mind why I was making this journey, but I recalled the dream I'd had so long ago, where the wind had whispered to me that peace, in some form or another, waited in the dark western cliffs.

As we walked, animals came to the entrances of their hollows to watch us. I felt the ground rumble gently with chanting that must have echoed through the halls: "Silent Warrior. Silent Warrior. Silent Warrior." I couldn't tell them I wasn't sure I would even fight Nivek. Their hope was too great. I didn't know what to say.

For several more long, uneventful days — or what I supposed were days, based on the times we slept and ate — we continued on through the underground tunnel. Families of those forced to live in the dark hollows watched us and chanted my name. We ate what we could find and spoke little. Each day was just like the last, and nothing ever seemed to change. I almost forgot what sunlight looked like, we were down in the dark for so long. The glowing fluorite was our only source of light. The patches were close enough together that you could faintly see the next one as soon as you exited the first, but the stretches of tunnel in-between were still incredibly dark. The straight path never seemed to end. I'd long lost count of the number of days we'd been traversing these secret passageways.

Then, one day, the earth trembled like never before.

The chanting of the animals from their hollows cut short. The ground shook, nearly throwing me from my feet. Rocks and clods of dirt fell all around us; dirt sifted down like rain. I felt the vibrations and knew this was no ordinary earthquake. This particular type of shaking could only be caused by one thing: the pounding of many feet, paws, and hooves on the surface. We stayed quietly where we were, clinging to each other for protection from the raining stones.

LI

When the vibrations died down and it seemed we were no longer in danger of being crushed, we brushed ourselves off and took a moment to breathe. The animals in their side tunnels watched me expectantly, too terrified to continue chanting my name.

"Al," I finally said, "would you dig up to the surface? We should investigate what just happened."

He nodded, then got to work. He started between two side tunnels, then dug with a steep upward slope. A pair of moles joined beside him to help him move faster. Before long, he broke through to the surface, and a beam of moonlight shone through the hole.

The first thing that struck me was the blinding full moon's light filling the frosty air. Once my eyes adjusted, I noticed two things: first, that the moon didn't shine as brightly as it should. Though it seemed intense compared to our time underground, it was shrouded by dark clouds so thick, it seemed Nivek himself filled the sky.

Second, I marked that I could see the shadows of hundreds of animals, traveling in the very direction we were headed: to the dark cliffs. The cliffs themselves were much larger now than they were when we were last above ground. I squinted to identify the hoard, then felt my eyes grow wide with terror and my heart fill with fear. There were humans and gigantic reptilian Beasts among them. The ancient monsters Spike had resurrected walked alongside the race that had previously held firm control over most of the world. Both were now walking directly into Nivek's grasp. Had he somehow recruited these powerful beings? As if to answer my question, the shadows themselves seemed to shift among the marching crowd, and I realized they were no normal shadows. It was the shroud, thick and heavy around their feet, curling up around their legs, and crawling into their mouths. None of them reacted... they'd already become one with the darkness. We were too late to save the race of humans.

As we watched the odd procession from the cover of the brush, an even greater darkness passed over us. It was the shadow vulture, Malvador. I'd never be able to forget the sight, so much more real than in my vision. It was an immense shadow with no body; its wingspan was longer than an oak was tall. It had blazing red eyes, and it brought with it a terrible feeling of cold, loss, hopelessness, and fear. Feelings far stronger than they should have been without some sort of magic. No wonder the creatures in the forest feared it over any other living thing — if it could even be considered alive. It certainly seemed Malvador was answering to Nivek.

We were very close now, so close that it was rather dangerous to continue, regardless of whether we were above or below ground. How would we get into the dark cliffs without being noticed, attacked, or captured? Exhausted and at a loss for a plan to continue, we built up a blockade of dirt and rocks around the new tunnel and rested there for the night.

Though I was tired, I couldn't fall asleep. I amused myself by watching Amery and Al in their slumber for a while, then grew tired of it and fell into deep thought. I was so close to the dark cliffs, but I still had no idea whether I was going there for revenge or power. A strong urge inside me pushed me to join Nivek, to have the strength he would certainly provide me and use my position to protect my friends… especially Amery. Yet each time I settled on this plan, a tiny but persistent feeling of hesitation kept me from finalizing it. The feeling was weak, as though subdued inside me, but it refused to give up. Something just would not let me join Nivek, no matter how badly I wanted to. The harder I tried to find its source, the more elusive it became.

Frustrated, I repositioned myself. I tried without success to settle down and sleep. I knew I wouldn't be able to reach a decision tonight. As I turned around again, uncomfortable and distressed, I noticed Amery was awake. She was watching me from the corner of her eye.

As soon as she saw I'd noticed her, she closed her eyes again and pretended to sleep. It had only been a moment, but I'd seen her, and that didn't help me sleep at all. I couldn't understand why she'd been watching me, and now I was even more uncomfortable. How long had she been watching before I noticed?

After hours engrossed in my own thoughts, I must have drifted to sleep. I dreamed of terrible shadow Beasts chasing me through the forest, into the dark western cliffs, straight into Nivek's lair. I could see a pair of eyes glinting in the darkness, and just as I drew near to where they were, I awoke, trembling.

When I woke, I realized I'd been deaf in my dream again. I hadn't heard a sound, in reality or a vision, for a very long time now. I couldn't even remember the last time I'd heard anything, nor could I recall what it was like. That made me sad. I missed the ability, even if it wasn't normally mine in waking hours. I'd completely forgotten what Amery's voice had sounded like so long ago, the one sound I'd enjoyed above all others, but now I couldn't remember any of them. If I could hear one single sound, just once more, it would be her voice. Even a single note.

Why am I thinking of such sad things? I wondered, but at the same time, I didn't regret it.

I struggled to make sense of what I was feeling; everything seemed to be in conflict. Part of me hated Amery because of it. But part of me wanted to be close to her, in the hopes that someday her voice would grace my dreams again. I closed my eyes as the night waned and fell into troubled sleep once more.

LII

Morning came, and with it, the choking scent of smoke. I wasn't shocked by it, noting how close we were to the destructive force of Nivek, but it was still a tough thing to wake up to. Amery, Al, and I peeked out from where we'd been burrowed, and no one was in sight. My companions turned their heads from side to side, listening. Al sniffed the air, and I closed my eyes and felt for vibrations in the ground. I could have conjured a vision, but what good would that have done? I couldn't hear in them anymore, and all it would've told me was that Nivek's power was growing. I could see that clearly, even without a vision.

We all looked at each other; nothing. We were alone. It was the calm before the storm, I was sure. A sense of dread settled in my heart and mind and refused to leave. I knew something was coming, but I still wasn't sure what to do about it.

Would I try to fight, despite my lack of powers, or even an army, and suffer the horrible death that would certainly follow? Would I turn myself in and hope Nivek was merciful enough to let my friends go? Or would I join him, as he wanted me to and as my own mind urged me to, even though I knew that was wrong, somewhere in the depths of my heart? I didn't seem to have any other options. We were drawing near, and I needed to make a decision. I looked at Amery and Al. I wasn't sure why they'd come this far, but I was grateful for their company.

We emerged into the forest, ever wary despite — or perhaps because of — the incredible stillness and emptiness. I was overcome with the sensation that I was absolutely parched, and the forest cried for water. It was as if the air itself was drawing moisture out of me. The ground was cracked and hard, the branches were brittle, and the leaves had all fallen and wasted away. The air itself was dry, and the sky was dark with the shroud. The forest echoed the dark times we were in. There was no hope, no growth, nothing pointing towards a better future. Everything was desolate, empty, hollow.

Except for one tree. One strong, persevering tree. Just ahead, I could see it through the mist. It had a few leaves, still green despite the fact that it was mid-winter. How had it survived? There was no water to feed it, no sunlight to bathe it, and spring was still a distant thought. Still, this one cherry tree bore leaves, and even blossoms. Though it was weak, and its growths were few and far between, it was distinctively stronger than the rest.

Drawn to it, we all approached the tree. If the forest was a mirror of Nivek's terror and reign, who then was the cherry tree? Why was it resisting, even when there seemed no reason or motivation to do so? I wished I were like the cherry tree, I realized — strong despite the cold and darkness, despite the despair all around.

Just then, I felt something. It was cold and wet. I looked up and saw clouds in the sky — real, gray clouds, intertwining with the black shroud of Nivek's power. They twisted through the darkness like vines, and rain began to fall. I flew up to one of the branches on the cherry tree, unable to take my eyes off the sky. How long had it been since rain had fallen?

Al bounced off in delight, hopping and scuffling around as the sprinkling became a drizzle. Amery flew and twirled, pure happiness in her eyes. Her beak opened in song, and for the first time, I felt no resentment. I only felt sadness, and longing to hear her voice.

It was then that I heard a ringing in my ears. It hurt to hear it, having been accustomed to silence for so long, and I doubled over with shock and pain… yet, a different kind of pain. Soon, the ringing evolved into a buzzing, and the buzzing softened to a strangely familiar sound. The sound of rain. Then the sweetest melody of all touched my ears, ever so softly, ever so gently, and I recognized it at once. The sound of it wiped away all fear of the rain, all distress for my future, all thoughts of anything but the sound itself.

I straightened, opened my eyes, and stared at Amery in disbelief. I was hearing her song. She noticed me and faltered. "No,"

I said quietly, stumbling over the words I could now hear coming from my beak. They sounded foreign, weak. "No, don't stop."

Her eyes sparkled, and she continued her song. I watched her, no longer in agony, listening with joy and bliss and amazement. Her voice rose and fell in sweet, happy calls. It was such a stark contrast to the times we were in, the sadness, and the despair.

Unable to help myself, and not entirely sure what I was doing, I was suddenly in the air with her. We danced together in flight, oblivious to all around us. As she continued to sing, I locked my eyes on hers; they were filled with surprise and joy. We twirled together in perfect harmony. This moment made the rest of my life seem useless, empty, and dark. This moment of light, of happiness, of joy and peace, brought everything else to shame. Nothing compared to this.

A certain despair I hadn't noticed before, I noticed now only as it left. I remained behind, even more elated than before, feeling freer than ever. My mind suddenly felt as clear as the clearest waters, as bright as the morning sky, and many different feelings washed over me, coming and leaving like waves.

I felt shock. Suddenly, I knew Nivek had never left my mind at all — until now, that is. He'd controlled me, influenced my thoughts and actions, for far too long. My memories from when he'd tortured me returned, and I knew it wasn't a dream. I'd only thought that because Nivek had wanted me to. But now my mind was purged of his evil influence. He had no control over me anymore.

I felt courageous, suddenly determined to do what I could to fight him. I wanted to save this good earth from his reign of terror and allow for more moments like this one. I no longer had any doubt, no lust for power, no lust for revenge. All of those things I now realized had been fueled by him, even if they'd started as seeds from my own mind.

I felt peace, happiness, joy, and for the first time in a long time, I was content. I wasn't worried about what lay ahead.

I felt strong again — a resurgence of a lovely familiar feeling inside me told me my powers had returned. I acknowledged them, but with caution. I knew how they could affect me now; I knew abusing them could corrupt my mind. Amery had been right. I'd save them for the last possible moment.

Amery's song was one of joy, of hope, and I knew at once it was related to the prophecy of old, the one I was meant to fulfill. She took its words and added to them; she took each sentence and made it its own beautiful stanza. She'd already finished singing of the fledgling sparrow with eyes of gold, broken in a tempest night. She'd sung with serious tones of the darkness, thick of smoke, which incited everlasting blight. Now she sung of the only hope against the scourge, the Silent Warrior, who must brave a battle more than might. I knew, now, what this part of the prophecy meant. I'd already been fighting the battle in my mind. It was time to finish it. Amery stopped, landing on a branch of the blossoming cherry tree to catch her breath. I followed beside her, my eyes still locked on hers.

"You have to finish the rest," she whispered.

I nodded. "The hero shall restore the light." At that moment, the strongest feeling of all washed over me, gentle but firm. I knew, with all my heart, that *this* was where I was meant to be. I wasn't thinking of my quest, or the forest, or the dark cliffs, though certainly my destiny would lead me there soon. I was thinking of right now, right here, gazing into Amery's eyes after dancing with her in the rain.

I noticed light coming in through the sky, and I tore my eyes regrettably away from Amery to look. Where the gray rain clouds met the black shroud, rays of sunlight were now filtering through, thin but hopeful. If I looked closely, I could see the colors of the rainbow glistening off the droplets.

After a while, the drizzle lightened to a sprinkling again. I heard and felt a breeze rustle the tree, whispering sweet words of hope. The sound was beautiful and gentle. I heard each and every small sound, new to my ears. The droplets of rain pattered on the ground, and flower petals from the cherry tree, taken up on the breeze, gently brushed our feathers, bringing us closer together. It felt like spring around us, even though it was nearly winter. I leaned my head

273

against Amery's and spoke through my heart something I'd just come to see… that I loved her.

"I love you, too, Sheer," she whispered, her eyes full of understanding. She looked at me, without speaking, and her eyes said everything I needed to know. "I always knew there was some good in you. I never lost hope in you. I knew the Silent Warrior would return to save his people."

"I promise…" I said, pausing briefly at the shock of hearing my voice again. "I promise that I'll stay with you, and protect you, and love you, as long as I live on this Earth. I won't ever let you down again. And I'm deeply sorry for all the pain I've caused you in the past, Amery. I really am. Would you forgive me?"

"I forgive you, Sheer."

I closed my eyes and breathed in her words, her sweet voice. I savored the sound and smell of the rain, and the feeling of her wing against mine. Finally, I was at peace.

LIII

While the breeze still encircled us, I heard it whispering to me. It didn't use words, but rather the language of color I'd grown to know. *Cielen*. As I remained still to listen, it told me all nature not yet taken under Nivek's control would come to our aid, summoned by the wind itself, and strengthened by power beyond my own. Nature itself wanted to help defeat this evil. I felt the trembling of the earth shake the branches of the tree as this already began to pass and animals traveled from far away at impossible speeds.

It was odd to be able to hear all the sounds around me, but not the source of the tremors. Not yet, anyway. My sense of the vibrations was far more concentrated than my hearing, thanks to the time I'd spent without use of my ears. I looked up and saw the rain clouds slowly drifting away. Right before the shroud took their place, I got a glimpse of sunlight. It was enough to tell it was about midday.

Amery shivered in the cold as darkness settled back in and the rain stopped. I held her close, listening to the beating of her heart and wrapping my wing around her. I knew these few hours may be our last together. I was thankful for her presence and perseverance despite all I'd done.

Al came back from his wandering around sunset, his eyes wide. Behind him, the first of the other animals were arriving, too. I watched them, sensing the duty of being their commander — of being the Silent Warrior. I was ready to live up to the status that had given me that name. I was ready to be the same Sheer that had led all of the thirteenth floor in the battle against Spike, the same Sheer that had led Samuel's family into battle against Finsternis. We would now face our greatest enemy yet. The wind had given them miraculous speed to arrive from all corners of the Earth, and it was now my job to lead them into the dark cliffs.

As an eastern wind rushed past me, it told me the tales of the western cliffs: that Nivek's army was massive; it was larger than ours, and more powerful. But we had nature and the wind on our side, and we were driven by hope rather than fear. I spoke to the great crowd of animals as it gathered; a few I knew, but most I'd never met.

"Greetings," I began. As attention drew to me, I heard many murmuring amongst themselves. My own ears heard the language of Montin as I knew from what Amery had spoken, though with several different accents. I listened for a while, just appreciating the intricacies of each animal's way of speaking, and from it I guessed each animal was hearing my words in their own language.

"Is zat ze Silent Varrior?"

"He can speak my language?"

"Ssh, I'm tryina listen!"

I waited for them to settle down so I could have their undivided attention, then continued. "As you probably know by now, we are on the brink of war. Nivek is strong. His armies are massive. But we must not let him win this. We must show him that we are not disposable creatures. We have hearts and minds and souls, and we have strength in hope and in each other."

After hearing several murmurs of agreement, I went on. "We will fight. We will win this war, and we will show Nivek once and for all who really has control of this Earth. We will show him that we are not afraid of him!" After the outburst of howls and calls of excitement, I ended my speech. "I have a plan."

I split the multitude into five groups; one to attack directly, and one on either side. The remaining two groups would come in after the battle had already started, as fresh reinforcements; one from behind, and one directly into the middle. I made sure each of the five groups had some animals who'd been trained to fight. Hope was powerful, but training was more effective. I trusted those who were stronger to look out for those who were weaker. Meanwhile, I'd have to find Nivek and defeat him. I knew I had to fulfill the prophecy, and I had to do this alone.

The wind called on the might of nature and provided new sprouts from the ground that satisfied us all. It may have seemed impossible, but the cherry tree was alive, wasn't it? I accepted that I didn't understand the might of nature and was grateful it was on our side. With full bellies, we rested to gain strength for the fight. I noticed this elusive force hadn't tried to prove itself to us; rather, it provided for us when we put our faith in it. I would no longer doubt this world was good at its core.

At the earliest break of dawn, the sun was barely visible past the shroud. I sent the first three armies silently on their way and nuzzled Amery one last time. I left her behind with Anna and a few other members of Samuel's family, who'd traveled from afar with the help of the wind. She would be part of one of the reinforcement troops. It was time for me to seek out Nivek.

As a group, we were all headed west, into even deeper darkness, directly into the sharp cliffs. I decided not to use my powers yet. Now that Nivek was no longer in my mind, he wouldn't know I'd recovered them, and I could use that to my advantage. I'd have to preserve myself, though, to last until I actually reached him. Instead, I'd do my best to guide my armies to the weakest points in the enemy's ranks as I made my way to Nivek's lair.

We didn't last long undiscovered. Soon, the great shadow of Malvador passed over us, raising a screeching cry to alert the others. Shortly after that, the battle began. The morning sun cast a glow over my first armies as they attacked from three angles. Now that I had an overhead view of what we were up against, I knew there was no chance we'd surround Nivek's massive militia. They easily outnumbered us ten to one. I cried out to the wind, asking it to help carry the message that we needed to change our formation to a more conservative one. It whipped around me in response, then rushed off to the two side groups I'd arranged. From my vantage point, I could see them shift more towards each other so they weren't as spread out. Still, even with a better tactic, I needed to find Nivek and end this war as quickly as possible.

I heard Malvador screech from behind me, and dove just in time to avoid its fiery talons. It swooped down into the crowd, snatched several of my troops in its grasp. It ripped them limb from limb, tossing burnt halves back with an ear-splitting shriek. I shuddered in disgust.

Forest animals and birds were clashing against their own kin, plus Nivek's accumulation of humans and Beasts. I noticed all the creatures under Nivek's control had completely black eyes... not even a hint of white or colored iris.

Did my eyes look that way when he was controlling me?

The humans wore primitive armor but carried weapons that seemed to be made of solid shadow. The beasts didn't need armor — their scales were as thick as stone, and they swung their mighty tails like spiked cedars.

All around me, the chaos was growing. My armies were losing, and it seemed somehow Nivek's was growing. But when I looked closer, my jaw dropped in shock. The slain animals from both sides were standing up again, eyes as black as night, fighting for Nivek. The dead had little coordination or strength; they flailed their arms and bodies limply at my troops. But what they lacked in power, they made up in numbers. The more animals died, the more were fighting for the enemy. Disgusted, I steered myself straight for the darkest cave. I dipped and dodged my assailants with determination, never losing sight of my goal. It was time to end this.

LIV

As soon as I entered, I was attacked. I had no time to react. The cold grasp didn't last long, but it pinned me in place, and I couldn't move. I used all my physical might against the magical bonds, but it was no use. I didn't want to use my powers yet, but I was sure they wouldn't help me get out of this thing holding me, anyway. Whatever it was, it was made of strong, dark magic. I couldn't see anything. It was pitch black.

An odd blue brilliance suddenly filled the room; I couldn't see its source. There was just enough light that I could barely see. I was thankful for my heightened senses from being deaf for so long. The shroud was absolutely dense in the cave, and I knew for certain I was in the presence of Nivek himself. I looked around me and found I was suspended in the air. The murky, pulsating shroud that was Nivek sifted around me, forming and dissolving itself. Finsternis had described him as a formless mass of dark spirits, but at its most condensed, it almost formed the shape of something that seemed vaguely familiar. I couldn't quite put a name to it.

I observed my surroundings, in case something might prove useful. The cave was rather small, but plenty large for a bird as tiny as me. Its shorter dimension was slightly longer than Samuel had been from his head to the tip of his tail; the longer was a little less than twice that. It wasn't a definite shape, but nearly rectangular, with jagged sides and corners. One corner, the one nearest me and furthest from the entrance, was so rough, it formed a small crevice near the ground just large enough that I might be able to squeeze my body inside it. The floor, oddly enough, was nearly flat, and the roof was sloped, with a hairline crack that spread halfway across the diagonal.

I was already beginning to formulate a plan when I was assaulted with a massive headache as Nivek tried to pound himself in again, but I was stronger now. I thought of my love for Amery and

279

my determination to fulfill the prophecy, and after a while, Nivek backed off without success. With multiple raspy, whispering voices, the shroud spoke, and I heard Nivek's booming voice in my head as well. I assumed he wasn't aware of my newfound ability to hear again.

"So, you have come to us," the shroud that was Nivek said as wisps of darkness encircled me. They prodded my body, as if looking for cracks. They felt cold and sharp. "How pleasant. We have been waiting quite some time to see you, sparrow, the one they call the Silent Warrior."

It cackled a terrible laugh. "You see, Sheer, we know all about you," it whispered. "You are connected to us. We wanted you in full, but even though you were still an egg when we passed by, something changed inside of you before we could fully possess your mind. You changed, and you fought back. We were forced to leave you, but not before one of us got inside of you. We've been trying to get it back ever since... but look where you are now! Soon, we shall be complete again!"

I gaped, but this new knowledge made everything come together. A piece of the darkness explained my powers, and Nivek's attempts to get it back explained everything else. Why I'd been targeted by Malvador with his fire when I lived with the squirrels, and why Nivek had been able to enter my mind.

"Have you ever wondered why fighting us was so difficult for you?" the shroud asked. "Why you have struggled with your own motives for so long? But you will not be able to keep it contained and subdued forever. It wants to rejoin us, and eventually, you will permit it. You will submit. You will give up."

"I will never let you control me, Nivek!" I shouted. "I will never give up. I'll fight until my death or yours."

The evil spirits swirling around me in darkness hissed at my reply. I struggled to identify something among them to focus on, especially since I could barely move my head. "We could not have you then," they continued, "but soon we will. When you pushed us away, we found instead another. He didn't resist. He welcomed us.

And now, he has become us. We may choose to reside in his form or in this one. He is no more. We are Nivek."

As I watched, the swirling dark spirits spun faster and faster in front of me, getting smaller and clearer until they coalesced into a form I'd long ago grown to love. A chickadee. Kevin. It was him, but at the same time, not him at all. It was the look in his eyes that made all the difference. When I looked into their depths, I saw only darkness.

"No... no, I can't believe it," I cried. "You can't be..."

"Oh, but I am," Kevin said, his sweet, innocent voice completely contradicting the story his eyes were telling — of lust for power. My sadness transformed into anger.

"You used me! You used my need for friendship to gain power."

"Of course I did," Kevin's form said. "And you helped us greatly. But there is still more we want, and you will help us get it."

"What more could someone like you possibly want?" I demanded. "You're the most powerful... thing... on the surface of the Earth, besides nature itself! Isn't that enough for you?"

"No!" He hissed, temporarily exploding into the multiple shards of darkness before regaining control of his bird form. "Nothing is ever enough. And besides, we are close to having the world, even without your help. We can control minds, but you... you took the piece that can control matter. You keep foiling our plans. Somehow, you released all three of our puppet tyrants. With your spirit back on our side, a major obstacle is removed. And with all our powers combined, together we will have the power to rule the universe."

I wasn't sure whether "we" meant Kevin and myself, or just the shroud, but I didn't care. I wasn't tempted by the offer anymore, but I had to find a flaw, something I could build off. Was it possible for me to rescue Kevin like I had the others? I had to try.

"And what of my friends?" I countered.

"Friends? You mean Amery — that useless little worm? Well, you may have her. She's yours. We want nothing to do with her. And Al, you can forget about him. If you really want him saved, he'll be protected, but does he really mean that much to you? Now, will you join us or not, Sheer?"

I tried to think of what to say. I wanted to come up with something to combat Nivek, but nothing came to mind. Nothing but the need to purge this evil from the world, once and for all. "I will not join you, Nivek. I will never stop fighting. I won't let you win."

"Well then, you'll just have to fight me, won't you?" With that, I found I could move again. But before I could do anything, Nivek was upon me. Half-chickadee, half-dark spirit, it was a terrible sight. It pinned me to the ground, and I felt icy blades piercing through me as shards of darkness constrained me. It felt as if my heart was being torn out, and I cried in agony.

My life flashed before my eyes, and I saw each of the lives that had touched my own. I saw Violet and Reika and was grateful for the time I'd been able to spend with my family, no matter how short. I saw Barrie and remembered his loyal friendship. I saw Nyoka, Spike, and Finsternis, and recalled all I'd learned in preparing to fight them. I saw Anna, and how she'd given me something to learn, and a way to help others. I saw Samuel and remembered fondly all he'd taught me, and how his kindness had given me hope. Last of all, I saw Amery. My love for her gave me strength to keep on, not to give up, to fulfill the prophecy… and end this evil, once and for all.

Using the muscular power of my legs given to me from weeks of walking, I pushed the half-bird, half-spirit form off me. With a shout, I ripped myself free of its deadly grip, but I slipped in the pool of my own blood and was attacked again in an instant. In that brief moment of freedom, however, I set my mind to a single task and didn't waver. The agony from Nivek's attack forced my mind to withdraw to endure it, but I maintained fierce concentration. I thought of Amery and focused on what I intended to do, retreating entirely from the physical world and entering a deeper state of mind than I ever had before.

Finally, a loud *crack* resounded through the cave, and I knew I'd succeeded. I'd shifted the roof of the cave, enough to collapse it. Nivek looked up, changing completely into bird form. The tugging inside me told me that the shroud needed the last sliver of spirit to stay outside a physical form for so long. While it was distracted, I used all my strength to feebly drag myself toward the small hollow in the wall nearest me. It felt as if I was going to split in two from pain, and the ground was slippery with my blood, but I pushed myself along with all the life I had left. I had to stay alive. For Amery. I had to see her again, to hear her voice, to tell her what I now knew.

I was mostly to the hollow when the roof caved in. Nivek — Kevin — disappeared under a mass of stone. Dust and rock filled the rest of the cave, falling on top of my feet, which were still exposed, and all around me. I saw no more.

LV

I floated above my body, through the walls of the cave, above the fight. Nivek's army stood, baffled, no longer fighting. They looked around in confusion, their eyes back to normal. The animals who had been the walking or flying dead were lying still and silent in the blood-red dust.

The darkness in the sky was dissipating, and a beam of moonlight filtered through. The air was still and quiet. There was no sign of Malvador. The dust settled and I could see a few thin wisps of fog drifting around the cave; all that was left of the shroud.

Anna stood near the collapsed cave, digging in the stones. "Amery!" she called. "Come quick!"

I saw her form fluttering quickly towards the rock pile; hundreds of humans, Beasts, and other animals were now gathering around. She flew over their heads and landed in the middle, next to Samuel's granddaughter.

As the dust continued to settle, I lowered myself down. Two bodies had been excavated from the rubble: Kevin's, and my own. My eyes were gray, and my broken feathers were stained with red, especially around a deep gash in my chest. My legs were a mangled mess from the cave-in. I knew that if I entered my body, I would feel its pain… but it was worth it, to speak to Amery one more time. I dove down, bracing myself for what was to come.

I coughed. Pain flared in my legs, my stomach, my chest, my head. Everything hurt. I struggled to open my eyes and located Amery peering over me.

"Sheer! Are you all right?"

"No," I moaned. Suddenly, I felt foolish for not checking whether the chickadee was truly dead. I didn't know whether I'd get another opportunity. "Is Nivek… Kevin…"

"Kevin's dead," she replied. "I'm sorry."

I sighed in relief; Amery's eyes flashed with surprise. "Good," I said simply.

"What? But I thought he was your friend?!"

"Kevin *is* Nivek, Amery," I said, trying to keep my explanation brief. I didn't have much time. "I'm so sorry. I never believed you. You were right. You… were always right." I shuddered, fighting the pain that tried to push me out again. I choked, and blood oozed out of my beak and broken chest. Amery stared, seeing for the first time the wounds where Nivek had tried to rip out my heart.

Amery closed her eyes and leaned down to support my head with hers, and we were quiet for a while. The pain surged with another slow heartbeat, and I groaned involuntarily. "Anna!" Amery called, "He needs…"

"No!" I cried, realizing what she was doing. "No, don't. He's not… gone forever." I struggled to get out the words. "Only… his physical body… was destroyed. It's still… here." I tried to move my wing, but I couldn't. Thankfully, Amery knew me well. She looked at me anxiously, afraid of what I was implying. Finally, my wheezing and coughing took over, and I was unable to speak for some time.

When the fit had subsided, I took several deep breaths. I fought to keep my hold on my body; I could feel my grip weakening. "I love you, Amery." I sighed, spending my last breath and closing my eyes. The last thread of life snapped, and my body expelled me once more. Beside it, I saw a badger taking Kevin's body to be buried. I was grateful. Though he was the enemy, I was glad Samuel's family — my family — wouldn't stoop to his level and leave him to the buzzards. Amery was watching him as well, but then she turned back to me. She saw the relaxed expression on my quiet face and stood quickly in panic.

"Sheer, wake up!" she cried.

Anna stroked Amery's head with her muzzle. "He's gone, dear. He was too badly hurt. His pain is gone now."

All she could do was cry miserably and whisper, "I love you, too, Sheer. I love you."

I know, I thought pleasantly. I wished I could still be with her, to comfort her, but I knew I'd done the right thing. When I was gone, so too would be the last shard of the evil shroud.

All around me, animals were bowing their heads in sorrow and respect for my sacrifice. Even though I would no longer live on this Earth, neither would the shroud. With the last sliver severed forever and its physical form crushed, it would never be whole, and it would never come back. Soft snow began to fall, coating my body and the stones around it with a thin white blanket, at first stained red, then fading. It hid my wounds and the blood around my body. A gentle breeze carried a single petal of a cherry blossom from afar, dancing softly in the air before it landed slowly and carefully on my still breast. The breeze picked up and whirled around the collapsed cave. *"Thank you,"* it whispered.

Amery's voice cracking with sorrow, she hummed the song she'd sung to me in the rain. That was when the true Sheer had come out, and I thought it was rather fitting that the same song would see my passing. Other animals and humans around listened to the whistling tune and joined along in wordless singing. Soon, the air reverberated with the voices of many creatures, all carried on the wind. As the snow fell, I let their voices carry me away, onward to wherever my spirit might go. I embraced it, thankful for my life and the time I'd spent on Earth, thankful for the many friends and allies I'd met along the way. I had fulfilled the prophecy; I had defeated the darkness. I knew Amery would be safe now, and that was enough to leave me with nothing but a deep feeling of peace.

If you enjoyed *A Song in the Rain*, please consider leaving a review!

Lydia Deyes has channeled her overactive imagination into writing since she was nine years old, and is excited to finally start sharing her words with the world fifteen years later. To learn more about Lydia and keep up with her writing shenanigans, follow her on social media (@LydiaDeyes) or visit www.LydiaDeyes.com!

www.ingramcontent.com/pod-product-compliance
Lightning Source LLC
Chambersburg PA
CBHW031649100726
47898CB00006B/2037